Mochos smoochos,
Mary B. Moore.
xxx

TALK FLIRTY TO ME

Katy Crew

Ever felt like you've had a crush on someone your whole life, but they never see you back? That's what it felt like with Jarrod Kline. I worked in the same building as him, I gave him his jobs, I took his order when I went out for lunch... but that was it.

Being shy didn't help either. I wanted to be like the other women around me – ballsy, a go-getter, confident... I wanted to be like Tabby, Jose, Rose, and the Townsend women.

One night, over margaritas, we hatched a plan – the 'Get Yo Man Plan', aka GYMP. Sober, I realize what we've called it, but by then it's too late. The GYMP is motion, and it's too late to turn back.

Jarrod

I was the longest baby the day I was born, the tallest in preschool, the tallest in kindergarten... you get the point, I've always stood out. The problem was, I was also uncomfortable with it. For once I wanted to not be seen, to do something and no one could see me doing it.

After Tabby made a joke about me becoming an audiobook narrator, I looked it up. It seemed easy enough, so I went for it and decided to live for the day. Now, I was a mechanic by day, audiobook narrator by night, except few people know about the last part.

Initially, it was uncomfortable reading some of the scenes, but then Katy starting working at the garage and they took on a whole new meaning. I just have one question, what the hell is GYMP?

DEDICATION

When I wrote Fireball last year, Jarrod was meant to be just a background character. All it took was two sentences into his first appearance and I was hooked. Ever since then, whenever he's popped into a book I've fallen deeper in love. Because of that, it was only right that I include a country that I love and partly grew up in, Jamaica, as well as my favorite place there – Port Royal. (Side note: if you ever go to Jamaica, you're missing out true beauty by not going to see it. It's where James Bond drove his car crazy near in Dr. No, y'all! Bond and Bond... you'll see the link soon enough).

I can't actually dedicate this to one person because too many people have wanted his story, so I'm going to dedicate it to some of the bands that made Jarrod who he was to me in this book.

Eric Clapton, CBE

George Harrison, MBE

Tom Petty

Red Hot Chili Peppers

Dan Vasc

Also to Henry Cavill who gave me hours of entertainment while I was writing this in 2019.

But mostly, I want to actually dedicate this outright to my parents. My song with my dad is My Father's Eyes, and as we drove down the Palisodoes/Norman Manley Highway, he'd be rocking out air guitaring. Even when we got to the roundabout, he'd be steering with one hand around it, then went straight back to it. My poor mum put up with a lot from us and she still laughs as we do our crazy things. She's also put up with years of us playing Eric Clapton, George Harrison, The Traveling Wilburys, Tom Petty and many others as we drove around the different countries we lived in. And yes, we air guitared in all of them.

xox

CHAPTER ONE

JARROD

It wasn't unheard of for a mechanic to have to reattach a bumper that had come off a car. It also wasn't unheard of to have to fix areas of a vehicle that had become twisted or dented because of an accident. What *was* unheard of was to have to remove pieces of metal that had been welded to the underside of the car – which had almost ripped a hole in the undercarriage – that had part of an industrial chain still attached to it, fix a new bumper to the vehicle because the other one looked like it had been hit by a semi, and also patch up nine holes that had gone straight through the bodywork of the car when the chain had snapped and whipped into it.

The question I had was – why was there a chain attached to the underside of the vehicle? And for that matter, why did it look like a Transformer had attacked the bumper?

And finally, *why* was Hurst Townsend standing next to his friend, Bill Richards, whose car was in the same condition, looking so guilty and worried?

Scratching the back of my neck, I tried to figure out how best to phrase it all, but there was only one thing for it. "It's fucked, Hurst. I mean, we can fix it, but I'm thinking insurance won't cover this."

Bill's body straightened up and stiffened at this and, with his head tipped back so he was looking at the ceiling, he hissed, "Shit!"

Avoiding my eyes, Hurst looked around us and then winced when he saw the damage to the cars again. "Uh, is there any way to do this like… well, off the books?"

Not understanding what he was asking for, I repeated, "Off the books?"

Clearing his throat, he gestured at his vehicle. "Yeah, so that no one knows."

Now it was my turn to look around us, but I did it with good reason. "Um, Hurst, we're standing in your grandson's garage. One of them will most likely end up working on this with me, but even if they didn't, they're going to recognize the car," I drawled, and then looked over at the other man who was now chewing on his lip. "And your grandson's a deputy here, so he probably knows y'all had an accident, right?"

Muttering something under his breath, Bill plastered a smile on his face and nodded. "Absolutely, of course he does. As soon as it happened we rang him and reported it. Didn't we, Hurst?"

Crossing my arms, I watched Hurst try to think of his addition to this merry tale. I wasn't buying it for a second – these two were trouble together, and this wasn't the first 'mishap' to their cars we'd had to fix.

Snapping his fingers, Hurst spun around with a smile on his face – although it had to be said it was one of relief. "Yup, sure did. As soon as it happened we rang through and he came out to inspect it and wrote it all down in his notepad."

"I see," I hummed, walking around to the other side of Bill's car and almost choking when I saw that the rear panel was completely missing and the chain attached to his car was now wrapped around the axle. "And what exactly happened?"

They exchanged a few glances, and then Bill shook his head and took a step back, leaving Hurst to answer the question.

"It was a hit and run?"

"What exactly hit you?"

"It was too dark for us to see."

Turning to face Bill, I watched him take a handkerchief out of his pocket and wipe his forehead. "How did it hit both of you at the same time?"

Sighing, he hunched his shoulders and looked at the floor. "Pure luck, I guess."

"And where did the chain come from?"

By this point the poor man was almost bent over in two as he repeated, "Pure luck, I guess."

Hearing a noise from the office that overlooked the garage, I glanced up and saw another person who confused me – albeit in a good way – Katy Crew. She was staring incredulously at the two vehicles until Hurst moved and caught her attention, then she rolled her eyes and shook her head, the questions in her mind over the type of damage answered immediately. Amen, babe, *amen*.

Dragging my attention back to the two old miscreants in front of me, I asked, "And what did Logan think about it all?"

"Um, not much. He just wrote in his little book and that was it."

Raising an eyebrow, I made to reach for the phone in my back pocket, making it clear what I was going to do.

"Ok, fine," Hurst snapped, throwing his arm out toward his friend. "Bill and me started having 'man night' every other Thursday three months ago."

Taking in a fidgeting Bill, I knew I'd kick myself for it, but I just had to know. "Man night?"

Oh, I knew what one of those was, absolutely, but Bill and Hurst were in their seventies so I was trying to figure out an age relevant version of the type I was familiar with.

Tilting his chin up slightly, Hurst narrowed his eyes at me. "Yeah, guys our age have those and it doesn't have to be playing Bridge or watching a black and white movie, ya know."

Nothing wrong with black and white movies, I loved them. I also loved the dubbed over martial arts movies, too, but to the best of my knowledge, no one had ever wrecked their cars because of them.

Seeing that I was still waiting, he sighed, "Ok, so we got to watching this movie with fast cars in it, and there was a scene where they stole a safe from a police station and drove it through Brazil."

Immediately my head dropped so that I was staring at the toes of my boots, knowing exactly which movie he was talking about. "You watched Fast Five, didn't you?"

Fast & Furious 5 was my favorite out of them all, but it tied with the sixth one where they went to the UK and found Letty. The one he was talking about involved Vin Diesel and Paul

Walker breaking a huge safe out of the police station in Brazil by attaching chains and dragging it out of a wall and through the streets with their cars. It was a fucking awesome movie and one of the smartest plots ever, but it was also impossible to do – as Bill and Hurst had apparently found out.

"That was the one," Bill muttered, looking at the cars and wincing. "I wanted to add some Noz to them and build a ten second car so we could race for pinks, but he," he nodded his head at Hurst, "wanted to do this."

Rubbing the back of my neck, torn between laughing and losing my shit, I tried to picture them dragging a big safe behind them. "What kind of safe did you use and where did you tear it out of?"

"That's irrelevant," Hurst mumbled, looking around the garage again, no doubt for one of his grandsons.

Apparently Bill was in a sharing mood, though, because he pulled his phone out and brought a photo up on the screen. "This was it. I had it in my shed out back, hidden behind a wooden wall. Can never be too safe even if you live in a small town like ours, so I went all out. It cost a fortune and weighs a ton, but it's good." He told me, and then added, "At least it *was* good. I'm not sure about it now."

The photo showed what looked like a standard safe, about five feet high and four feet across, obviously taken before they'd dragged it behind their cars.

"You got one that shows it now?"

Sliding his finger across the screen a couple of times, he stopped on one that showed that the safe was in fact still shut tight, but the outside walls of it looked like a supernatural creature had been at them.

Rubbing my face with my hands now, I muttered, "Jesus."

Before I could ask any more questions, though, Cole Townsend walked through the side door of the garage and burst out laughing when he saw his grandad standing there. "I'd be hiding too if I was you, old man. Gammy is pissed, and when I say pissed, I mean the last time I saw her she was talking about staking you down so the bull could get at you."

Hurst's face went almost gray hearing this, and he swung around to face me again. "You've gotta fix the cars. If you do that, I can deny all of it."

A disbelieving whistle came from the door, and this time Ren walked through it and headed in our direction. "You're in so much shit, Gramps. I just came from…" he stopped as he saw the cars, his mouth opening and closing a couple of times.

Walking around to see what his brother was staring at, Cole made a choking noise when he saw it. "What the fuck?"

Deciding that the safest thing to do would be to make a break for it, Hurst got one step into his run when a big arm shot out in front of him, and Coleman snickered, "Oh no, not this time."

Seeing that everyone was focused on Hurst now, Bill started inching toward the door, realizing that his path to freedom was wide open. Or at least it had been, until Tom Townsend stopped in the doorway with his arms over his chest, Logan Richards at his back giving his grandpa the same look the Townsends were now giving Hurst.

Apparently his solution to the look was to act like he hadn't seen Logan in years, so that's what he did. "Hey, son, you look like you've grown two inches since I last saw you. How're your parents? They good? I should probably pop round and see them, you know. It's been a long time."

Moving past Tom who was still in the doorway, Logan straightened to his full height and glared down at Bill. "You saw them yesterday, I'm thinking before you and your friend decided to rip up the road with a safe, leave it embedded in the road with chains still attached to it and part of y'all's cars. Am I right?"

Shaking his head, Bill went straight into denial. "Nope, nuh unh. I'm seventy-six, Hurst's seventy-three, we're too old to do that. I mean, where'd we get the chains? We're living on our pensions, which means Ramen noodles and bread for dinner."

"From the barn," Ren clipped. "And don't give me that shit about pensions and Ramen noodles. Both y'all eat just fine and worked hard enough not to have to rely on your pensions to survive."

Nodding his head like the source he'd gotten the chains from was plausible and ignoring the comment about his pension, Bill then retorted, "Ok, where'd we get the stuff to attach them to the safe and cars then?"

Leaning into the open trunk of one of the vehicles, Cole pulled out the welding machine that Ren had bought for the garage two months previously. I knew it was the same one because it had the label he'd printed out for it that read: *This cost a fucking whack. You break it, you replace it. RT.* And it had cost a whack, roughly four thousand whacks.

Seeing something else, Cole let out a frustrated growl and reached in for it, coming back out with a pair of Oakley's dangling from his finger.

"You used these to protect your eyes? Seriously? You only just gave me these last week for my birthday."

My eyes flicked to Logan when he looked back at his own grandpa and growled, "Is that why you borrowed my Ray-Bans?"

Totally unsympathetic to the misuse of their sunglasses, Ren ground out, "You stole my welding machine to attach a safe to your car?"

"Yeah, but I followed the what you put on the label and didn't break it. In fact, we looked after it and kept it on us the whole time," Hurst replied with an innocent smile on his face.

Jesus take the wheel. In fact, take all four of the wheels on both cars so they'd never drive them again.

Taking a step closer to his grandad, Ren growled, "You did that by putting it in the back of your car which was attached to a safe - a safe you dragged for half a mile behind those cars until it got stuck in the road and ripped your cars apart."

"But it was still safe," Hurst pointed out. "No pun intended."

That was when Ren lost his shit. "The trunk of the fucking car doesn't even close because half of what it needs to do that is still attached to the fucking safe." Hurst wisely didn't respond to that verbally, although the blush on his cheeks said it all. "And it's not about the welding machine, it's about the danger you put yourselves and anyone driving along that road in."

Leaning around his grandson, Bill offered, "We weren't in any danger, Ren. We welded roll bars in the car like in the movie." All of our heads snapped to look back at the cars, not seeing any of the bars mentioned. "They came off when we got loose from the safe, but Hurst said that was 'cos the welding machine was shit, not 'cos…'" he stopped when Ren turned the full force of his glare on him. "Shutting up now."

Figuring now was the best time to leave the men to deal with their grandfathers, I shifted away from them and toward the stairs that led to the office. After this, I needed coffee, preferably with rum in it. Lots of rum.

Opening the door, I shut it softly behind me, not wanting to scare Katy who was standing at the coffee machine herself, staring at something on the wall in front of her. "Yo!"

It wasn't yelled, it wasn't snapped, it sounded like I'd said it gently to my ears, but she jumped and then let out a noise like a yelpy squeak as she looked over her shoulder at me. Katy Crew, aka Katarianne Crew, was the quintessential 'sweet girl' as my mom called them. That didn't mean she was boring, homely, or anything like that – it meant that she was so damn pretty that you'd never expect her to have the beautiful personality that she had. Katy would give you the shirt off her back if you needed it, and everything she did let you know this. My mom calling it the 'sweet girl syndrome' purely meant that she was as sweet on the outside as she was on the inside. I was of the mind that it should be 'fucking awesome girl' syndrome, but my ma wasn't big on cussing, so I kept that one to myself.

Right now, seeing her wide blue eyes on me, I was even more adamant that fucking awesome should be the terminology used to describe her. The center of her eyes were a medium blue color, but they had an even darker blue ring around the edge of them and were framed with long dark brown lashes, the same color as her hair.

Jerking to look at something in front of her, she then glanced back at me. "Hey, sorry, I didn't hear you coming up the steps."

I was a big guy – six foot seven inches tall – but I'd learned to tread lightly as a kid so that I could either get the drop on one of my brothers, or sneak out the house without waking my parents up. I didn't see the point in stomping or treading heavily as an adult, regardless of where I was, because that expended energy that I didn't want to waste. Noise also drew attention to you, and I hated doing that, so I tried to minimize anything that would get people's focus on me unless it was necessary.

I'd always been tall, even in kindergarten, and it had drawn people's attention. I also had greeny hazel eyes that had a dark ring of blue around my pupils, so they got people's attention, too, because being half Jamaican they stood out even more. In high school I'd bought colored contacts to hide them, but once I got them in my eyes the first time I couldn't get them back out again. It took my brothers holding my head still for Dad to get them out, after which he'd flushed them down the toilet. My brothers had similarly colored eyes, so they'd got it, but Dad had sat us down and lectured us about loving what the good Lord had given us and how we were to use it to make us who we were going to be through life.

That advice had stuck with me and on the whole that's what I did, but I still tried to fade into the background as much as I could. Part of that fading included walking softly, and I'd managed to scare Katy just now without meaning to. "I'm sorry if I scared you. I came up to get some coffee and get away from that," I pointed over my shoulder at where the men - who were now arguing - were.

The side of her mouth tilted up slightly when we heard Tom yell something, the noise echoing inside the garage. "Yeah, I saw that. I'm not going to ask what they did because it's Hurst. That man is a law unto himself." With her back still facing me, she took a couple of steps sideways away from the coffee machine. "Help yourself, I just opened a new box of pods for it."

Moving to where she'd just been, I reached for a cup and saw a puddle of coffee on the counter as I placed it in the machine. That wasn't unusual, and she'd probably been about to clean it up, so I wiped it with paper towels while my cup filled so she had one less thing to do. The guys here were slobs, that's the only way to put it. They spilled, they dropped, they did whatever, and rarely did they go back to try to clean up after themselves unless it was to put tools back. Hell, most of the paperwork was covered in oily fingerprints because they didn't wipe their hands off first. I was guilty of that myself, but I wasn't guilty of not picking up my shit, and I knew Katy had OCD tendencies so it had to drive her crazy.

Once the coffee was done, I threw the towels in the trash, grabbed my cup and gave her a chin lift as I turned back to the door. I wasn't immune to Katy Crew, in fact far from it, but because she always left me feeling off center, I tried to keep our interactions quick and casual. It wasn't because I was shy, I just didn't know what to say or do around her, so it was easier this way.

Closing the door quietly behind me, I blew out a breath and made my way back down the steps toward the car I'd been working on before Hurst and Bill had arrived. The Townsends were still arguing it out, so I resigned myself as I got back to work to the fact that it was going to be another eventful day. Fucking joy!

Katy

As soon as the door shut behind Jarrod, I pulled my coffee drenched top away from my boobs and let out the little squeal I'd done my best to smother when I'd jumped and tipped the hot coffee on them as he'd said yo.

"Hot tits, hot tits!"

Moving quickly to the small bathroom, I grabbed a chunk of paper towels and wet them with cold water, lifted my t-shirt up and placed them on the red skin. Fortunately, I had a change of clothes with me seeing as how getting dirty here was a common occurrence, but that didn't stop me worrying about long lasting damage to the area the hot water had landed on.

Lifting the wet towels up, I looked at the skin and figured I'd probably get away without needing to bandage my entire chest, which would mean having to explain it to someone here because it started at my collarbones and they'd see the dressings. That would mean I'd probably be known as the chick with burned boobies, something I'd really rather not happen.

Slightly burned boobies, though, *that* I could live with.

CHAPTER TWO

KATY

I'd only just dried my bra out with the hand drier and changed my t-shirt when the door to the office opened and in came some of the Townsend women. When I'd started working here six months ago, they'd all come in and introduced themselves to me and we'd become friends, so I had coffee with at least one of them every day while I was working.

"Hey, babe, what's shaking," Ren's wife Maya called as she plonked her ass down on one of the chairs in the room. With her were her sister-in-laws Ebru, Sabine, and Layla, and Isla Montgomery who was married to Luke Montgomery and who was a close family friend of the Townsends.

Sweeping my hand in a wave at them all, I moved back behind my desk and dropped down into my chair, shaking my head. "Jarrod came in twenty minutes ago and when I jumped because he walks like a ghost on those stairs so I hadn't heard him, I got coffee all over me," I gestured to my boob area, nodding when they all winced. "Freshly made coffee, too, so I've just had to get changed."

Resting one butt cheek on the edge of my desk, Layla grinned down at me. "Bet you gave him the wet t-shirt shot of his dreams. What color was your top? You got lace on under it today?"

Leaning away from her, I ruined her excited vibe. "I hid it from him because I didn't want to look like a dick."

I mean, how the hell could spilling coffee and burning your boobs equal a sexy wet t-shirt shot? It was coffee, this was a garage, they were my boobs, so they definitely didn't fit into the sexy category (more like boringly average), and Jarrod would probably have preferred a Playboy style bunny doing it. With water. And huge gadunkadunks that screamed 'these are for you, Jarrod Kline'. I was only just a C cup, I was me, I was also only five foot seven with heels on – and even then that was pushing it because I was probably only five foot six with them on a good day – and I wasn't even close to a Jarrod Kline level of woman.

Eyes narrowed on me, Layla took me in, no doubt trying to think of something to say to make me feel better. What she said instead made my stomach drop into my big toe. "Ok, don't take this the wrong way, but this has to be said. I get that humans are fickle, even I'm guilty of that a lot of the time, but men want what men want and if you think that Jarrod doesn't see what we see," she shook her head looking over at the others who were nodding back. Taking a deep breath in, she turned back to me. "Katy, babe, you've got it going on. You've got beautiful hair, your face looks like someone drew it for a fairytale, you have all that," she gestured at my body, making me look down to it even though I knew it better than anyone. "And you have the advantage of being a height that makes men melt. They see this pretty petite babe, hair that's fucking outrageously beautiful, and it brings out their alpha protective rawr side." The word was accompanied by a slashing of her nails through the air like a tiger.

"Add in the shyness with an edge of nerd to it and you have major alpha protective rawr," Maya added, getting a head nod from Layla and making me shift uncomfortably.

"I think we need a girls' night out," Ebru mused, watching me closely and no doubt reading me perfectly.

Before any of them could say anything, I repeated, "A girls' night?"

Leaning so that she could see me around Layla's back, Sabine nodded. "I'm in agreement with this suggestion. I think you need a night out with us. One that involves cocktails and getting drunk."

Before I could say anything else, they all started throwing out suggestions. Some of them freaked me out – especially when they said things like going to a strip club could wait until the next night out – and some of them left me confused.

"So, it's decided. Saturday we're going to Sheeves, so you need to get out a little black dress and get your dazzle on," Layla informed me, grinning widely.

"But I've just moved into my new place so I was going to unpack some more boxes."

This was an unnecessary reminder of my recent move into my new place, the first one I'd ever lived in that was just mine, seeing as how they'd all helped me do it two weekends ago. They'd also seen how bad my OCD could get when the guys had started putting boxes in whatever room they wanted to, totally ignoring the room marked on them. I hadn't lost it when I'd discovered it, but it didn't take a genius to see the immediate anxiety that had hit me when I had. Being the great people that they were, after that they'd made sure they all went in the right place. For a moment, old insecurities about it had hit me, but the Townsends had glossed over it like it wasn't a big deal. Moving was hard for someone who liked everything in the right place, so them reacting like they had meant more to me than I could put into words.

And with that in mind, I decided not to be rude and say no. "Actually, you're right – I need a night out with the girls. I've already unpacked my clothes and shoes," and they were all organized perfectly in my walk-in, I didn't add, "so let's do it."

I had two nights to unpack after work before it happened which meant I'd only have about five boxes of books left to unpack on Sunday. I'd deliberately left my books until last because it always took me a while to organize them. I was still undecided if I wanted to put them in the bookcases in alphabetical order based on the author or the title, or if I wanted them done by color. My bookcases were white and split into square boxes, so organizing them by color would look awesome. Then again, organizing them alphabetically was what I was used to for them, whereas color was what I used in my wardrobe… it was a tough choice.

While I'd been musing through this dilemma, the girls had apparently been making more plans, because I heard Maya say, "Get da man plan."

"Nah," Ebru snorted, waving her hand. "That's lame. We'll think up something better."

If I'd known they were talking about me, I probably would have thrown myself down the steps in front of my office to get out of it. Instead, I figured they'd been talking about someone else or even Layla, so I laughed with the rest of them.

Stupid books!

"OK, OK," MAYA SNICKERED, WOBBLING ON HER STOOL. "GYMP!"

Finishing off my drink, I lowered the glass back to the table with more force than I'd meant to. *Damn Sex on the Beach cocktails were freaking fine!*

"Who's the gimp?" Layla slurred, reaching for the pitcher and frowning when she saw it was empty. In fact, all seven of them were empty. "Bar keep," she called, waving her hand in the air and giggling when Ethan turned around and glared at her. "Yoo hoo, we need more of your wares."

Rolling his eyes, he leaned over the bar to the guy who'd been making the drinks for us all night and said something as he gestured with his thumb at us. The guy – who was actually kind of hot – burst out laughing and nodded, before moving off to do something that hopefully involved more cocktails.

Slowly – or that could have been the alcohol giving the world a *Matrix* style vibe – Ethan turned back and walked over to where we were, coming to a stop right behind my stool.

"If you cause any damage to my property or get on the karaoke machine," he aimed this at Tabby, the sheriff's wife who had the most beautiful pink hair, "you're banned."

Ignoring the hot owner of the club, Ebru cupped her hands around her mouth and called out, "Yo, Joe!" Before stopping and bursting out laughing. "Holy shit, that rhymes."

All of us started laughing with her - probably harder than the situation warranted, but, ya know, alcohol - and I realized how happy I was that I hadn't thrown myself down the steps and caused an injury that would have prevented me from enjoying tonight.

Remembering what she wanted, Ebru called out asking for more cherries for our glasses and if we could have more shots, too. That's how the mess had started when we'd first entered Sheeve's. We'd looked at the cocktail menu, decided on shots but seeing as how we all wanted different ones we'd done them in waves. By that I mean, we'd all had choice number one, then the next round was the next person's choice and so on. After that, we'd wobbled to a table, sat down, and stuck to our pitchers of Sex on the Beach.

Big hands landing on my shoulders distracted me from the discussion on which shot we should have, and I tipped my head back on my shoulders so that I was looking at the owner of the hands upside down. Because of that and the alcohol consumption, it took a moment for me to recognize the owner of them.

Grinning widely, I greeted, "Hey!"

I think Ethan's mouth smiled back, but it could have been a frown. Alcohol and understanding upside down directions were apparently incompatible. "Hey, Katy. How's your brother?"

My brother…

I had two of them and I hadn't even thought about them tonight, so again it took time for me to figure out what he was asking. Initially it was a question of – I have a brother? Then it went to – oh my god, I have two brothers! How awesome is that? That was quickly followed by – aw man, I love my brothers.

Finally, it ended on – "I have two brothers who are the bombdiggidy. I mean, they were mean when we were little and

18

cut bangs on me that started here," I put my hand halfway across the top of my head to show how far back they went, "and were like this," I moved it up and down like a wave because what they'd done looked just like that. "Then they got Mom's hairspray and sprayed it so it stuck up like this," I lifted my hand up into the air, high above my head, still making a wave like motion with it. "And then Jonny Dobson dumped me the next day because he said I looked like a donkey."

I faintly acknowledged the fact his shoulders were shaking, but that could just have been me shaking with the movement my hand was still making until I dropped it just then.

Looking away from him, I muttered, "It was a shame because I was really into Jonny Dobson, he was seriously hot. Hey, do you know Jonny? I need to show him my new bangs so he doesn't think I look like a donkey now."

That was a genius idea.

Shaking his head, he replied in a voice that sounded like he was being strangled for some reason. "No, I don't know Jonny, but that sounds like it sucked. How old were you?"

"Totally broke my heart, bruh," I sighed. "I was seven, but you never get over heart break. I learned a lesson from it, though, so now I make sure no donkey has wonky bangs, and if they do I trim 'em in straight line and feather them a bit. Nothing worse than wonky donkey bangs."

His head disappeared from his shoulders - which was the coolest and freakiest trick I'd ever seen - and the sound of his laughter drowned out the voices around me. When it reappeared, his face was bright red and he was wiping under his eyes. "I was talking about your brother Major."

A flood of love hit me hearing my brother's name. "I love Major," I breathed, trying to figure his face out. He had eyes on his chin and a mouth on his forehead, and even when I closed one eye to check his nose was upside down. "He's like the best big brother in the world. I've got another one called Ammon and a sister called Aura, you know?"

"That I did know."

"Hey, Katy," one of the girls called, and I remembered where I was. "We've got slippery nipples."

Glancing quickly at their chests, I tipped my head back again. I'm not sure what Ethan saw on my face at the image that popped into my brain hearing those words, but whatever it was I heard him laughing for a long time after I watched him walk away and hold onto the bar while his body shook as he laughed.

Looking back at the girls who were all holding up shot glasses, I shrugged and lifted the one in front of me.

"Here's to GYMP," Ebru called, and we all shot them back at the same time and slammed the glasses back down on the tabletop.

They kept calling someone a gimp, so excusing myself, I made my way toward the ladies bathrooms, and looked up what one was while I was doing my business. It would be fair to say that I struggled to look at any of them in the eye when I got back to them, knowing that one of them was into that sort of stuff. I also couldn't figure out which one, and that was bugging me.

All of this was cured by more shots and cocktails, though, and then they came up with the 'Get Yo' Man Plan' which was also called GYMP. *How ironic was that.* And this plan was a list of things that I needed to do to get Jarrod Kline.

With the alcohol beating through my body and ruling my brain, this seemed like the best idea in the world. However, also knowing that alcohol could cause memory blanks, we wrote the plan down on napkins so that I wouldn't forget.

EIGHT HOURS LATER...

Apparently on my way home I'd taken a detour to the ocean and set sail on a raft. That ocean was currently being hit by a hurricane which was making it go up and down, up and down, up and... taking in a gulp of air, I did my best to stop the contents of my stomach making a bid for freedom, and then took another one.

Then the raft changed into a rollercoaster that was chugging up the tracks to three thousand feet above the ground, and then it just let rip with no warning and plummeted back down, taking a sharp right before we could hit the floor, a sharp left, going up and down...

And that's when I jumped out of the taboggan looking rollercoaster car that I was sitting in, opened my eyes, recognized my home, and blindly stumbled to the nearest bathroom to wave goodbye to what I'd been trying to persuade to stay inside me. I had never, not once, been sick after a night out, and I never ever, not once, wanted to do it again. Every heave felt like I had a gorilla trying to break out my skull, while two anacondas blocked off my airway and a porcupine rolled around inside my stomach.

Seventy-four-thousand heaves later it was all over and I was left curled in a ball on the bathroom floor, trying to remember the last time I'd cleaned it and if anyone had come over and used it since. I knew my toilet habits so I was safe with the knowledge that if I was the only one who'd used it, the floor I was lying on was clean. Anyone else's toilet habits, though, then I needed to go and boil myself in the shower with bleach.

Thankfully my memory – what little of it I had – pulled up a replay of me cleaning the place yesterday afternoon and the fact that no one else had used it since. I still needed to boil myself because it was a toilet so *eww*, but I didn't need to use bleach so that was a relief.

Pulling myself up using the edge of the sink, I leaned my head on the countertop and aimed a weak hand swipe at my toothbrush and toothpaste. So long as I kept my movements slow, small, and lived basically from now on, I'd survive the hell going on inside my body. Also, so long as I brushed my teeth four times and gargled with mouthwash I wouldn't throw up again. So that's what I did.

I was just drying my face when my phone started ringing in my bedroom, making me groan at the thought of moving.

Looking at the blurry person in the mirror, I moaned, "I'm not ready."

Apparently the person calling agreed with this because the phone stopped ringing. Sinking back down on the floor, I rested my head on the cool tiles, and my moans this time were because that just felt freaking awesome.

Until the phone started ringing again… then again…

Whimpering, I crawled back through to the bedroom and tugged on the white cord that was responsible for juicing up the device from Satan, letting it drop from the bedside table onto the rug before answering it.

I didn't put it to my ear because that would involve movement and co-ordination. Instead, I hit the green button and immediately hit the speakerphone one. "What?"

A voice that sounded equally as rough as mine croaked, "Are you dying too?"

Lowering so that I was face down on my new rug, I groaned, "Yes."

"I've never felt this bad in my life, and I pushed a baby out my vagina."

That was a weird thing for a random voice to say, but I couldn't even begin to analyze it, not when I had the inhabitants of a heavy metal mosh pit headbanging inside my skull. "Did that happen last night?"

I didn't remember someone doing that, but we'd been drinking pretty heavily so who knew what was going on under the table?

Just then a baby started crying in the background and I heard a deep voice say, "I'll get her," as the person on the phone started making crying whining noises too.

"I swear when she does that it feels like an axe murderer is attacking my brain," it wailed, which then made me start whimpering because I felt her pain.

I wanted to let her know that and that she had my full sympathy, but the words just wouldn't form. At last, after what felt like seventy years of pain, the baby settled, and both of us let out relieved sighs at the same time.

"So are you ready to go?" the voice asked, and I slowly lowered my head to look at what I was wearing, not once lifting it up from the rug or noticing the abrasiveness of the fabric on my cheek. I was in a tank top and panties, that was it, and I wasn't sure what we were doing, but I was sure that my current outfit wasn't suitable for public consumption.

"Not really."

"I'm gonna crawl in the shower," she croaked, "then crawl

back out of it. Then I'm gonna beg him to put clothes on me so I can leave the house. Then…"

As interesting as the breakdown was of her future plans, I interrupted her anyway. "Who is this?"

"Tabby," she croaked. "Who's this?"

"Hey, Tabby, it's Kat. Where are we going?"

"The writing on my hand says, 'call Kat, get dog'. I thought it meant I needed to call my cat and then go get my dog, by the cat has a K like your name, so I guess we're getting a dog."

Groaning, I got up onto my knees, keeping my head on the floor until the last second, and then slowly lifted my upper body up too. "Ok, I'm getting in the shower."

Tabby just got out a, "See you soon," before she hung up, and I dragged myself back to the bathroom for a shower, praying throughout the whole thing that I didn't drown.

TWO HOURS LATER…

In all my life, not once had I felt the pain I felt when I opened the door after she knocked on it and I got the sunlight in my eyes. I'd broken my arm and my ankle, and the pain they'd caused didn't even come close to that sunlight. Grabbing my sunglasses out of my purse, I pushed them up my nose and squinted at Tabby who was wearing a cap and sunglasses as she used my door frame to hold herself up.

"Car. Now."

With my hands cupped around my eyes, I stumbled behind her, only just remembering to close the door behind me and lock it. When I turned back, I took one step and heard, "Yo, Tab, Kat."

With my hands still up, I turned and saw a group of guys from work moving things into the house next to mine. I'd rented one of the newly built houses on the outskirts of Piersville after falling in love with it on first sight. They were small and they were close enough to town that I didn't have to wake up at the crack of dawn to get to work, but far enough away that I had peace and privacy.

Or at least I had had privacy until a group of men moved in next door who knew my name.

Tabby called, "Hey... Oh, hey, *Jarrod*!"

Before I could ask her where she was looking to see him because I couldn't see him at all, she grabbed my hands away from my face and tugged me to the car, waving over her shoulder. Fortunately neither of us were driving because we were more than likely still over the limit and I wasn't even sure what hand-eye coordination was and you needed that to drive, so I sat in the front next to Dave as Tabby got in the back with her daughter, Sheena, and we headed to the Dog Rescue place Dave knew that about twenty minutes away.

As Tabby and I got out of the vehicle, I warned her, "I need to cover my eyes because the second I make eye contact with a dog I'll want to take it home."

"You said last night it had to be a small dog so you can put it in your purse. This place has them sectioned out in small, medium and large breeds, so just cover your eyes until I say you're safe."

I'd just reached out for the handle of the door that said ENTRANCE in huge letters, when she said it and it all became clear. "Wait, *I'm* the one getting the dog?"

"Yup, girls are out getting what you need for it, so we just have to take it back."

"Tabby, I don't think…"

Ignoring the fact my hand was on the handle, she tugged the door open and gestured inside. "Good, because I can't think right now. I'm never drinking with you guys again."

Following along behind her, I was in full agreement with her on that one.

"It's unlikely they'd let me take the dog home today anyway," I muttered to the back of her bright pink head – hair that normally made me jealous, but right now was killing me. "They've got to do background checks, checks on your…"

"Why, Katy Crew, I'm so excited to have you here for your first puppy!" A voice screeched from the office and made it clear I was totally screwed because I would be taking the dog home with me today. "Whatever she wants, Beth, Katy gets. She's totally clear on all the checks."

And why was that? Because I didn't realize that my parents neighbor was the director of this rescue center.

Ten minutes later…

I had my hands over my eyes as Tabby pulled me along behind her. I wasn't exaggerating, I was terrible when it came to dogs. My uncle now had three because when I'd gone with him to adopt one from a place near where he lived, I'd dropped a hand to cover my mouth so I could cough and had made eye contact with a dog. Then, I'd tripped over a bucket and put both hands out to catch myself, and made eye contact with another dog. Then he'd pointed the one out that he'd actually wanted to adopt while he was filling in the paperwork for the other two… and he ended up with it, too. We'd also had four dogs in the house when I was a kid because of that exact reason. I was the worst person to ever go dog adopting with.

"One second, she's just moving a bag of food," Tabby told me as we stopped.

A high pitched, heart breaking whine came from beside me, and without thinking I dropped my hands and stared into the prettiest eyes I'd ever seen in my life – apart from Jarrod's. They were also not that much lower than where my own eyes were while I was standing up. As if that wasn't bad enough, the dog then raised a paw and scratched at the cage in front of me, whining the whole time.

"Uh, Katy…" Tabby murmured beside me. "That's not a little dog."

No, it was the size of a fucking horse, but it was love at first sight and we'd made eye contact.

Looking around her, I got Beth's attention. "This one."

CHAPTER THREE

JARROD

My couch had never felt so good as it did at that moment as I leaned back and took a sip of my beer. I was moved into my new place and it was frigging awesome. I had peace, quiet, my house was the shit, and I could focus on my secret without anyone finding out.

Groaning as he raised the footrest on my recliner, Ren got comfy with his own beer. "So, Katy Crew's your neighbor, man," he snickered, wiggling his eyebrows as the others joined us. "How's that for luck."

"Who's Katy Crew?" My brother Bond asked as he sat beside me, with my other brother Canon beside him.

"Christ, it's like looking at three different versions of Jarrod," Cole muttered as he sat in the other recliner, leaving my last brother, Reid, to sit in my desk chair which was currently parked beside where I was sitting. When he did, Cole added, "Make that four different versions of him."

Yeah, we all looked a lot alike, with the main differences

being the colors of our eyes. I had green, hazel and blue in mine, Bond's were a lighter blue, Canon's were a dark green, and Reid's were a mixture of green and brown – as in, both colors seemed to twirl around his irises together. Freaky bastard.

"Ok, I gotta ask," Ren said, leaning forward in his chair now. "Who's the oldest, and how did y'all get the eyes. Brother," he directed at me, "your eyes have been a topic of conversation in the Townsend houses for a long time…"

"No shit," Cole agreed. "My wife won't quit talking about them and his voice."

"So if my wife or the other ladies see all y'all together, I think they're gonna melt on the spot," Ren continued like his brother hadn't said anything.

Glaring at him, Cole growled, "Apart from my wife, because she likes my eyes just fine."

"That's where you're wrong, man. My wife worships the ground I walk on and loves every part of me, but as much as they love us, the second he looks at any of the women they legit turn into giggling schoolgirls."

"Is that a fact?" Bond asked before Cole could argue back. "I see you've been holding back on us, J."

In actual fact, I hadn't been because what Ren said wasn't true. At least, I didn't think it was true?

Ignoring all of it, I pointed at Bond, "He's the oldest at thirty-one, Canon's next at twenty-nine, as you know I'm twenty-seven, and Reid is the baby at twenty-four."

Both men's mouths opened slightly hearing how close in age we were – again, something we got a lot.

"Whoa, your parents were on a roll, weren't they?" Cole

muttered, getting a glare from all four of us. "Are your parents giants, too?"

"Dad's six foot seven," Reid told him, pausing for effect. "Mom's five foot four."

Ironically, if I had to take a guess, that was the difference in heights between me and my new neighbor if she wasn't wearing heels, too.

If they looked shocked before, the looks on their faces now were downright hilarious.

"Five foot four?" Cole clarified. When we all nodded, he stood up and looked at us all. "Bullshit. No way can an ittle bitty squeeze out four behemoths back to back like that. No fucking way."

He was right on one part of that — we were all behemoths. Bond and Canon were six foot six, and me and Reid were six foot seven, but she'd definitely given birth to all four of us which was why we spoiled her on Mother's Day.

"Jesus," Ren mumbled, looking at us all and ignoring his brother's outburst again. "That's impressive. What about the eye thing?"

"The quirky quirks of DNA, man," Canon replied, putting his empty bottle on the coffee table. "Mom's from Jamaica, Dad's family are German. You'd think we'd get Mom's eyes, but somehow we all have a mixture of green and blue. I read up on it somewhere and the dominant gene should be her brown eyes, but sometimes there can be blue eyed DNA further back that mix with the blue of this parent. I'm not sure if that's right because I'm not a geneticist and I hated biology, so I'm not sure the exact reasons."

Normally people went quiet when we explained it, like they were trying to figure it out or were uncomfortable discussing it, but Townsends were unpredictable, which was proven when Cole nodded and said, "A friend of our family in Gonzales County has white parents but she's black. They did DNA tests on her and it's something to do with DNA related phenomenon called atavism, which is when a dormant gene from centuries ago reactivates itself and becomes a dominant one."

"Holy shit. Is she hot?" Reid asked, rubbing his hands together.

Taking a quick look at his brother, Ren snickered, "She's our cousin's." Making Reid sit back in his chair like he was disappointed.

I knew the Townsend family well and I'd heard all about Archer and Bonnie. I wasn't sure if I'd say she was his, but with how determined the Townsend species was, I didn't doubt he'd make sure that it ended up being the case.

"So, who's Katy Crew?" Canon asked, bringing up a subject that I'd hoped would stay buried after our trip down DNA lane.

"She's the hot chick who lives next door," Cole grinned, winking at me. "And she works with Jarrod, too."

Looking at each other, Bond and Canon stood up and made their way to the window that faced out the front of the house.

"Exactly how hot is hot?" Bond asked over his shoulder.

Holding his hands up in front of him, Ren shook his head. "I'm her boss so I can't talk."

"I can," Cole offered. "Out of ten she's a twenty. Petite, beautiful face, brunette hair, long, bangs that go like this," he moved his hand in a sweep across one eye. "She's got that innocent doe vibe about her, teamed with the slightly nerdy chick."

"That's fucking hot," Reid mumbled as he got up and went to join them at the window.

"Yeah," Cole nodded. "And even better, she doesn't fucking know it."

By the time he was done, I'd peeled the label off my bottle and was getting ready to throw it at one of their heads – the bottle, not the label - mainly Cole's.

"You hitting that, J?" Reid asked, his attention focused on the road in front of the house.

That's when I got up and was across the room before they knew it. Grabbing Reid by the collar of his t-shirt, I pulled him behind me. "Don't talk about her like that, asshole," I growled, letting him go and pointing at the chairs. "Sit your ass down."

I was about to give the same order to Bond and Canon, when Canon ran to the door, opened it, and was outside before I could stop him. Following behind him was Bond who glared at me before he cleared it. "You lucky bastard!"

"Ah, it appears she's home," Cole informed me unnecessarily from where he was now standing at the window Reid had been looking out of. "And it appears she has company."

Katy

How had this happened? I mean, I knew how it had happened – eye contact – but *how*. This morning I'd been so close to death that the grim reaper had added me to his Christmas card list, now I was walking toward my door with my new dog. Oh, and that dog was a freaking Great Dane.

How. Did. This. Happen?

Dave figured I weighed the same as my dog - which he'd imparted when he'd helped me get Duke in the back of the vehicle - and I wasn't sure he wasn't close to the truth on that one. I'd decided on a little dog and come out with a horse, who I'm pretty certain was walking *me* across the grass in front of my house.

I was so screwed.

"The girls say they're ten minutes out," Tabby told me, walking behind me with Dave who was carrying their daughter. "I told them while we were in there that whatever they got needed to be suitable for a dog the size of Dave, but they didn't believe me until I sent them the photo of him sitting on top of you on the floor while you filled in the form."

That was the other problem, the second I'd sat down Duke had wanted to sit on me. With anyone else he was happy to sit on the floor or just walk around, but not with me. I had a Dane who thought he was a lapdog.

Did I say I was screwed?

Looking down at the front page of the pack the center had given me about him, I looked over the behavioral and mannerism observations section of it, worried that maybe they'd missed something when we'd gone through it all there. None of it was new news, including where it said he had excessive excitement and obsession with playing with a ball. As the poor guy had been neutered, I assumed it was actual game balls and not his own so maybe he was compensating?

A hard tug on his leash almost knocked me over and when I followed where he was staring, I saw two Jarrods watching me.

"Lord have mercy," I whispered, getting an, "Amen," back from Tabby who'd also stopped to take in the view.

Then two more joined them, so I blindly reached out and

grabbed her hand for strength and support. "Are we still drunk?"

"I don't think so, and they're all wearing different t-shirts," she whispered back, pointing out something I hadn't noticed.

"I was stuck on their faces, I didn't even notice they had bodies." But now that she mentioned it, there was Jarrod facial and body hotness times four. "Sweet Jesus."

"Amen."

"Hey, Katy," three of them called out at once and I swear my knees buckled.

"They know your name," Tabby mumbled out of the corner of her mouth, her hand tightening its hold on mine. "Say something."

Instead, I just raised my hand as much as Duke's leash would allow and gave a pitiful wave to them. When I lowered it, I figured that wrapping it around my wrist instead would stop me from ever doing that again, so I did it, anchoring myself to my horse dog.

One of the Jarrods broke away from the group and picked something up off the ground. Then, reaching back as far as he could, he yelled, "Fetch," and launched it through the air.

Tabby and I both turned to watch the item sail through the air past Dave, but before we could look back at them or even ask why they were throwing things (so beautifully), my arm was almost wrenched out of its socket and I was running behind my horse who was chasing after whatever it was. I swear my legs had never moved so fast in their lives, not even on a bike, and I had a thought that I was going to die and this would be the last memory of me alive, when my foot went into a hole and I was being dragged across the grass on my front.

"SERIOUSLY," TABBY howled, USING DAVE'S ARM TO KEEP her standing upright. "He went off like a rocket and she's running behind him…" she broke off and squeezed her knees together. "Little legs," she wheezed.

"Why didn't you just let the lead go?" Maya asked in disbelief.

Looking down at the red mark on my wrist, I decided to hold it up instead of using words to answer the question.

After I'd been dragged across the ground by my wrist, Duke had managed to catch up with the ball, which meant that the four Kline men and Dave had managed to catch up with me. After being carried into my home by who I assumed was Jarrod, I'd limped into the shower, cleaned myself off, and I was now sitting in a pair of short pajama shorts and a t-shirt, having been unable to put my cut off jean shorts and tank back on seeing as how they were covered in mud and grass.

Taking one look at me, I'd been ordered to sit on my couch while one of the Klines ran next door for a first aid kit, and now the grazes that went from my shins to just above my knees were clean and had gook on them, and my ankle that had twisted when I'd stepped in the hole was strapped up and had a bag of peas on it. Oh, and my horse dog was sitting on the floor with the top half of his body between my legs because he wasn't allowed to jump on top of me.

All of this while four male members of the Kline family watched at me. Great! Actually, make that three members of the Kline family, because as soon as I held my wrist up to answer the question just now, one had broken away and walked to the kitchen.

"I'm so sorry, babe," one winced. "I didn't realize he'd react like that when I threw the ball."

Shrugging a shoulder and almost groaning when I remembered it almost being yanked out of its socket, I tried to not look like the loser I felt. "It's cool. He just needs a bit of training, I guess."

An arm appeared over my head with a bag of frozen carrots in it, then placed it on top of my wrist. "That should help."

Tabby was only just able to get oxygen properly into her lungs, and the sound of her deep breathing was the only noise in the room while everyone continued to stare at me. Looking desperately at Ren and Cole and begging them with my eyes to do something, I groaned when they both shrugged looking totally bemused by it all.

Then Cole said something that started it all off again. "So, did you do long distance running or something in school?"

Tabby fell to her knees and even Dave choked as he turned around to face the door, with Ren walking up beside him to do the same thing. Chancing a glance at the four Klines, I saw one of them looking at the ceiling, one of them looking at his boots, one of them who I knew was Jarrod because of the eyes was looking at me worriedly, and the last one looked like he felt like shit because he'd thrown a frigging ball.

Picking up on his new mama's emotions, Duke turned back and rested his chin right on my cookie muffin and stared at me with sad eyes like he was saying sorry.

Scratching behind his ear I sighed. "It's ok, baby."

"I feel, like, really bad, too," the Kline who'd thrown the ball said. "Can I put my head on you to get an ear rub? It'll make me feel so much..." he broke off as Jarrod smacked him around the head. "Yo, you kill off brain cells every time you do that," he snapped, rubbing where he'd been hit. "All I'm saying is that the guilt is eating me up inside, and a snuggle and head rub would make it feel better."

The one who'd been staring at the ceiling shook his head as Jarrod swiped out again. "He'll keep on about it until she gives in."

Glaring at his brother over his shoulder, Jarrod growled, "He's not putting his fucking head in her lap, Bond."

The world stopped spinning at those words, I swear. One second it was spinning like it always did, deciding sun/moon/stars, and the next it had screeched to a halt as we all got our heads around the name he'd said.

"Your name is Bond?" I breathed, staring at him.

Not realizing the effect this information had on the female occupants of the room, he nodded and walked over with his hand out. "Yeah, Bond Kline. Pleased to meet you, Katy."

I shook his hand, managing not to pass out, and then looked at his other brothers. "Please tell me that one of you is called Bourne!"

I was always the one who was so quiet she almost mute, but this information was *huge*.

One by one, the other two brothers came up and introduced themselves to me.

"Afraid not. I'm Canon," the next one said with a huge smile on his face.

"Reid, and I got all the good genes," the one who'd thrown the ball told me as he shook my hand. "Now will you rub behind my ear?"

In the space of twenty-four hours, I'd gotten hammered, thrown up, become a horse dog mama, been dragged behind the horse dog in front of four of the best looking men I'd ever seen in my life, almost died of embarrassment, been saved by them, had first aid applied by Jarrod, and only then can I say my world was blown into little tiny pieces and glued back together again by meeting his brothers and learning their kick ass names.

For someone who liked to live in her own world with books and a lot of gaming thrown in, I wasn't sure how much more I could take.

CHAPTER FOUR

KATY

Last year I'd bought a second hand, three door Mini Cooper convertible. I loved the car and the fact I didn't have any issues reaching the pedals, I could parallel park with no problems, in the summer I could lower the roof and sing my heart out, and it was reliable and had hardly had any mileage on it because the lady who'd owned it hadn't really used it.

Getting Duke in it to drive to work, though, had been problematic. In the end, I'd had to push the passenger seat back so he could sit on the floor in front of it or pop his booty in it and lean forward. The fact he wasn't strapped in had also meant I'd driven to work like an old woman, so it had taken me twice as long to get here. In the end, I'd lowered his window halfway, and had eventually managed to relax a bit as he enjoyed the ride with his head out of it in the wind.

Parking up at the side of the garage, I got out and waved at Cole who was standing talking to Jarrod beside a car.

"Why didn't you just put the roof down?" he yelled as Jarrod walked toward me, then opened the passenger door to let my dog out and made a fuss of him. Lucky big bugger!

"Because I couldn't get the seatbelt around him so I wasn't sure if he'd jump out while I was driving," I shouted back and looked at Jarrod who was still focused on Duke. "Thanks, Jarrod."

Shooting me a smile, he made his way back to Cole as I limped to the entrance with Duke beside me.

"I put a cup of coffee on your desk two minutes ago, Katy, so it'll still be hot, and you need to use the ice packs on your ankle and wrist," he ordered, then turned back and resumed talking to Cole, leaving me staring at his back and wondering if the world had started spinning again after his brothers had stopped it with their names.

OK, SO LINDA TOWNSEND WAS ON A TEAR ABOUT HURST'S car and the damage he'd caused to it – as in, she wanted photos so she could beat him around the head with them. That meant I had to warn Ren and Cole that their grandma was coming in to take those photos so she could carry out the beating.

Carefully making my way down the steps, I stopped at the bottom to give my ankle a second to adjust. It wasn't bad as in screaming my head off bad, but it wasn't great as in skipping and hopping around great. Once it had settled down and the piercing pain was a bit easier I started off walking, once again upset that I couldn't wear heels to work today. I'd been wearing heels and wedges for as long as I could remember because as the shortest of four kids I'd had to so that I didn't get sat on. By that I mean literally sat on because my brothers never once failed to do it and say they hadn't seen me there when I made a noise because they weighed a ton. I was also the shortest in my grade throughout the whole time I was at school and that'd sucked even more. I wasn't even *that* short, it's just that everyone else was so much taller. Unless it was flip flops, wearing flat shoes was a hell no for me.

I kept my eyes on the ground as I walked across the garage to where Hurst's car was, making sure I didn't step on anything or accidentally kick something. Flip flops in a garage wasn't a smart thing to do, in fact it was a health and safety hazard, but I didn't own any other flat shoes so I'd had to wear them. Seeing that they'd moved his car from the bay furthest away, I turned to walk out of the door to the lot and had to bite back the groan when I saw who Ren was talking to – Shane Perkins.

Shane was someone my sister had dated for all of three dates until she'd dumped him because he was a skeezy phlegm wad. Plus, she'd been eighteen and he'd been twenty-six at the time, so my dad hadn't exactly been over the moon about it. I'd had the misfortune to be there when he'd collected her for the first two dates, and on the third date he'd told her he wanted a threesome with her and me. After that, every time I saw him, he found a way to make me feel uncomfortable and dirty so I avoided him as much as I could. Added onto that was the fact that he knew my cousin Effie and even though I loved her, she was a total wreck and hung out with the wrong crowd. Him being part of that crowd wasn't a surprise, it was a disappointment. When Aura had dumped him, I swear I'd almost cried big, fat happy tears because I figured it meant I'd never have to see him again. Sadly, that wasn't the case. He kept popping up in the weirdest places, and I could have sworn I'd seen him walking down a street near my house on the development this morning even though he didn't live there.

Before I could say anything to Ren, Shane gave me a slow dirty look over and grinned when he saw my shoes. "Hey, sexy. If you go running in those, it'll sound like what I'm gonna do to you later."

Thinking about the noise my flip flops made when I walked and imagining it happening at a faster rate, it was obvious what he meant. I only just managed to hold onto the contents of my stomach for Ren's sake and ignored him.

Ren, however, didn't. "You want my fist in your face, Shane?"

"Don't tell me you don't wanna do her," he laughed, throwing his arm in my direction. "Fuck, bet she's tighter than…"

He didn't say anything else because Jarrod had appeared out of nowhere and had him by the neck of his t-shirt. "You've been warned once by Ren and now you'll be warned once by me – shut the fuck up. She doesn't exist for you, you hear me?"

"She wants it, man. Did her sister and it was ok, but Katy? Fuck yeah."

He was lying because Aura hadn't let him do anything with her, not even when he tried to kiss her. But at the thought of him 'doing' me, nothing could have held back the gag that hit me as he said that, not one thing, and it was loud, too, and got all of their eyes on me. Covering my mouth with a hand and choking back the next one, I mumbled, "Sorry."

"Go back to your office for a minute, honey, ok?" Ren called as he looked back at Shane. "We'll be up in a bit."

Not needing to be told twice, I carefully turned around and limped back from whence I came. Five minutes later, Ren walked in and sat down heavily in the chair in front of my desk.

"I fucking hate that guy," he growled. "I'd call him a dick but that's offensive to dicks."

"He really is. My sister Aura only went out with him three times and on the third date he told her he wanted a threesome with me. I think she was trying to figure out how to dump him anyway, so that gave her what she needed to do it, but still."

Shuddering, he pulled himself together. "What can I do you for, Katykins?"

Let me just add at this juncture that I adored my boss. Not in a gross way, but as in he was one of the best guys I'd ever met in my life. His wife was also one of the best women I'd ever met in my life, so spending time with them was never ever a hardship. He'd heard my dad call me that when he'd dropped in to say hi two weeks ago, and since then every now and then he'd call me the nickname.

"Linda says she's coming in to get photos of Hurst's car, and then she's going to beat him around the head with them."

Not looking at all surprised by this, he chuckled, "I expected that."

That may be the case, but there was something else. "She said she's also looking for you and Cole because you didn't tell her what he'd done."

That got a reaction from him. Sitting straight in the chair, he ran his hand through his hair and looked at the door to the office. "When did she say she was coming in?"

"She called ten minutes ago and said she was leaving after she hung up."

Looking at his watch, he jumped up and made his way quickly to the door. "Gotta go for lunch. Let me know if you want anything." And then he was gone.

45

Roughly five minutes later, the door to my office opened and Jarrod was there with Linda behind him. "Hey, Linda's looking for dumb and dumber."

"Lunch," I snickered and then leaned my head to the side to smile at Linda. "Guess you just missed them."

With a twinkle in her eye, she turned back to the stairs and called over her shoulder, "Yeah, but I know where they live."

Flashing me another grin, Jarrod followed behind her and I heard his deep laugh as it carried across the building. The man was porn for all of your senses, and this I could say without hesitation or exaggeration.

First up, if you didn't hear or see him, you smelled him - and by that I meant the guy smelled fucking outstanding. I wasn't sure what cologne he used or if he was just born smelling like that but holy shit. I had mental images of nurses coming into the room while his mother recovered from the arduous task of giving birth to a six foot baby and sniffing him.

Second, his voice – it was deep, rumbly and growly, had a lot of bass to it, and when he spoke it gave me goosebumps. In fact, most women stood staring at him with open mouths when he spoke because of that (and the way he looked, I'm not gonna lie on that). When he laughed it was goosebumps and Skittle nipples all the way so I had to wear padded bras to work. And if that wasn't bad enough, the man could sing. Trying to think of someone he sounded like was impossible because he was literally pitch perfect, but in the deepest way, and again it was filled with bass.

Last but not least came the third Jarrod Kline porn sense hit – visually. Tall, shoulders I swear I could sit on one side of, not overly built in an 'I'm gonna eat a shark' way but in a natural 'I'm just this built' way. He wore thin white t-shirts to work and you could see certain muscle bumps when they tightened across his abdomen. Then there were the moments when he reached up for something and the t-shirt would lift enough to see the sexy hot V muscle thing that only sexy hot men got... again, hallelujah for padded bras. Add onto that his thighs, his butt, and his beautiful face and eyes – he was total porn for your senses.

I lied about there only being three, because there was definitely a fourth sense hit – his personality. Almost shy, quiet, hella loyal, and serious, but then something would happen and a playful side would come out that would melt you down to goo. When he joked around or let out his playful side, it was better than Christmas. I'd heard many a lady, even Linda Townsend, whimper when he did it around them, that's how awesome it was. Any woman who was lucky enough to win the heart of Jarrod Kline would know that he would be her strength, protect her, stay loyal to her and also give her a life of laughter and hot sex (because I refused to believe that in any world he wasn't a king in bed).

All of that porn fodder made working around him a bit hard, but I lived for it. In fact, it was my incentive for getting out of bed every morning, no matter what the weather was. We could be hit by a tornado and if I heard that he was in work, I'd crawl through that twister using my nails in the mud to get in just to see him. At least, that was until he moved in next door to me. Now all I had to do was take the trash out, open my door, go to my car, walk Duke, decide the noise I heard was a yellow jacket so I had motive to run out the front door, and things like that – not that I did that seeing as how I had a horse dog to walk now, but hey.

Seeing the time, I picked up the keys for the BMW that was ready to be collected, and took them down to the man in question with Duke following behind me. As soon as I opened the door I heard him singing something that I didn't recognize, and it pained me to interrupt him, but the guy would be here in two minutes.

Hearing something about a Witcher and tossing coins, I got closer to him and called, "Jarrod?"

His head appeared over the top of the vehicle he was working on and his beautiful eyes focused on me. "You good, Katy?"

Shifting from one foot to the other slightly, I held up the keys. "Mr. Warren is coming in to collect the BMW in a second, so I figured I'd give you his keys. The paperwork's on the passenger seat so you can go through it with him."

Straightening to his full height, he walked around the back of the vehicle and reached his hand out for them. "Cool, I'll deal with it."

Deciding it was all best left at that, I dropped the keys and turned to go back to my safe place in the office, forgetting somehow about the pain in my ankle. On the first twist it felt like someone had shot me in it, so I compensated as subtly as I could by putting most of my weight on my good foot and reaching out to hold onto Duke.

I'd only taken one step like that when I was swept off my feet, screaming as my legs lifted into the air.

"You're good, honey," Jarrod mumbled next to my ear. "I'll carry you up. If you need to come back down, shout out or text me and I can do that, too."

Being carried around by Jarrod? *Freaking sign me up!* Is what I thought, but what I said out loud was, "Oh, you don't have to do that."

I didn't mean one word of it, though. I was all for being carried around by him.

"I'm doing it," he insisted, tightening his arm that was around my back. "Now put your arm around my neck and hold on."

Doing as I was told, I uttered a little something to the big man above. *God, if you can hear me – thank you! I am now a believer. Love, Katarianne Crew.*

As he got to the stairs, I asked what I figured was a pertinent question. "What's a Witcher and why would I toss a coin to it?"

Hearing a chuckle from him, I turned my head and realized just how close our faces were. Seeing Jarrod smile or laugh from a distance was far from shabby, but up close while I was being carried by him? Whole different ball game.

"It's from the Netflix series called *The Witcher*, you haven't seen it?"

"I've played a game called *The Witcher*, but I haven't seen the series."

Taking the steps like he wasn't carrying around an extra one hundred and twenty-eight pounds of human, he explained, "That's what it's based on. I've never played the game but I love the series, and that song's stuck in my head."

"I love the game, I used to play it all the time. The character Geralt of Rivia in it is hot, and there's this part where he gets in a tiny wooden tub and…" I broke off when I saw he was grinning even wider.

"Does that in the TV series, too."

Well shit! "Who plays the character?"

Bending to open the door of the office, he walked in and lowered me gently into my chair. *Holy shit that was a nice move.*

"You know the dude who was *Superman*, Henry Cavill?"

Picking my phone up off the desk, I opened the IMDB app on it and looked it up. When I saw the guy looking just like the character in the game and some of the shots from the series I about died. That's what I was going to blame what I said next on, the shock.

"Holy shit, I dunno about tossing coins, but I would totally make it rain for him," I breathed, skimming through the gallery of photos and making a plan to cancel anything and everything I had to do after work so that I could go home and watch it.

A deep rumble of laughter got my attention off the screen, and then I was wondering if I could record him laughing and watch that instead.

When it left him, he looked down at me with a huge smile on his face and said something that I swear will stick with me until the day I die. "I used to think working with you was the highlight of every day, but now I live next to you, too, so I have you 24/7. I don't think life could get much richer than that."

It's probably just as well that I wasn't standing up because I would most likely have dropped to my knees and begged him to take me home with him. Instead, with chin almost hitting my desk, I watched him turn and walk back out again – his ass in faded denim taunting me.

Looking over at Duke who was watching us both with his head tilted, I whispered, "If I die, find a way to type out exactly what happened so that people understand why I combusted."

Just then my phone beeped with a text from Maya.

Maya: *Phase 1 complete. Time for phase 2 to commence.*

Confused, I replied to it.

Me: *What do you mean phase 1 complete? What are we talking about?*

Maya: *GYMP – Get Yo' Man Plan.*

My memories of our night out were a bit fuzzy, but that was ringing a bell. Reaching into my purse, I pulled out a wad of napkins with writing all over them. Sure enough, there it all was, all though there was absolutely nothing in phase one about getting a dog.

Me: *How does getting a dog fit into phase 1?*

Maya: *You've got his attention. Cole told Ebru that the dog was all over him this morning and he even opened the door of your car for him. Now stop arguing and start planning phase 2.*

Me: *Someone spilled their drink on the napkin and I can't read the writing. What's phase 2?*

Maya: *Bonding over a common interest. I don't know what that is just now, but we'll think of something.*

Me: *We discussed* The Witcher *just now while he carried me back up the stairs to the office. Does that count?*

Maya: *Well shit. Onto phase 3 then. And Henry Cavill is outstanding in* The Witcher.

Me: *Never watched it, but I've played the game and the dude in that would have you sliding off your chair.*

Maya: *Welp, I just became a gamer.*

Me: *Before you dive into the depths of* The Witcher *gaming hotness, what's phase 3?*

Maya: *You got his attention over a common interest, now you need to* *get it onto you. Walk sexy, act intriguing, engage with him, don't go overboard, but be a magnet for his brain.*

Me: *That sounds weird...*

Maya: *No weirder than us finding a game character sexy as hell.*

Me: *Point taken.*

Now what the hell was I meant to do for phase three? I was just me, there was nothing sexy or intriguing about me!

CHAPTER FIVE

JARROD

It felt like something had changed between me and Katy since I'd moved in yesterday. The two people who'd danced around each other and who hardly spoke were now talking to each other, and I was carrying her up the stairs so she didn't hurt her ankle even more. I hadn't seen her much the rest of the day even though I'd been listening out for her in case she needed help down the stairs, and when the time had come to go home, Ren had given her a piggyback down them as he lectured her on how to look after sprains.

When I'd pulled into my driveway after going to the store, I'd noticed the lights were on in her house and I'd been tempted to check on her, but I didn't want to make her feel awkward so I left it and came in to unpack a bit more. Now it was ten o'clock and I was lying out on the couch with the television on, but I wasn't watching it. Instead, I was thinking about what I'd seen in Katy's house and how she organized things.

OCD intrigued me. I understood the need for things to be laid out in a way that you were happy with, but the fact that she was compulsive about things was what got to me the most. I'd looked it up earlier to try and understand it a bit more, and was relieved when I saw she wasn't high on the scale of OCD tendencies, but it also made me feel for people who were. From what I could see, Katy liked to lay things out in terms of size, color and subject which wasn't all that unusual because I did that, too. The difference was, I knew that she got stressed and anxious when shit was moved about at work, so now that I understood it better I needed to try and make sure the guys didn't mess it all around. That was going to start first thing in the morning.

I didn't expect the knock on my door right then, but figuring it was one of my brothers I got up and answered it, shocked when I saw Katy standing in a pair of shorts and a huge hoodie that almost swallowed her up.

"My Netflix has stopped working, and I've only just started the third episode. Help!"

Taking a step back and opening the door wider so she could come in, I chuckled as she limped to the couch with Duke right behind her. "Make yourselves at home."

Shooting me a smile, she dropped onto her right side and curled up on the sofa, pointing at the TV. "*The Witcher*, please."

I'd watched that shit at least ten times but it was no hardship to watch an episode again, so I took the opposite side of the couch, stretched out with my legs running behind hers, and navigated through the menu on my TV until I got to what she wanted.

"Addictive, isn't it?"

The opening scenes of the episode had only just begun, but

already she was engrossed in what was happening. "That song's never going to leave my head."

After that she didn't say another word unless it was a reaction to what was happening. The third episode moved into the forth, and when it hit midnight we were still watching it. Curled up on a couch with little Katy Crew was far from being a hardship for me I realized. In fact, I enjoyed every fucking second.

IT FELT LIKE I COULD HARDLY BREATHE AND MY BODY WAS being held down by a giant as I woke up. I tried moving my legs, but there was a heavy weight across my shins and feet that didn't move when I did. Then, when I tried to move the top of my body whatever was on it held on tight. Blinking in the soft glow coming from the television, I looked down and saw Katy curled up on me, fast asleep. Lifting my head, I lifted my head up to look over her shoulder and saw Duke on my legs - both of which explained a lot.

Wrapping my arms around her, I rolled onto my side as best I could, and positioned her so that she was against the back of the couch with her front pressed against mine. She wiggled a couple of times, wrapped an arm around my back and that was that. Carefully, I managed to lift one leg out from under Duke and used it to change the position of my lower half and get more comfortable.

And I fell straight back to sleep with the scent of Katy's hair in my nose, her head tucked under my chin, her body wrapped around me, and her dog on my leg.

It might sound like it would be uncomfortable, but it was the best night's sleep I'd ever had.

Katy

Drip.

Drip.

Drip.

In my dream there was a huge flower above me, dripping water on my cheek. So, in my dream I shifted forward into the cuddly teddy bear that had eyes like Jarrod's, and nuzzled my face into its chest. The cuddly teddy bear wrapped its arms around me and rubbed its chin on my hair. I loved being in the forest where the teddy bears lived.

"Try dropping it on him now," a voice whispered in the forest. Probably another teddy bear.

"I think we should just dump the whole glass on them and see what happens," one of the other teddy bears replied.

I was too comfortable and happy where I was to open my eyes and see what they were talking about, until my teddy bear growled, "I will pull your underwear so high up your ass, you'll feel it in your eyeballs if you do that."

Frowning, I blinked my eyes open and saw nothing but a wall of t-shirt seeing as how my nose was pressed up against it. Teddy bears wore t-shirts?

Leaning back slightly, I tilted my head back to see what teddy was angry about, and about shit my pants when I saw Jarrod glaring at something over our heads.

"Ah, the princess is awake," a voice chuckled. "Morning, Katy."

Tilting my head further back, I saw three Jarrod's looking down at me with matching smiles on their faces as they dangled a glass of water above us.

"I thought you were nice when I first met you, now I just think your assh…" I was cut off by the mouthful of water that I got when the glass was tipped over us.

Sitting up, I did what I'd do if it was my brothers who'd done it, and reached for the first thing I could get my hands on – which just so happened to be the remote – and started hitting whatever human I could reach with it.

"Jesus, I thought she was nice and quiet when we met her," one of them yelped as he jumped back. "She's like one of those little psycho dogs that…" he broke off on a squeal as Jarrod launched himself over the back of the couch and went after him.

Figuring he'd inflict more pain than I could with a remote, I sat back down. "Huh, that's what you get."

The two Klines that had escaped their brother's wrath stood looking at me in shock. "Seriously, you were so cute when we met you. What happened?"

Looking around me, it started to sink in that I was in Jarrod's home, that I'd fallen asleep with him on the couch, I'd probably drooled on his chest in my sleep, and I'd been woken up by his brothers pouring a glass of water over me. The screen on my watch said it was coming up to five o'clock in the morning and that confused me even more.

"Why are you guys here?"

Focusing in more closely, I looked at the eye colors to figure out who was who and saw it was Bond and Reid that I was talking to.

Looking quickly at each other and then back at me, Bond explained slowly, "Because our brother lives here."

"But why are you here at five in the morning?"

"Because we're on our way to work and wanted to piss him off," Reid replied.

"And because I'm hangry," Bond muttered, rubbing his stomach and looking around him. "Do you think he's killed Canon already so I can go in the kitchen?"

Looking in the same direction, Reid mumbled, "I dunno. Remember when we took the last original glazed donuts that time. It took Mom twenty minutes to stop it."

The mental image of the four of them fighting as kids was admittedly adorable. "Now that you're adults it'll be different. I used to fight with my brothers and sister when we were little all the time, but now we do it in different ways. You're probably good to go in and get something."

"This happened three weeks ago," Reid told me distractedly, moving closer to the doorway to the kitchen. He only just reached it when he jumped and ran back again, hurdling the back of the couch like his brother had done, and sitting down before pulling me into his lap. "I didn't do anything, and you can't hit me because you'll get Katy," he yelled as Jarrod came back into the room.

Seeing that his brother hadn't settled, Bond jumped over and sat beside us, lifting my legs over his. Unfortunately, he forgot about the sore ankle and just dropped that leg, meaning that my foot hit the remote I'd beaten him with. I didn't make a noise, but I did tip my head back and practice my breathing – if it worked for pregnant women, it would work for this. Also unfortunately, Jarrod read this perfectly and realized that his brother had caused me pain, and in the next second he was pulling Bond over the back of the couch.

"Kick your legs and hurt her sore ankle again and I'll tell Mom what you really did with Jenny Baker in your room," he growled.

Bond's eyes widened and he held his arms up in the air. "I give up! White flag waved, brother. Jesus!"

Before anything else could happen or be said, Canon came wandering in from the kitchen with a donut in his hand. "We ready to go or what?"

And that's when chaos truly hit as Jarrod saw what he was doing. "That was my last donut, you little shit!"

Hearing this news, even Bond and Reid joined their brother when they jumped at Canon. It was like every woman's biggest fantasy watching them all roll around the floor. Seeing as how I still had another hour and a half to sleep, though, I committed the five seconds of it I'd seen to memory, lay back down and closed my eyes.

THREE HOURS LATER...

Driving into work with the window open for Duke, I had to admit that the song from *The Witcher* seriously was addictive and played it on repeat singing along with it. As I pulled into my normal parking space at the side of the garage, I pulled out my phone and sent a text to Maya.

Me: *Spent the night at Jarrod's and got to watch him and his brothers rolling around the floor together.*

I was just letting Duke out when my phone beeped in my hand with a response.

Maya: *You lucky bitch]*

Yes, yes I was. Because of this, I limped into work with a huge grin on my face, waved at everyone and then lifted my leg to make my way up the stairs before I was swept off my feet. Obviously I had to hum the song, which turned out to be a good choice because Jarrod tipped his head back and burst out laughing when he heard it.

Best morning ever!

CHAPTER SIX

KATY

T*wo hours later...*

That high flying feeling plummeted only two hours later. One second I was riding the breeze over the happy clouds, the next I was caught in a storm.

I'd just completed two invoices and was about to send an email to one of our suppliers when I heard a voice I knew well in the garage.

"She'll come down if she knows it's me," it said. "All's I have to do is just call for her, so you don't have to waste your energy going up those steps, son."

I heard Jarrod say something back, and then the door opened and he was standing there looking like he was going to burst out laughing.

Sighing, I tipped my head back and looked up at the ceiling. "It's ok, I know you want to. Just go ahead and let it all out."

I was five words away from the end of the last sentence when his deep laughter started. By the time I'd finished it, he was fully engrossed in his laughter endeavors to the point it took him a good while to stop.

"Your grandma's a hoot," he wheezed. "Came in and started talking to Ren and Cole like she saw them every day of their lives." Yup, sounds about right. The old biddy had never met a stranger. "When Ren asked if they were working on her vehicle, she told them her car was fifteen years old and hadn't even had an oil change, it was that reliable. His face..." he broke off, gasping in a breath. "I was in the back room," he nodded at the wall that separated my office from the small stationery supply room next door, "but I heard every word."

I didn't reply, mostly because at that exact moment she called up, "Katarianne Joslyn Crew, get your butt down here and let me see you."

Knowing that if I didn't she'd just keep shouting for me, I got up and moved slowly to the door. I'd only just opened it when Jarrod swept me off my feet and started carrying me toward the stairs. She looked confused when she saw that I wasn't walking, but by the second step her eyes were like saucers in her head. There was very little in life that could shut my grandmother up, but apparently the hotness that was Jarrod carrying her granddaughter down some stairs to her was one of them – good to know.

We were halfway down them when I called out, "Hey, Maude!"

Her hand lifted and grabbed a fistful of the neck of her top. "Have mercy."

Ignoring that, I continued, "Just so you know, I hurt my ankle over the weekend when Duke dragged me behind him when he was chasing a ball and I stepped in a hole. It's only a sprain, so that's good."

Looking behind me she asked, "Are you Duke?"

Jarrod's laughter rocked my world again, but this time it was mainly because the movement made the arms holding me shake. "No, ma'am."

"This is Jarrod. He's my neighbor, but he's also my elevator as you can see."

Her head nodded slowly, and she said, "That looks like some ride. Lord have mercy."

When we were four feet away from her, he gently lowered me to the ground, and then moved forward to shake her hand. "Nice to meet you. I live next door to Katy, too, so I'm sure I'll see you around a lot."

I swear he had to tear his hand out of her grip, and when he did, she reached out like she was going to hold on tight. In case it wasn't clear, my grandmother had no shame.

"I'm thinking my Katarianne left some things out when we last spoke," she muttered, shooting me a glare before she turned back to him. That's when I knew she'd seen his eyes because she gasped and started fanning herself. "Sweet Jesus, heard about it, but never believed in the big man in the sky loving someone enough to make them into all that's you."

Jarrod tipped his head down and awkwardly rubbed the back of his neck while I looked around me wondering if there was a hole I could fall into and stay in this time.

Cole chose that moment to break his silence (which had consisted of him standing with his mouth open while he listened to Maude talk, most probably thanking everything Holy that there was a grandparent worse than Hurst in the world). "He's got three brothers who are identical to him, too."

Hearing this news, her legs wobbled like her knees had given out and she walked over to pick up one of the clipboards with a worksheet attached to it from one of the counters. We all watched this, our heads moving at the same speed as she moved, confused as to why she was doing it. Welp, that lasted all of ten seconds because she started fanning herself in wide sweeps. I would say her hair moved with the big breeze those sweeps caused, but Maude Crew had been a hairdresser back in the day, and her brand of hair do was stuck back in the sixties. This meant that it was big – *oh so fucking big* – and not even a hurricane could make it move with the amount of hairspray she used.

"There's four of them?" she asked Cole. When he nodded, her eyes rolled so she was looking at the ceiling of the building and she muttered, "Thank you, Jesus."

Still feeling generous with information, Cole added, "They've got kick ass names, too. Bond, Canon and Reid."

She stopped fanning herself with the clipboard and looked at Jarrod. "I'm writing to the President to get him to make a medal and honor just for your parents. After that, I'm going to church and I'm telling them about the proof I've just seen that God loves some people more than others, and that's ok because we end up with people who look like you in the world, which is far from being a hardship. After that, I'm making posters and taking out ads across the country with your photo on them so that any non-believers start believing in Him," she paused and thought about something. "Wait, his brothers look just like him?" she asked Cole who was her source of information, apparently. When he nodded, she started fanning again, her hand now moving in jerky sweeps. "In that case, I'm putting all four of them on it because that's even more proof of all of that. Lord have mercy."

Taking pity on Jarrod, who was now rubbing his face with his hands, I moved toward Maude and gave her a hug. "Not that I'm not glad to see you, but what are you doing here?"

"Well, my beautiful grandbaby hasn't called me in over two weeks, so I figured I'd go to her to check on her with my own two eyes," she muttered, her eyes skimming my face as she held me away from her and checked me over. "Mind, I didn't expect the reason for her silence to be down to the perfection that just carried her down the stairs to me."

Both Ren and Cole made choking noises behind me, but Maude wasn't finished. Leaning in, she whispered loudly, "Good choice. Now I get to brag at the ladies' luncheon about the hotness in my beautiful Katarianne's life. Jane Priestly was all about her grandson's photo going viral on the interweb and the girls calling him gorgeous. That boy's nowhere near what my Katy's got."

I was about to tell her that it wasn't like that between us, when Ren told her, "You want him to take you to that luncheon, Mizz Maude, you tell me when and Jarrod can have the time off paid. I'll even throw in his brothers."

Shooting him a glare, I then looked over at Jarrod to make sure he was ok, only to see him biting his lip and looking up at the ceiling. Almost like he felt me looking at him, he lowered his head and I was relieved to see he was trying not to laugh instead of trying not to cry – which was how I felt.

Maude started discussing plans and dates with Ren, but cut off when she saw something behind me. "What the hell is that?"

Turning around, I saw Duke sitting watching us all with his head tilted slightly. "That's my dog Duke."

Bursting out laughing like I'd told the best joke in the world, she gave my shoulder a shove – which for a woman in her early eighties had some force behind it.

"That's what dragged her behind it when he went chasing after a ball," Ren told her and pointed at my ankle.

That stopped her laughing. "You're serious? That's your dog?"

Like he knew we were talking about him, he padded down the stairs and walked up behind me. I thought maybe he'd lie down or even head outside to go potty, but instead he shoved his head between my legs, moved forward so that I was balanced on his shoulders, and then he stood up to full height meaning that my toes were only just skimming the floor.

"He feels bad about her ankle," Cole snickered.

On the outside I made a face like this whole thing was dumb, but on the inside I'm not gonna lie – I was doing cartwheels over the fact I could ride my dog. How cool was that?

And then Maude said something that made my mood plummet. "Uh, not sure if you know, but another reason for me coming to visit was to tell you that Effie took off again, and your Uncle Leo needs help with Elodie. Not sure how that's all gonna work out with your dog, honey."

I felt all the happiness leach out of me at hearing that. My fucking, fucking cousin. She got caught up in bad shit, did bad shit, got knocked up, did more bad shit, had a precious baby girl who was the definition of beauty, did more shit, took off, came back, and it was up to the rest of us to make sure Elodie was kept safe until it suited Effie to come home to her again.

No one knew how messy that part of my family was because we kept it quiet, but anyone who knew of Effie had to see that she was hardly ever around. My other cousin Neo, her brother, was the total opposite, and he adored his niece, but he lived two hours away so he couldn't take her all that much. My uncle was an awesome guy, but he already provided for Elodie financially and he couldn't take her to work with him. This all meant that the rest fell on my family, and because I had such a great bond with the baby, it was no hardship at all to take her. In fact, that's why I had more bedrooms than I needed in my new house – so that she had one of her own to stay in whenever she wanted to.

What was pissing me off was that the last time Effie had come back, she'd gone into rehab and had sworn that it would be the last time. It wasn't the first time she'd said that, but even her counselors had told us they thought she meant it this time. What a big, fat stinking lie.

"Duke will be fine," I muttered, knowing that I was right on that. "What time do you need me to come and get her?"

With a smile that looked like it was forced out of her because Maude was definitely feeling the same way that I was, she told me my uncle would drop Elodie over tonight. That gave me an hour after work to go to the store to get what I needed for her, get home and put together the bed I hadn't built for her yet, make the bed, tidy her room, make sure that everything else was out of the way of tiny curious hands, and do some more organizing. It also gave me only an hour to figure out who was going to look after her while I was at work every day.

As my brother used to say when he was little and didn't want to get into trouble for cussing: Sofa. King. Great. Say it all at the same time and you had that right. As an aside, we still said it around her now so that we didn't get into trouble and made other versions up, too.

Now, with what felt like a suffocating amount of weight on my shoulders, I walked back to the stairs so that I could get into the safety of my office and either panic, breakdown, or get my shit together and create miracles.

I'd only just grabbed onto the handrail when Jarrod picked me up and started up the stairs. This sadly didn't give me the feeling of ecstasy that it normally did because I was so deep in my emotional crash zone that it would take more than that to pull me out of it.

Placing me gently on my desk, he squatted down in front of me. "I need you to explain so that I can help you, Katy."

If it had been anyone other than Jarrod or the two men who were still downstairs quizzing me about it just now at work, I'd have said it was all great and there were no problems, but the three men I worked with most of the time had something different about them. They genuinely cared, they were genuinely good guys, and I trusted them.

So, I started at the beginning. "That was my grandma Maude. She didn't want to be called grandma because she said that was her mother's title, and no way in hell could she ever live up to that level of greatness. There were other variations available, obviously, but she hated them all including the Italian versions seeing as how she's of Italian descent. Her real name is Marianne, but her family all called her by her nickname, which is Maude. My Uncle Leo is so fricking awesome it hurts and his wife died of cancer two years ago. He has a son, Neo, who's three years older than me and one of the best men I know. My Uncle Leo is also the reason my parents and Maude moved here four years ago, to be closer to him. Then there's his daughter Effie who even before her mom died was an off the rails delinquent. She was born with a brain set on mayhem, causing people hell, grand theft auto, being known to the police, and testing the boundaries of her father's sanity."

Drawing as much oxygen in as I could, I forged on. "Thirteen months ago, Effie gave birth to Elodie. We didn't know she was pregnant and, from the way she tells it, *she* didn't know she was pregnant. She just felt some cramping and apparently out the baby came – even though she had enough time and concern to get to hospital, so at least she was born in a sterile place and not somewhere littered with needles and heroine spoons."

"Jesus," Jarrod growled, looking almost sick at the thought.

Newsflash, that shit happened, and those poor precious babies suffered for it.

"Yeah. The hospital rang Leo and told him he had a granddaughter and that her mom had disappeared, so he went and got her. Two months later Effie came back claiming that she wanted to be a mom, and that things were different this time. For the last year, that's happened eight times."

Picking me up, Jarrod carried me across the room to one of the chairs and sat down with me on his lap. "Where does she go when she disappears?"

Shrugging, I kept my focus on the windows where I could see the tops of some trees moving slightly with the breeze. "No one knows because she never calls while she's away, but it most definitely involves drugs."

"Who has custody of Elodie?"

"That was the one thing Effie did for her daughter that was good – she awarded custody to her dad. But that means that Leo needs a break, he can't always find someone to look after her when he's busy at work, and it also means he's got dreams of his retirement and he's looking after a baby. Neo helps out as much as he can, but his job has him living two hours away so it makes it difficult."

"So your family helps out?"

All the stiffness I'd had that had been holding my body upright and like I was carved from stone left me. "Yeah. That little girl is the world that my family lives for, Jarrod. She's the most beautiful baby ever made, and I'm not just saying that because she's related to me. The first time I held her, she opened her eyes, and I felt like someone had inflated my heart. She can be teething or feeling like shit, but the second someone holds her she settles and uses the love to erase her pain. Looking after her isn't a hardship, every second sticks with me, but what cuts me is that her own mother can't see what she's created and use the pure innocent beauty of Elodie Crew as an incentive to get clean and stick around. I just don't understand it."

His arms tightened for a second, and then he bent his neck so that his chin was on my shoulder, meaning his mouth was roughly an inch away from my ear. "Sometimes, Katy, people are so caught up in whatever their brains are telling them to do that they miss the beauty around them. I'm not that informed on drug addiction and the reasons why it happens, but it's a disease that's so hard to kick. Lots of people get a hold of it once they have a baby, some don't. The thing is, that little girl is not going without love, and she's going to grow up knowing that she has a lot of people around her who care, which will make her feel safe and precious. She'll also know that she has an aunt who thinks she hung the moon, because I don't doubt for one fucking' second that you're ever going to think or act otherwise. So, now what we do is figure out how to make this work for the time that you've got Elodie, which leads me to ask, what do you need help with, honey?"

Everything.

"I need to get to the store to stock up for her, I need to build the bed I bought her for her room in my house, I need to make sure her toys are put away and her books are next to her bed so I can read them to her. I also need to make sure there's nothing around that'll hurt her, figure out how I'm going to work with a baby every day..." I trailed off and thought about something else. "She's also at the age where she can cogitate now, Jarrod. That means that she knows who her mom is and more than likely understands when she disappears. How do I protect her from the pain that's causing her?"

His reply might have sounded dismissive if he hadn't said it with the emotion that he used. It was an emotion that said he understood, he hurt for a little girl he'd never met, and that he was determined to make sure she was ok. "I don't know the answer to the last bit, baby, but I do know how to get the first done. Do you trust me?"

I fucking hated that question when people asked me it. My ex in high school had asked me that once when I'd found out he'd cheated on me with one of the cheerleaders. On that occasion I'd replied with a no immediately. With Jarrod, I didn't know him enough to fully trust him because having a heavy crush on someone didn't mean you knew all of them, so I guess I trusted *some* of him, so that's what I went with.

"From what I know about you, yes, but there's a lot of you that I don't know."

His lips twitched at my answer, and he didn't even look slightly offended by it. "Ok, in that case let me reword it. Do you trust me to help you get this done and that I will get it done by the time Elodie arrives tonight?"

Now that was easier. "Absolutely."

And then he blew my mind far away from my problems by giving me a peck on the tip of my nose, before he got up and started ordering me around as he placed me on the chair behind my desk. "First up, shut down your computer, get your shit and I'll carry you to your car. Do you have spare keys to your house?"

"Not on me," I choked out.

"Right, give me your keys and I'll make sure I'm at the house when you're done. I'll call Bond to get him to help you out at the store so that you're not carrying a lot of shit and hurting your ankle more," he told me, holding his hand out.

And what was a girl to do when a six foot seven hottie was asking for the keys to her house? Well, if she had any sense, she'd drop to her knees and thank the man Maude had been thanking only thirty minutes ago, unless she was crazy and said no to him. I don't think there was one woman alive who'd say no, though, but it was possible.

Because I couldn't fall to my knees, I opened the drawer and got my keys out, dropping them in his hand. I had a second to take in the fact his hands were huge and as beautiful as the rest of him before he clenched his fist around them and started walking to the door.

"I'll be back to take you to your car in two minutes, Katy," he told me over his shoulder, before he walked out and started organizing whatever he had planned.

I went into automatic mode as I saved and shut everything down. It was only when I was looking at the black screen of the computer and Duke let out a whine next to me that I whispered, "What the hell just happened?"

Jarrod

There was one thing to be said about Piersville, and that was when you made the call for help everyone answered. Mine and Katy's houses weren't small, but they also weren't huge, so having a majority of the Townsend family as well as Tabby, Jose, Rose and their men dropping in periodically to help out… her home was almost busting at the seams.

That said, Elodie's bed was done and the furniture in her room had been laid out in a way that Maya thought was perfect for her. Unfortunately, stuff that Katy might need for the baby was scattered everywhere, and any semblance of order and organization that Katy had was now shot to shit.

Picking up some of the packaging that the bed frame had been in, I went downstairs to take it outside and stopped when I saw Luke Montgomery's twins moving things around in one of the shelving units in the living room. It took a lot not to tell them to stop so that Katy wouldn't have what I'd learned was like a miniature anxiety attack because the careful order that made sense to her had been screwed up, and the reason I didn't do it was because babies were a big weakness for me. Every time I heard Jose and Ellis's daughter Olivia cry it broke my heart and holding her was the highlight of the day it happened on, so doing something like telling off two toddlers, that was a hard limit for me.

The longer I stood watching them, though, the more I realized they weren't just touching things or messing around with them. Far from it. In fact, they'd recognized the way Katy had put them in order and were helping her out.

I was so caught up in that realization that I didn't notice Hurst standing beside me eating a donut and whispered, "Fuck me."

Tossing it onto the table, Hurst groaned, "I didn't think anything could put me off food, but the mental image of me fucking you did it."

Walking up beside her husband, Linda snapped, "Why do you always have to sink so low, Hurst? Seriously, anyone else would ask what the issue was, but not you."

Thankfully, there was a knock at the door that interrupted them before the argument could escalate further, although when I saw who it was I did an internal groan. Katy's grandmother was a trip, and if her comments hadn't been directed at me, I'd have been laughing my ass off at the person they were intended for. Sadly, they had been directed at me, and here she was again.

Shaking it off, I shot her a grin. "Hey, Maude. We're almost done getting things together for Elodie."

Looking around the room, her eyes wide as all the men stopped and waved at her at the same time, she mumbled, "I'm seeing that."

Before anyone could introduce themselves to her, my brothers arrived carrying bags of shit.

"Yo, we've got pink fluffy crap, girly stuff, a teddy bear that was giving sad eyes, lacy underwear for Katy, edible body glitter, and..." Bond broke off when he saw everyone watching him, including two toddlers who were smarter than people knew. "Damn, how come every time we come to Katy's it's full of people. It's like party central."

Maude spun around to look at the newcomers and her hand shot up to the neckline of her t-shirt like it had earlier. "Sweet Jesus."

Giving her one of his signature grins, Canon winked. "Name's Canon Kline. I'm Jarrod's favorite brother."

Thus started the fanning. "Sweet Lord."

Not to be outdone, Reid reached around and held his hand out. "Reid Kline, Jarrod's best looking brother."

Slowly Maude reached her own hand out and about fainted when he kissed the top of it. Total Reid.

With a cocky grin tipping up one side of his mouth, Bond leaned down and gave her a peck on the cheek. "Name's Bond."

Maude tipped slightly when he straightened back up again and breathed, "Holy Mary in a manger."

Figuring that I'd help her out before she started going through every name in the bible, I called, "That's Katy's grandma, Maude. Maude, those are my brothers, and if you'd like I can introduce you to all the other people helping out?"

Twisting to look back at me and taking in the guys standing behind me, Maude started fanning herself harder than before. "Katy's got three bedrooms, I'm thinking I feel the need to move in. I'm at that age, you know, the one where I need assistance."

Holding his arm out to her, Bond said, "Well let me escort you into your new home, beautiful lady."

I swear I saw her shudder slightly as she reached out to take it. "Jesus take the wheel and drive me to heaven."

"Don't go leaving us too soon now, beautiful Maude, you hear?" Bond frowned down at her playfully, making a blush burn on her cheeks.

"Oh, they're good," Linda muttered, watching it all. "I mean, they're good to look at, but when it comes to charming the granny panties off an old woman, they're *really* good."

"That working on your granny panties, too?" Hurst asked, chuckling at the look on his wife's face.

Shooting him a glare, she snapped, "I don't wear granny panties, Townsend, something you know well."

Ok, now I wanted Jesus to take the wheel and drive me away from that information. We could crash and burn and I'd be ok with that.

The sound of car doors closing came from outside the house and I looked around wondering who else it could possibly be. If anyone else turned up, the walls between our homes would probably collapse. Thankfully, this time it was Katy who'd arrived home, and who was carrying in bags of groceries with her eyes looking at the floor. Crossing the room, I was almost at her when she lifted her head and froze in place when she saw everyone.

Reaching down, I took some bags from her. "We got it all done, but people have brought some shit over they thought you might need for Elodie. I'm not sure where you want it to go, but if you tell us, we'll get on that now."

"Holy shit," she whispered, looking around. I wasn't sure if it was anxiety because people were in her place and moving her stuff, or if it was shock that there were so many of us there.

"I made some calls and asked for help, but Ren and Cole had also made some calls and asked for help..." I trailed off, trying to explain it all.

"Mom sent us shopping to get girl shit," Canon announced as he walked past us to go outside again. "It's on the side in the kitchen. I'll just go get the rest of your bags out the car."

With that he walked out, leaving Katy watching him with her mouth open. "Holy shit."

"Katarianne," Maude called, getting her focus back on the room. "Neo's the one bringing Elodie over, so I said I'd be here to get kisses from my son and grandbaby. I was going to offer to help, but the hotties seem to have done that anyway, so now I'm free to just sit and watch," she announced, sitting down on the couch next to where Linda was now sitting. "Oh, it's such a good day."

"Your grandmother says she's moving in," Bond told Katy as he carried out one of the boxes from upstairs. "Gotta say, at this rate I'll be moving in, too."

That brought her out of whatever haze she was in. "You're not moving in, Maude," she snapped, leaning around to see behind me. "Every time you come to stay, I wake up with rollers in my hair that you've already sprayed with that cement mix you call hairspray. Last time it took five shampoos to get it out."

Patting the side of her bouffant nonchalantly, Maude shrugged, "It's a good look, I can't help it if you want boring flat hair because you have no taste."

Straightening back up again, Katy whispered, "She teased my hair so much that I had to sit with conditioner on it for an hour just to get a brush through it. It was out to here." She held her hands about a foot away from her head.

Judging by the height that the lady had going on with her own hair, I didn't doubt that there was no exaggeration on this at all.

Bond and Canon came back in, both of them loaded down with bags, and the ladies all appeared from where they'd been upstairs and started working on sorting it out in the kitchen.

Watching it all, Katy kept her voice low. "How many people are in my house?"

"I don't know the answer to that," I muttered back. "It's a lot, though."

Hearing this, she drew in a shaky breath and then looked around the place again, stopping when she saw the twins still working on their creation. It looked like she was about to freak out, but then her head tipped to the side. "Holy shit, I couldn't figure out why that was bugging me so much. I had them in order of color and author in the individual sections, but something was really wrong with it. It's the heights of the books I should have gone with, not the author."

See, those guys *had* figured it out. Watching them, they stood back and nodded at each other and then turned and moved toward the stairs. My hope was that they were headed to the bedroom we'd just set up to work on the shit waiting to be put away.

"Knock, knock," a deep voice called from the doorway, and I saw a tall guy holding a little girl with dark brown ringlets. "Someone's come for a sleepover with her Katy."

Hearing the name, the girl looked up from where she'd been playing with the collar of the man's shirt and searched the room, stopping on 'her Katy'. The smile that took over her face would have melted even an iron heart, and I didn't have one of those, so I swear mine took flight. She was gorgeous!

"'Lodie," Katy cooed, walking up to her and catching her just as the little girl launched herself out of who I presumed was her uncle's arms. Bringing her close to her chest and leaning her face into the baby's neck, she sighed, "There's my precious 'Lodie."

A big hand clamped down on my shoulder and Reid muttered, "Shit, man, I'm gonna cry. I don't have ovaries, but even mine are screaming out right now."

My brother was a goof, but he wasn't wrong.

Five hours later...

We'd left Katy and Elodie to do their thing two hours ago after ordering in enough pizza to feed Nairobi, and now I was looking at the work I did outside of the garage and wondering if Katy knew about it. It was unlikely seeing as how I'd only told Tabby and Jose about it, but never say never.

"So, we're going to go through chapters five to nine tonight,"

Karen, the female narrator for the book told me. "We're slightly behind so we have to catch up. You good with that?"

This was the first time I'd ever done a narration with someone and so far it had been ok, but now we were getting into the sex scenes of this book and I'd been dreading it. When Tabby had made the joke about me being an erotic book narrator, I'd laughed it off, but over a matter of days the idea had stuck and I'd looked into it. In the space of eighteen months, I'd narrated seven books, with this being my eighth, and I enjoyed it. I also liked the fact that few people knew I was doing it, and for once I didn't have eyes watching me.

This was one of my biggest hang-ups, and I knew it was something that my brothers sometimes had issues with, too. For as far back as I could remember, I had eyes on me. I was the longest baby the hospital had ever had when I was born and it had made the newspapers. I was the tallest kid in my class throughout school. I had a deep voice and liked to sing – something I did without realizing it – so again, attention. I had eyes that drew attention, too. And I hated it. I wasn't comfortable with it at all and never had been. When all the guys in my class were planning which girls they were going to ask out, I was thinking of ways to turn dates down. I just didn't see what they saw and when things were pointed out about my appearance or singing to me, it made me feel awkward and unsure.

That didn't mean I'd lived like a monk, hell no. I'd had girlfriends, some great - some not so great, but they were all females who were clever, quiet, and who didn't go out looking for attention. All I wanted was peace.

So having this secret, I could do something for me that no one knew about.

"Ok," I agreed, pulling up the book in front of me.

I currently had my computer on with the recording equipment and software ready to go, my iPad, which was what had the book on it, and my phone that was on speakerphone with Karen.

"We're going to switch to the dual recording function, so you'll be able to hear me while I read, but you can hang your phone up," she said, and I heard the sound of rustling after it.

Agreeing and going into the recording file, I hung up and got ready to go.

This should be easy enough. I was the main voice for this chapter and she would read the female parts, then she was the main voice for the next chapter and I'd read the male parts. How hard could it be?

Katy

Elodie was finally asleep in her bed in her kick-ass room, so I went about getting ready in my own room. It had been a freaking long day, and I was now running on fumes, so the only thing I wanted was my comfy bed that felt like I was sleeping on a cloud.

Padding across the rug, I'd just sat down when I heard the deep tones of Jarrod through the wall. That was unusual because I was certain he'd said his study was the room I shared a wall with, and it sounded like he was talking to someone.

Leaning closer and trying not to breathe so I could hear it, I listened in. And this is where the saying curiosity killed the cat most likely came from – but it was curiosity killed the Katy heart.

I shouldn't have listened in, or I should have put the last episode of *The Witcher* on seeing as how I'd fallen asleep during it when I'd watched it at Jarrod's.

"You're going to take five from my hand, baby," his deep voice said. "Once you've had your punishment, I'm going to eat you and fuck you."

"I don't think I earned five," a female voice argued.

"Keep going and I'll double it. Now take your punishment and you'll get your rewards."

"Yes, Master."

What. The. Fuck.

There was a pause and then he said, "I love my baby's pussy. It's so tight, hot, wet... fucking sweet. Never had pussy like it, never."

There was another pause, and then, "Harder, Master. Baby wants it hard."

Ever felt like someone had stuck a spoon in your chest, one of those soup ladle ones, and just ripped your heart out? That's what I felt at that moment. Not only was the crush I'd had on Jarrod shattered, but he was fucking someone in the room next to mine. Did he know I could hear it? Was he doing it to make a point?

Curling up on my side, I put my pillow over my head and struggled to breathe through the tears that were coming. They were at that point where it felt like you had a tidal wave coming up from your chest, so much so that your sinuses were clogged, you couldn't swallow around it, but you hadn't even shed a tear yet.

I'd gone from flying high to crashing to the ground in twenty-four hours, as had my hopes and dreams that were based on Jarrod Kline.

CHAPTER SEVEN

Jarrod

I t was fair to say I disliked dual narration books. It might be different if we read the scenes independently and meshed them together, but at the same time? Total dislike.

Closing my front door behind me, I stepped over the short fence that separated my garden from Katy's and walked to her front door. I'd said I'd watch Elodie while she showered until they established a routine, so that's what I was doing now.

Knocking on the door, I waited, then knocked again. Finally, it opened, and I saw Katy in a hoodie and shorts with Elodie waving at me on her hip.

"Morning, ladies," I held my hands out to the baby and waited to see what she'd do. After a short assessment, she held her own out to me, so I leaned in and picked her up. "Have you had breakfast, Miss Elodie?"

She gave back some giggles and head nods as Katy moved

back from the door - further than she normally would - to let me in.

"What about Miss Katy, have you had your breakfast?"

Closing the door, she kept her head down and started moving toward the stairs. "I'll just shower."

Looking back at the baby who was watching her aunt, I moved to the kitchen and saw the remnants of toast on the tray attached to her highchair. "Did you keep your aunt up all night, young lady? Poor Aunt Katy's tired."

With a wiggle of her body that indicated that she wanted to be let free to roam, I popped her booty on the ground and got myself a cup of coffee from the machine while I watched her. She seemed small for age, but then from the two Crew females that I'd met, height wasn't really something that they had, so maybe it was normal. Elodie shared the same hair color as her aunt, but instead of the thick, straight sheets that Katy had, Elodie had what looked like hundreds of tiny curls on hers. She also had dark brown eyes, unlike her aunt's blue ones.

What stood out was that the girl was *smart*. She went straight to a box that had toys in it, picked out a shape sorting one and was finished in about thirty seconds. Then she picked out one that had a maze of wires on it with beads and had them around the maze faster than I could do it. After that, she picked up a book and sat with it like she was actually reading it.

Moving closer to her, I sat on the couch and put my cup on the coffee table. "Hey, Elodie girl, are you a genius?"

Swear to god that little baby looked at me, grinned, shrugged in a 'what can I say' way, and then went back to it.

I was the definition of confused with how things were between me and Katy. Ever since she'd gotten Elodie, she'd been aloof and distant. I'd wondered initially if she was adjusting or doing it for her niece's sake, but when she'd acted like normal with everyone aside from me and even my brothers, I'd realized it was more than that. She wasn't rude or anything, just reserved and quiet with us all, and even they were confused by it.

Sighing as I pulled my truck into my drive, I was relieved that today was over. The author of the book I was working on had asked for it to be completed sooner, so I'd been working on it until the middle of the night for the last three nights. I was drained.

Looking over at Katy's house, I saw four vehicles that I didn't recognize, and one that I did – Canon's. My brothers weren't quitters, and the more Katy withdrew, the more they'd push for her to give in, which was what they were doing now. Hopefully, if they figured it out, they could help me fix whatever the problem was between us.

Climbing out, I thought about going over, but I was too tired. All I wanted to do was drag my ass to my couch, lie out on it, put something on television that didn't require any brain function and pass out.

Katy

"So, what did he do?" Bond asked, scooping some salsa up with a chip. "Was it bad? Do you want us to hurt him, 'cos we'll do it for you, Katy. You just say the word."

I'd come home to find my brothers, my sister, my parents and the Kline brothers at my house with dinner ready and waiting, instead of the peace I was looking for. I hadn't slept properly for the last three nights, listening to Jarrod with his woman or even women for all I knew.

Seeing how tired I was, Mom had taken Elodie for her bath while Dad and Aura cleaned up the kitchen and my brothers did 'man shit' in the backyard, leaving me with Things One to Three.

"Who are we talking about?" I asked, curling up in a little ball in the best part of my sectional – the middle bit where it curved round.

Sitting down heavily beside me, Canon threw his arm around my shoulders. "Our brother. It's obvious he's done something, so tell us, we'll hurt him and make him cry, and then it'll all be good again."

My ability to find comfort was now gone, so I twisted until I was sitting normally on the cushions. "He didn't do anything."

"Sure he did," Reid argued, sitting on the coffee table in front of me and stretching his long legs out either side of mine. "Did he forget your birthday?"

"No, asshole, because if he did that then we forgot her birthday, and we wouldn't do that," Canon snapped, and then turned around to look at me in a panic. "Shit, we didn't forget your birthday, did we?"

Chuckling at how smoothly they interacted with each other, I shook my head. "No, it's on May fourth."

There was a moment's silence while they mulled that over, but it was Bond who figured it out. "That's freaking awesome," he chuckled, double dipping his chip in the salsa. *Ew!* "May the fourth be with you."

There was always one. In fact, there was normally more than one.

Once they'd laughed it out, Canon gave me a quick squeeze and then positioned himself so he was now facing me head on. "Tell us what he did."

"It wasn't what he did," I tried to explain, "and it's going to sound really lame."

"Katy, it's not going to be lame," Bond argued. "Jarrod likes you and we think you'd be great for him. We also like you and know he'd treat you like the princess you are. So if we can sort this shit out and get him to fix his fuck up that's bothering you, then how's that lame?"

I wasn't sure what to say, and then it became a case of being physically unable to speak let alone breathe when a voice yelled, "Incoming!" And the full weight of my asshole brother landed on me as he jumped over the back of the couch.

Wiggling around like he was trying to get comfortable, he looked at the three Klines who were staring at him like he was a freak show. "What are we talking about?"

Wheezing, I dug my nails into Major's shoulder to try to get him to move, but he didn't even flinch.

"Man, you're crushing your sister," one of the Klines snapped, and I saw Bond's face squeeze between the cushion and Major's back. "You ok, honey?"

"My sister? Where is she?" Major asked as innocently as he could, considering he was squeezing the life out of me and he knew it. "She needs to get a new couch, this one's all lumpy."

There was only one thing that would get him moving, and that was a small area of hair that always grew longer than the rest, which was seriously sensitive. We didn't know why it grew like that or why it made him freak out when it was pulled, but it had been the last resort for the rest of us since we'd made the discovery when we were little. Reaching up, I caught hold and yanked as hard as I could, making sure I did it better than I'd ever done before.

Letting out a shriek, Major jumped off me, but I wasn't letting that hair go. This was now war.

"Get her off, get her off!"

"Say sorry," I growled, yanking even harder on it. "And that you'll only do that to Aura from this second on."

"I'm sorry and I'll only do that to Aura," he whined, still trying to get free. "Holy shit, let go, you Satanic turtle."

"I hate those things," Aura screeched from the top of the stairs.

"Shit, wrong sister," Major muttered, finally getting a grip on the hand I had holding the lock of hair. "Ok, I promise never to do it again, now *let go*."

I released the hair and sat back with my arms crossed on my chest, glaring at the big shit brain who was rubbing the area and glaring right back.

"I thought we were bad," Bond snickered, looking between us.

"You haven't seen it when Major and Ammon both sit on me at the same time," I snapped, looking around to make sure the other one wasn't sneaking up on me, and spying him sitting on the couch beside Canon.

That sobered the Kline men up. "Man, your sister is one of the tiniest things I've ever seen," Reid growled, and I struggled not to take offense at that or roll my eyes. I really wasn't *that* little. "And y'all are at least a foot taller and a hundred pounds heavier than her."

"We didn't want sisters," Ammon sniffed, looking down at his nails. He was also talking out his ass because he adored the two he'd been given and we knew it. "We wanted a dog."

Bond's head snapped around to look at me. "Whatever Jarrod did can't be anywhere near the level of assholery coming off these two. Now, let us fix it before I make it unfixable when I drown one of them in the bathroom behind me. You've got five seconds…"

"Wait, who upset you?" Major asked, looking pissed.

"Five…"

Ignoring my brother and trying to stop Bond counting, I looked at Canon. "Help me."

"No way, little one. I'm with my brother on this."

"Four…"

"It really isn't that bad," I tried, watching Reid get up from the table and look at Major like he was going to jump on him.

"Three…"

"Why don't we have a cup of tea or coffee, something nice like that and discuss it like adults?"

"Two…"

Standing up, I threw my hands in the air. "Ok, all right. You say he likes me," I pointed at Bond, "but I can't be with someone who brings women home every night and does what he's doing to them. I mean, it's not what he's doing to them that's the problem – if I'm honest. It's the fact that I can hear it through my wall, and that just isn't nice, ya know? And I don't know if it's the same woman, a different woman, or hell if he has a whole line of them down the hallway every night that he goes through like one of those restaurants with the sushi on the conveyor belt."

When I ran out of steam and pushed my bangs agitatedly off my forehead, I looked between Jarrod's brothers, watching them blink while they processed this. *Yeah, think how I feel hearing it, boys.*

Looking at his brother, Canon asked, "He's doing sex things with women at night, you say?"

"Yeah."

"Every night?" he clarified.

"Yeah. Last night was the longest one, and he didn't finish 'til four."

His eyes widened at this. "And you're sure it's Jarrod?"

"Yes."

"Ah, but are you sure it's Jarrod's wall and not your other neighbor's?" Reid asked, looking like he'd solved the puzzle.

"Considering it's only our two houses that are joined together – yes."

Frowning over at Canon, Bond asked, "Did we ever have the sex talk with Jarrod to explain what it was?"

None of them had an answer for this and just looked at each other expectantly.

"And you're sure you heard a woman's voice in there with him? While he was doing the sex stuff?" Reid asked, sounding like I was talking about something impossible.

"Yes!"

This time when they looked at each other, there was a glint in their eyes.

"Shotgun," Bond yelled, jumping up from his seat and running toward my door with the other two behind him. The only issue was when they all tried to run through the doorway at the same time and it ended up with them pushing, shoving, and slapping each other.

Watching all of this from his space beside me now, Ammon mused, "I'm glad we're not as weird as they are." And then followed it up by shifting so that most of his body was lying across my lap. "Scratch my back, sissy."

I wasn't sure my uncle had made the right call entrusting me with Elodie, even if it was on and off until he sorted out a long-term plan. With the way it was going, she was going to end up scarred for life.

Jarrod

I was just falling asleep when it sounded like fifty hands were hammering on my front door at the same time. I'd thought moving here would get me away from that shit and give me a peaceful life, but I was wrong.

Getting up, I crossed over to the front door and had only just unlocked it when it burst open and my three cretin siblings fell through it.

Catching himself before he landed, Canon shot up and pointed a finger in my face. "You've got the best one I've ever met in my life, and you're doing that shit to her? What the hell is wrong with you?"

Not going for words, Reid and Bond jumped on me and we went down on the floor in a tangle of long limbs. While Bond was trying to find a spot on my abdomen to hit, Reid was wrapping himself around me like a sloth, trying to get a chokehold on me.

It went without saying that we'd fought a lot – *a lot*, a lot – over the years. Some of it was understandable, some of it was fueled by hormones, some of it was just because we needed to blow off steam, but not once had I been left wondering what the hell was going on.

"She can hear all of it through the walls, you stupid son of a bitch," Bond growled, finally landing a hit beside my belly button but not with enough force to wind me.

"You just insulted Mom," I wheezed, reaching over my head to find Reid's and pulling it. "And I've got no fucking idea why."

Using his foot to find purchase on the floor, Bond tipped me so that I was now on my back on top of Reid and jumped on top of me. Reid started panicking at the extra four hundred pounds pushing down on his chest and tried waving at Bond to let him up. Not that it made a difference – he was a man on a mission.

"Katy," Bond snapped, punching me in the ribs and inadvertently bouncing at the same time, which made Reid gasp. "You're bringing bitches back to do sex shit with them, and she hears all of it. Way she said it, it could be a number of bitches all lined up waiting."

"I've not had anyone back here," I yelled, jerking my torso to get him off and getting a huge amount of satisfaction when Reid groaned as we landed on him. *There you go, fucker!*

Throughout all of it, Canon had been pacing around us, but at this he swung back. "She heard it, Jarrod. Fucking heard all of it, so don't lie."

"I'm not lying!"

"What, are you renting out rooms by the hour then?" Bond sneered and then sat up and looked around the place. "I mean, I'm not sure how much you'd get for that, but it doesn't seem like a bad way to make some extra income."

Using this distraction, I shoved on his chest as hard as I could, and grinned when I heard the thud and groan that came out of him when he hit the ground. As a final fuck you to Reid, I went to stand up, and then dropped straight back down on him.

"Fucker," he rasped, rolling to the side and holding his stomach when I got to my knees beside him.

Standing up, I turned to Canon now. "I haven't had a woman back here, man, not one. I'm not sure what she's heard…" and then it hit me. "Oh, fuck!"

Still in pain, Reid rolled to face me and only just managed to ask, "Is it porn?"

How to answer that. Technically, no it wasn't, but on another technicality it was word porn, so if I said no was that a lie?

"Dude, if you're doing porn in your home, that counts as having a woman back," Bond said as he got to his feet beside me. "Either way, Katy deserves better than that."

Walking over to the couch, I flopped down on it and covered my face with my hands. This was such a monumental fuck up. I didn't want to explain it to these three, but I was going to have to say something.

Unfortunately, the only thing I could come up with was, "It's not what you think, or what she apparently thinks."

Jesus, a line of women in the hallway? What the fuck?

"Well, what is it? If you explain it to us we can help you translate it into words that'll work with a woman like Katy," Reid suggested as he crawled across the floor to one of the recliners. I wanted to say he was being dramatic, but I'd been in his predicament many times and that shit took a while to get over. He'd be feeling it for days.

Groaning at the prospect of telling them what I was doing on the side and thus ending the dream of having something that was just mine, I tried to stall. "She really thinks I've got women here every night? In the room next to hers?"

"Yup," Bond said seriously as he joined me on the couch.

"But that's my study."

They all looked at each other, but it was Bond and Reid who had the 'what the hell does that matter' looks on their faces.

Not losing focus, Canon leaned forward with his elbows on his knees. "Well?"

In for a penny... "I narrate books and this week I had a dual narration job, which means that I was reading my parts while a woman called Karen was reading hers. That's what Katy must have heard."

Sitting back, he crossed his arms and glared at me. "Well, if you're not going to tell the truth then your fucked. I like Katy, I'll take her."

"I'll fight you for her," Reid snapped, bracing for Canon to say the word go.

"We all know she's into me," Bond shrugged. "And she gave me her number earlier."

And this was why I wanted peace and quiet. This was why I wanted something that was just mine. I'd spent the last twenty-seven years with this shit, and as much as I loved my brothers, I just wanted less of the crap that came with it.

Standing up, Canon started walking to the door. "Y'all are such amateurs. You don't text a woman like Katy, you court her. Courting means treating her like a princess, making her feel appreciated, giving her the time and attention she deserves – all of which none of you can do."

As soon as he got the last word out, he swung open the door and I realized I had to move now. For once I let my age drop so that I was at the same level of maturity as them, and I hurdled the recliner that Reid was getting out of and pushed Canon out of the way. Once I was outside, I did the same with the little fence and got to Katy's door.

Not knowing what to say to explain it didn't matter at all, what mattered was getting Katy. So I knocked on her door, doing my best not to sound like a maniac. Fortunately, she was the one who opened it with Elodie on her hip.

In a split second I knew what I had to do, and I did something I'd never done before. I put myself out there big time and leaned in and kissed her, doing my best not to crush the baby. Initially Katy froze and her mouth was unyielding against mine, but the second I lifted my hand to the back of her neck with my thumb on her pulse, she melted and it opened, giving me access which I took advantage of. As soon as the taste of her hit me, I wanted to take it further, but… Elodie.

In fact, she's why I pulled away in the end, seeing as how she'd grabbed onto my ear and was tugging on it as hard as she could. It was hard, but I managed to do it even though I didn't move too far away from Katy.

"It's not what you think," I whispered, watching as her eyes opened slowly and she looked at me in confusion. "Tomorrow, I want to take you out, just you and me so I can explain. Can someone babysit for you?"

"I…" she whispered back, breaking off and looking behind her where her brothers were standing next to her dad. "I'll have to ask."

Lips twitching at how obvious her ability to do that at this exact moment was, I waited for her to realize it herself. When it did, she blushed and bit down on her lip, almost making me groan.

"Oops, I forgot they were there," she breathed, and then turned to look at them. "Can someone babysit Elodie for me tomorrow night?"

A face peeked around the corner of the stairs with a big grin on it – Katy's mom, Katherine. "Your dad and I will do it."

Katy's dad, Paul, glared over his shoulder at his wife, and then turned back to glare at me. "Have her back by nine."

"Paul, she's an adult," Katherine snapped, then smiled at the two of us. "We'll keep Elodie at ours for the night, so long as we bring her teddy she'll be fine."

That was something that was true. The only thing Elodie's mom had ever given her was an ugly purple teddy bear, but she took it everywhere with her and fell asleep cuddling it. I wanted to get her a Steiff or something special, but apparently she had to have this one.

"Nine," Paul growled, glaring at his wife until she mouthed something to him that I couldn't read and he turned around with a deep blush on his face. "Fine."

Katy had the day off tomorrow seeing as how Ren was worried she hadn't had enough sleep, so I leaned back in and gave her a quick lip touch. It wasn't even a kiss or anything close to it, just a skim. "I'll pick you up at six, ok?"

"Ok," she breathed, and then looked over my shoulder and blushed. "Hey, guys."

Glancing back at my brothers, I saw them all standing in the exact same positions as hers were still standing behind her, and wearing identical expressions. Christ!

"Later, baby."

As I turned to walk back to my front door, ideas of where to take her rolling around in my head, I heard her mutter, "What just happened?"

CHAPTER EIGHT

KATY

I'd finally slept. In fact, I'd gone to bed at the same time as Elodie – nine o'clock – and I'd slept all through the night until nine o'clock this morning. She'd always been a good sleeper, so I wasn't worried that I'd missed her, she just liked to sleep in – something I was supremely grateful for this morning.

Rolling out of bed, I frowned when I noticed that the three jewelry boxes I had on my dresser were at weird angles. My family knew not to come into my room given that they'd grown up with my OCD issues, and I was certain that no one else would have come into it, so why weren't they in the right place?

Looking around the room, I checked to see if anything else was out of place, and saw the frames that I'd carefully hung on the wall were at angles instead of perfectly flat as well. Fixing them, I walked toward Elodie's room and noticed that all the frames in the hallway were at strange angles, too. In fact, one of the photos was upside down. I must have been so tired last night that I hadn't noticed it because it was unlikely I'd have slept through someone doing it. I'd been tired, but I was still a light sleeper, especially when I had my niece with me.

Leaning over the bars that surrounded her bed and kept her safe, I smiled when I saw her sucking her thumb, waiting patiently to be picked up.

"Morning, beautiful 'Lodie," I cooed, lifting her off the mattress and up to my chest. "You're such a good girl for me. Auntie Katy was exhaaausted," I said dramatically, making her giggle. "We're gonna put a fresh diaper on your booty, make you smell like a precious baby again, and then have some breakfast, girl, ok?"

"Da!" she nodded and pointed where the diapers were.

"Clever girl, that's exactly where they are."

Once she was clean and smelling fresh, we went downstairs and I looked around to see if anything else was out of place. I wasn't sure what it was, but something was seriously off in my house. *Was it like this last night?*

Popping her in her highchair, I sliced a raspberry bagel in half and put it in the toaster while I waited for the coffee to finish its magic.

"Aunty Katy's just going to call Aunty Katherine, baby. I'm right here making breakfast, though," I reassured her, and reached for the phone that was sitting in its charger.

Hitting the button for the last number dialed, it rang twice and Mom answered.

"Hey, Katykins. How are you and the precious baby this morning?"

"Slept twelve hours, and she was a gem. I'm just making her breakfast," I told her as I got the creamer out of the fridge along with the juice that she liked. "Hey, Mom, did you notice if anything was out of place in my house last night?"

I was so focused on what I was talking about that I started pouring creamer in Elodie's sippy cup instead of my coffee. *Sofa. King. Great.*

Dumping it in my cup, I tossed hers in the sink to wash up afterward and got a fresh one out. This time I got it right, and she ended up with her juice and not creamer.

"No, honey, I don't think so. Like what?"

"Were the pictures on the wall at weird angles or anything?"

There was a pause while she thought about it. "No, I remember checking a couple in case they'd shifted. It happens to ours sometimes, they just start to drop slightly, and it's a pain in the ass when you realize. In some countries, they actually tilt the frames slightly to stop bad spirits resting on them, you know."

I'd definitely had some bad spirits on mine then. "Did the boys come upstairs to mess with me?"

"By moving your frames? Oh, hell no. None of us has forgotten the night Major got pissed at you and rearranged your CDs. I don't even think the ER doctor has forgotten that night seeing as how you kept attacking him even when they were stitching his eyebrow up." On a technicality, that injury wasn't my fault. I'd thrown one of the CDs in question at his head, he'd deflected it in the wrong direction i.e. towards his head, and it had cut his eyebrow up. It's not like it was even an issue seeing as how he said the chicks totally dug the split eyebrow look. "They don't go upstairs, Katykins, so I don't think they did."

That was true. After that mishap, my new house rules were that none of my siblings could go near my room – which in this house was extended to the whole upstairs level – without express permission from me. It didn't matter if the house was on fire or I was being attacked by a Yeti – none of them was allowed upstairs unless I said so, and that included screaming it.

"That's weird," I muttered, placing the bagel down in front of Elodie. "Maybe we had a tremor or something?"

"Oh, shoot, your dad needs a hand with something so I've got to go. I'll see you later when we come to pick up the baby," she blurted and then hung up.

Picking my cup up and moving to sit next to Elodie at the table, I checked online to see if there was any record of even a small tremor in the area and found nothing. Tapping my phone on the table, I watched Elodie tear the bagel apart and throw chunks of it to Duke who was in doggy heaven having her around. Every time she ate, she threw him food. At this rate, he'd be as wide as he was tall. In fact, now that I thought of it, where was Duke last night? Normally he slept in the hallway or in my room, and I didn't remember seeing him when I got up.

This was turning into a strange morning for me, so I relied on the power of coffee to help me figure it out and focused on drinking what I had. Just as I finished my first cup and was getting up to get the next one – because seriously, who just has one cup of coffee – my phone beeped with a text.

Ebru: *Girl, you've totally annihilated the GYMP. There was a plan, and you've left it in the dust. Total pro ho! What you wearing tonight?*

Me: *What do you mean?*

Ebru: *Your Jarrod date. If he talks dirty to you in that deep voice, can you record it for me? I swear I'll love you for life.*

It took a hot second to filter through all the other shit I had whirling around my brain, but when it finally made sense, I almost dropped my phone in the sink.

Oh jumping through shit on a pogo stick – I had a date with Jarrod tonight.

Jarrod

"You," Maya snapped as she stormed across the lot in front of the garage. "You fucked up the GYMP."

A quick glance behind me told me that Ren was the one who'd fucked up with a gimp, so I asked, "What gimp did he fuck?"

"The G, Y, M, P. The Get Yo' Man Plan that we came up with so Katy could get you," she said, stopping with her hands on her hips.

I will not deny the fact that I grinned wider than I've ever grinned in my life. Swear to shit, the Cheshire Cat had nothing on what I did hearing this. "She had a plan to get me?"

"Well d'uh. And now you've gone totally off script, and she's not following it at all. How am I gonna get y'all together if you can't follow simple directions?"

"I've got a date with her tonight, Maya. It's all good," I told her, cleaning my hands off on the rag that was hanging out my back pocket and enjoying the way her mouth open and closed a couple times while this sank in.

"You have a date?" she asked quietly, looking around us. "Like a just you and her date?"

"Yup, just me and her going out together."

Throwing her arms up in the air, she let out a piercing scream, "Yass!" As quickly as she did it, she dropped her hands and grabbed my arm to pull me closer. "Ok, what's your plan?"

Leaning in like I was about to tell her, I whispered, "It's a secret," and backed away, also enjoying the fact that she now looked like she was going to throttle me.

Before she could do that, my phone beeped in my pocket and I pulled it out to see that I had a message from Reid.

Reid: *Did you know that Mom can sniff out information on us a mile away? She's like a shark. So I need to tell you that she knows about Katy, she knows about all of it, and she's at Katy's right now. Sorry!*

The little shit stain had told Mom?

And she was at Katy's?

"Yo, Ren," I yelled, running toward my truck. "Need you to cover for me, I'll be an hour."

Not looking pissed or upset, he raised a hand and walked over to see his wife, only just realizing that she was there. For once I didn't smile when I saw the soft looks they gave each other when he leaned down to give her a kiss. Instead, I was trying to figure out how I was going to drive without having an accident to get to Katy's before Mom could do her thing.

And again, I'll point out – this was why I'd wanted some space.

I was going to fucking kill Reid.

Katy

Jarrod Kline's mom was in my house. She was sitting on my couch with my niece on her lap, drinking coffee from one of my cups. *What in the hell was happening?*

When I'd heard the knocks on the door, I'd expected a delivery guy or the mailman, not his mom. Smooth as anything, she'd held her hand out, introduced herself as Gloria Kline, and had then melted and held her hands out for Elodie - who'd of course gone to her. Know the most stupid part? It wasn't until she was sat down with a cup of coffee and had said the words, "I hear you're dating my son," that I'd actually realized she was his mom.

There were so many issues with this. The first was that I'd let a stranger into my home and had let her hold my niece. I was such a shitty aunt. The second was that she had the name Kline – the same name as Jarrod – and I hadn't figured it out. The third was that I'd put on a Hooters tank thinking that it was just us girls today, so that's what I was currently wearing while I was talking to her. And trust me, there was no disguising the fact that it said Hooters, San Diego, on it. The fourth was that I hadn't dried my hair, so I probably looked like Mufasa while she looked like a team of beauticians had worked on her. The fifth… I don't even know what the fifth issue was, but the list was fucking long.

"My boys have all told me such great things about you, Katy," she murmured, letting Elodie jump around like a maniac on her knees. "And I see they're all true."

What did you say to that? I'd never even met a guy's parents before. Well, unless you counted the parent-teacher evenings at school where I'd bumped into my boyfriend's parents. Did that count?

Totally lost for a response, I whispered weakly, "That's very kind of you."

We were both watching Elodie doing her thing on her new friend when she said, "You're probably wondering why I'm here."

It wasn't a question or even a statement, it was just a thing that was now dangling between us. Did I nod and say yes, or did I say she was always welcome to come over? I had no freaking clue what to do.

Thankfully, she didn't wait for me to figure it out.

"My Jarrod is special," she told me, reading Elodie's new movements perfectly and putting her on the floor. "He's always been the quietest one out of my boys, the one who thinks more than talks. He's also the one who is more grounded, reliable and sturdy." Thinking about all four of the Klines, I had to disagree. They were all built like flipping buildings, so they were all sturdy if you asked me. "All of them have something in their own unique way – just like you with your siblings – but Jarrod… he truly is something rare," she told me, and then picked up her cup and took a sip of her coffee.

"He was born on a Sunday, and from the second he entered the world he started screaming his head off," she chuckled. "My mother had been listening to something on the radio while I was pushing, a Sunday church service that was being broadcast live, and when they passed him to her, she turned it up louder to hear what was being said, but a gospel group were singing *Swing Low, Sweet Chariot* for one of their members who'd passed away. The second he heard it, he stopped trying to burst his little lungs and went silent. After that, whenever he was sick, upset, angry, feeling low, he'd either hum it or he'd listen to something else."

I was trying to picture a little Jarrod doing that, but it just didn't compute for me. I mean, I knew he used music to destress, but I didn't know it was as deeply ingrained in him as this.

"At the age of eight, he came home from school, bursting with news about a guy who was teaching kids the guitar. He picked that instrument up and boom, he could play like that," she clicked her fingers.

"Jarrod plays the guitar?" I asked, strangely not feeling uncomfortable anymore.

"Like he was Mozart with a piano," she sighed, and then leaned into me. "But he's rubbish at reading music," she whispered. "You put sheet music in front of him and he can't do a thing."

"So how does he play the guitar?"

"He listens and figures it out on the guitar himself and then memorizes it so he can play the full song."

Holy shit, that was freaking cool.

"And his voice," she sighed, looking at the window. "His voice when he sings is the most beautiful thing I've ever heard."

She had that right. I got to hear it every day while he was working, even if he tried to keep it as quiet as he could, and I never got tired of it – which is what I told her, too.

After I'd done that, she sat and took me in more carefully. "My son is a special gift, Katy. He's quiet, and he has no confidence, but he has so much that makes him the special gift that he is. The man everyone sees out there," she waved at the window, "isn't the one that's inside him. If he gives you even a hint of the true depths of who he is, you'll see that the world has a truly amazing man helping to make it the magic it is."

Looking back over at the window she'd gestured to, I whispered, "I'm starting to see that."

"He's shown you parts of it then, I take it," she said over the rim of her cup, her eyes smiling at me.

"I think so."

Lowering the cup so that it was on her knee, she used her free hand to take the one of mine that was closest to her. "Then hold on, because you're going to experience true happiness with him. It goes without saying that all of my sons have something to them, and God willing, when the time comes I'll be able to share that with the women they choose to make permanent in their lives, too. But Jarrod holds everything deep, even music, and has always used it to establish his own rhythm and beauty."

What could you say to that? *Oh, Mrs. Kline, I get that. He's the hottest guy I've ever met and I can't wait to feel his rhythm?* That was all kinds of wrong… but true. I wondered what kind of rhythm he had in…

"I see I've got you thinking now," she chuckled, putting the cup back down on the table. "Well, let me just say, when my boys called me and told me Jarrod had someone special, I was shocked. He's had girlfriends before, but not once have they involved me in it. Heck, one of them he had for two years and I never met her," she muttered, her tone making it clear she still wasn't happy about that. "Then they told me he was making a mess of it with you…" I'm thinking they'd used different words for mess, ones that included 'fucking it up', but ok, "and that I needed to fix it." She looked at me out of the corner of her eye, "I didn't come here to fix it, I came to figure out if you were worth as much as they were making out."

I stopped breathing, not even realizing I'd done it until my brain started screaming at me to sort my shit out.

When I did, I whispered, "What?"

I mean, she was really nice, and she'd been that way since she'd come in. At no point did I think the visit was that deep. Then again, what did I know? I wasn't a parent, and I'd never done the boyfriend/girlfriend parent thing, even with my ex in college. So this news made me panic that she was just being nice and that the second she left she'd tell her son to move the hell on and find someone better. That would not only mean losing Jarrod – even though I was still ticked at him about what I'd heard and didn't understand it at all – but it would mean losing her other sons who I liked a lot also.

How the hell was a woman meant to breathe during a time like that? The answer to that would be: only if she had balls of steel and was hella secure with her man, and as I didn't have either of those I was at an impasse. Basically, I was screwed.

Her eyes scanned my face as I thought this, and then her face softened. "Katy, I've only just met you, but I'm thinking that you're perfect for him. If I had to dream up a woman for him, it would be everything I see sitting in front of me right now."

Holy shit. Holy fucking shit. *Holy, holy fucking shit.*

"I…" I started and then shook my head. "I don't know what to say."

Seeing that I was having an internal freak out – although I wasn't sure I wasn't having an external one, too – she relaxed into her seat. "Say ok and then we'll get to know each other. I'll start by telling you about me and my husband. What do you know about Jamaica?" she asked, changing the subject so quickly it felt like I had whiplash.

"Um, it's in the Caribbean?"

Throwing her hands in the air and making the row of bangles she had on her wrist tinkle, she launched into a story that by the end of it had me thinking about when I could next take a break and head to Jamaica.

Holy shit again.

Jarrod

How I got home without crashing was a miracle, and it wasn't until I pulled into my driveway and got out to go to Katy's that I realized I should have just called one of them on the way. Instead, I'd spent the last twenty minutes imagining Mom putting her through a gamut of tests and trials, like an 'are you fit to date my son' assault course.

My mom was awesome, but she was fiercely protective of us.

Hurdling the fence between our gardens was now something I was used to, so I cleared it easily and was in front of her door in seconds. Then I was knocking, praying to the man Maude kept talking to all the time that Mom hadn't ruined the fragile something that Katy and I had. I had a lot of explaining to do, and for someone who'd never had to do that and wasn't good with words, this was a big problem. Add on trying to repair any damage Mom had done… I was freaking out.

I was just about to knock again when the door opened and Katy was looking up at me wide eyed, and then Duke was excitedly head butting my thighs.

With our differences in height, I had a clear shot of Mom sitting on the couch with Elodie, watching me with a smile on her face.

"Ma…"

Not mistaking my tone – not that anyone could seeing as how I was frustrated as hell and struggling to hide it – she just shot me a grin back. "Nice to see you, Jarrod. I was just telling your Katy all about Port Royal."

Port Royal – where her family was from in Jamaica. Was I fooled that that's all she'd spoken about? No. She'd definitely said more before she'd moved onto home.

Looking down, I tried to read Katy's current mood, but she was just watching me like she was waiting for something. "Are you ok, baby?"

A hiccupy sigh came from the couch and Mom muttered to Elodie, "He calls her baby."

Fuck my life.

Fortunately, Mom's dramatic reaction made one corner of Katy's mouth tip up in a grin. "Your mom's a trip," she snickered, and then sobered. "She can never meet Maude, though."

That wasn't something that I hadn't realized the second I'd met Maude... Those two together would be a huge mistake for the entire world.

"Who's Maude?" Mom asked, not even hiding that she was listening in now.

Moving out of the door so that I could get in, Katy threw over her shoulder, "My grandmother. She's a walking holiday, but she's totally crazy."

Mom's head jerked slightly, and she looked up at me in shock. "You've met her grandmother?"

Shit.

"Yeah," I sighed, resigning myself to the fact that I really was screwed now. "And the rest of Katy's family." It was only a small exaggeration given that I'd met her parents and sister for all of ten seconds the night before, but I'd met her brothers for slightly longer so it was the truth and lying to Mom about it was just shitty.

A determined look replaced the shock, and she clapped her hands together. "Well, then we'll have dinner at ours. No, no, no lip," she snapped, holding her palm out to me when I went to interrupt. "Call your family and tell them they're coming to ours. You said you wanted to try the food I was telling you about, so that's what I'll make," she told Katy, getting up and looping her purse over her shoulder. "How many of you are there?"

Katy looked up at me like she was pleading for help, but if she hadn't gotten it by now, she soon would. There was no stopping Gloria Kline when she made her mind up.

"Just go with it, honey," I muttered, shoving my hands in the pockets of my jeans for something to cover up the awkward feeling I had now.

I'd wanted this with Katy, but we had a lot of work to do to fix the fragile link we'd had that had been broken by a misconception. I couldn't do that while my family were around, and I knew my nosy brothers would be watching everything tonight. Basically, this was a fucking nightmare.

"Invite this Maude, too," Mom ordered, still waiting for the guest number from Katy.

No, now *this* was a fucking nightmare.

"There's eight of us," Katy whispered, then bit down on her lower lip. "Elodie's super cool about food, though, and eats anything. Her favorite is Mexican that borders on being too spicy for anyone else."

"I'd heard all about her from my boys," Mom said through a grin, tickling the baby and making a face at her. "And they were right when they said she was beautiful."

And there it was – all the tension went out of Katy at the thought of the little girl who technically wasn't her niece, but who she'd claimed with her whole heart. "Yeah, she's the most awesome little girl in the world. I've been looking after her because her mom – my cousin – isn't around, but I love every second of it."

One of Mom's hands flew to her chest. "This poor baby's mother died?"

Katy looked up at me for help, and I knew what she wanted help with was explaining her cousin's addiction in a way that wouldn't bring judgement on her family. Not that Mom would, she wasn't that narrowminded, but I could understand why Katy would be worried about it.

Pulling her into my side, I explained, "Elodie's mother has an addiction problem, Ma. She has for years, so Katy's family all help with Elodie, making sure she has everything she needs and grows up healthy. She's got a strong bond with Katy, so she's alternating keeping her with her uncle who can't always get time off or find someone he trusts with her."

Telling her this wasn't a mistake, far from it, and I knew that the second she looked at Katy even more determinedly. "Well, you just found someone else who'll help out. Bring her with you tonight and we'll set up some more time together next week, too. Once she's used to me and you're comfortable with me and trust me with the precious, I can step in to help you out, too."

Shit. "Katy has her family who can help, Ma…" I reminded her, but it was no use.

"Babies need love from a variety of people, and you can never have too many people to hand. You yourself help Jose out with her little Olivia, don't you?" She had me there. "So I can help out with Elodie." She finished and then started tapping her lip. "I need to get some toys, perhaps." Looking around the room, she took in the box in the corner. "Huh, that maze with the beads would keep your brothers and father entertained for hours."

"It has," Katy choked out, and then clarified, "I mean, it's entertained your sons, not your husband, obviously."

Rolling her eyes, Mom crossed over to us still carrying Elodie. "Right, little one. You go to your auntie, and Auntie Gloria will see you later."

She didn't want her aunt, though, she wanted me, which she made clear when she lunged out of Mom's arms to me. Fortunately, I knew to expect it by now, so I'd been ready just in case she'd done it.

Bringing her around onto my hip, I tucked Elodie in close. "One of these days, the person you do that to isn't going to be ready, little precious. Then we'll have an Elodie pancake and your auntie's gonna be sad all day."

Staring up at me with big eyes, she stuck out her lower lip and let it tremble as her nose started to turn pink.

"Ok," Mom croaked, fanning her face with her hand. "I've got to go to the store. Jarrod, I'll check what time the boys can make it and text you a time to tell Katy's parents."

"What if they've got plans, Ma?" A bit like we'd had plans that now weren't going to happen, but I was going to take the rest of the day off to sort shit out with Katy and then I could plan something better to do with her tomorrow night. So in a way it wasn't actually that bad of a situation – unless you counted the woman you wanted a relationship with meeting your crazy family with her crazier (although, that was a matter of opinion) family.

"Then we move it to tomorrow or just you and your girls come," she shrugged, giving Katy a hug and leaning in to give Elodie a kiss on the top of her curly head.

I was beginning to think she was going to leave without doing it, but just as she started to walk past, she pounced. Grabbing my cheeks, she used them to pull my face closer to hers, gave them a shake, and then furiously kissed back and forth between them. When that was done, she patted my left cheek loudly twice, and then walked out, leaving Katy staring at me and trying not to laugh. Elodie didn't have that control because she kept giggling even after the door shut behind twister Gloria.

Peace... apparently even distance wasn't going to give me that.

Looking back at Katy who was watching Ma go out to her car, she whispered, "I guess I need to call my family."

Lifting my hand to the back of Elodie's head – who was now rubbing her face in my chest – I managed to get out the words that almost choked me. "Don't forget Maude."

The scared look she gave me would have been funny if it wasn't for a good reason. In my mind I heard an explosion and realized that it had come from the hopes and dreams of peace and quiet I'd had.

But strangely enough, holding Elodie and watching Katy, realizing how special she was and how much I wanted this to happen... I didn't mind the explosion.

CHAPTER NINE

KATY

As I'd picked up my cell to call my family, Elodie had started whining and wouldn't stop rubbing her face on Jarrod's chest – lucky duck – so he'd taken her upstairs to put her down for a nap.

Now I was done, the calls had been made and my family were now free. My parents would meet us there and still take the baby for the night so that I could have a break. Seeing as how she had a room at their house so that they could help out whichever one of Leo and I had her, and also loved being with them, this was a relief. I'm also not gonna lie – I was freaking looking forward to the lie in tomorrow.

Seeing that Jarrod wasn't down yet and that I'd left the monitor in my bedroom, I climbed the stairs, stopping when I heard his deep voice singing softly. Describing it was one of the hardest things ever, which was frustrating because its beauty was unreal. Then again, there weren't many things in life that were so beautiful they were indescribable, and Jarrod had quite a few of those.

Straining to hear the song, I almost melted when I figured it out. Was it a song written for kids? Hell no, but his deep baritone voice and the way he was singing it could have made and song sound like it was.

But Metallica's *Nothing Else Matters*? When I listened to it normally, it struck me as an almost angrily, aggressive, sad song. But how he was singing it, those words turned into something that was almost touching and heart wrenching.

Tip toeing closer to the door, I peeked around the frame and saw him sitting on the huge bean bag I'd put next to her bed. He was leaning back with her on his chest, his big hand holding her in place on her back, while she looked up at him and listened.

How wrong was it to be jealous of a baby?

Beside him on the floor was Duke, lying face down with his legs spread out like a star. He was also watching him and periodically wagged his tail whenever Jarrod got to the chorus.

Going with the idea that hit me, I reached into my pocket, pulled out my phone and took a photo. That was totally going to be my wallpaper.

As the song came to an end, he softened his voice until it was a whisper. Elodie's eyes fluttered a couple of times, and then they stayed shut. She was out.

I was so engrossed in them that I didn't realize he was talking to me until he said my name.

"Katy?"

Raising my eyes off my niece, I watched as his face split into a huge grin. "Sorry, what?"

"I said, I think she's got another tooth coming through. I

noticed her chewing on her fist when Ma was holding her, but she's been rubbing her face on me since I got her and her cheeks are warm."

Shit, I'd noticed it, but it hadn't occurred to me that she might be in pain. I was seriously such a bad aunt.

Closing the distance between us, I leaned over and put the back of my hand against her cheek like Mom used to do to us when we were little. Sure enough, she was warmer than usual. "Does she need some Tylenol?"

In the months since she'd been born, not once had she been unwell when I'd had her. In fact, I couldn't even recall a time when my uncle said she'd been properly sick.

Running his hand over the top of her head, he asked, "Do you have one of those kid thermometers?"

I did a mental run through of the contents of my first aid kit and then realized I did in fact have one. Holding my finger up to him, I sprinted through to the bathroom that was attached to my bedroom, opened the drawer that I'd dedicated to all things medicine, and looked at the second drawer in the organizer box that had bigger items in it like bandages and a bottle of that shit that burns when you pour it on a cut. Sure enough, beside it was the thermometer I'd bought the first time I'd taken care of her.

Pulling it out, I made sure the battery wasn't dead and took it through to where she was now lying on her bed with Jarrod standing watching her.

"It's a forehead one. You just press the button and it reads it," I whispered, holding it up for him to see.

When I didn't move to use it, he gestured at her with his head. "You gonna use it, babe?"

That was a good point.

Leaning over her, I pressed it gently on her forehead and put my thumb on the button. In a matter of seconds it beeped, and I lifted it to look at the screen. "Ok, if your temperature is meant to be around ninety-eight, that means that literally just under one hundred is high, right?"

Frowning at this, Jarrod walked around and gently pulled me out of her room and into my room.

Now was the time for me to embrace my inner Maude. *Sweet Jesus, I had Jarrod Kline in my bedroom. Jesus needed to take that wheel and drive!*

"Ma," he said into his phone, something I hadn't seen him using until he spoke. "'Lodie's got a fever. Yeah, almost one hundred. No, just chewing and rubbing her face on me. Her cheeks are pink and warm, but she wasn't sweaty. Hang on, I'll ask her." Raising his head to look at me, he asked, "How's she been with eating and drinking, honey? Any issues?"

Thinking back, I did a quick analysis of how she'd been eating. "No, she was fine. Fed Duke like normal, was chewing ok, but she was thirsty this morning."

Focus back on his phone, he asked, "Did you hear that? Yeah, that's what I'm thinking, too. Ok, we'll do that. Thanks, Ma. Yeah, later."

"What did she say?"

Putting his phone back in his back pocket, he blew out a breath. "She says it's probably teething, but if anything changes to call the doctor. She also said she used to check our temperatures every hour when we were sick, just so she was aware if anything changed."

That was a good idea. "I'll do that for sure."

"How do you feel about giving her some Tylenol right now, just to see if that helps?" he asked, his head tilting to the side as he watched me.

That question made me freak out. I'd never given her any medication before and, honestly, after her mom being addicted, the thought of doing it was terrifying.

I don't know what he saw on my face, but he definitely would have been able to read my fear. "What's going through your mind, Katy?"

Wringing my hands in front of me, I laid it out. "Her mom's an addict, but I don't know enough about addiction to see if kids can inherit it. I know that they learn by viewing, but addiction is addiction, it's a disease that a lot of people can't help, Jarrod. Giving Elodie a medication, even if it's only baby Tylenol, when Effie has that..."

Closing the distance between us, he lifted his hand and cupped the side of my neck. "Baby, she'll be ok with Tylenol, especially the baby stuff you've got for her. After that, you need to speak to a doctor and do some research so that you understand it better, and so that in the future you can help Elodie understand what her mom's going through."

"Ok," I breathed, my freak out slightly calming.

"Now, get the stuff and look at how much she needs to have. Do you want to hold her, or do you want me to do it while you give her the Tylenol?"

How did he know so much? I hadn't even gotten to that stage of the process in my mind. I was still stuck on the part where I went to get it.

Knowing she'd wake up when she was picked up, even if it was only for a second, I made my choice. "I'll hold her, you give it to her."

Smiling at my choice, he gave me a gently nudge. "Ok, baby, go get it then."

After his kiss last night and order that he was taking me out tonight, I hadn't been sure if I could do it. I knew he wanted to talk to me and explain about what I'd heard, but seriously – that discussion could have gone in any direction, including the one where he was just 'getting it out of his system' before anything happened between us. That would have sucked balls.

Him helping me with this, though, chipped away at the wall I'd built around me two nights ago. This was the Jarrod I knew, the Jarrod who I'd semi fallen in love with months ago. This was the Jarrod that I understood.

So, having this Jarrod in front of me, helping me with my niece, the awkwardness and wariness that I'd still been feeling for him lessened.

Jarrod

After we'd given Elodie her Tylenol, and she was settled back down again with her ugly ass purple bear in her arms, we went back through to the room we'd been in before, and that's when I took in what was in it and realized it was Katy's bedroom. I'd known it would be given that our houses were identical, but I'd been so focused on the problem at hand that I hadn't actually put two and two together.

Now I was, so I was going to try to get some more clues about Katy. I wanted to know everything I could about her, and this was a great place to start. It also had her bed. The bed that Katy slept in at night. I wonder if she wore something, or if she slept naked? Looking behind me, I saw a tall drawer unit… Which drawer had her panties and bras?

Katy came in and closed the door slightly behind her. "Ok,

she's out. I've set a timer on my phone for an hour so I can take her temperature again."

Making my way over to her bed, I sat down on the edge and patted the space beside me. It was time. "That was a good idea. Come and sit for a second, baby."

She didn't play any games or try to delay it at all, not Katy Crew. Instead, she walked over and dropped down, her attention on the countdown display on her phone.

"Katy," I called, trying to get her attention with her bangs now in her face.

Lifting her head up, she blew out a big puff of air that lifted them. Somehow, through some follicle miracle, they landed in the right spot, the one that they were always in when I saw her – swept to the side, covering her eyebrow, and framing her gorgeous eye.

"While we're waiting, I want to have the talk with you I was going to have tonight. Is that ok?" When she nodded, but her expression turned wary, I shot her a smile and reached out for her hand. "What you heard most sure as shit wasn't me with another woman. I mean, I was with another woman, but that's not what you heard." When she froze and stiffened up, I hissed, "Shit, I'm fucking this up." Turning her hand around so that I could lace my fingers with hers, I started gently rubbing the area of her hand that was accessible to my thumb. "A while back, I was in a cell at the Police Department. While I was in there, I started singing to get my mind off the shit I'd been involved in – which, just to say, wasn't my fault. A man was beating on his woman and I stopped it – and Tabby was in the cell next door."

Nodding at me, she whispered, "I'd heard about that, and you did the right thing. So did Dave when he put you in there so that the asshole wouldn't come after you."

That he was, Dave was a great guy. "Agreed. But while I was singing, Tabby said I should narrate erotic books because of my voice. It was a joke for a while, and then it wasn't a joke."

I'd expected to see disgust, disappointment, confusion, anything other than what I saw on her face when she heard this. "Oh shit, that's so freaking cool. You're narrating audible books?"

"That I am. And for the last however many days, I was doing my first dual narration where I did it at the same time as the female narrator for the book."

"How does that work?" she asked, no doubt wondering if the chick had been in my house.

"You go online together and record at the same time. We have a special program that does it for us, and we also have a copy of the book that's highlighted in different colors to tell us who says what."

"That's pretty handy," she mumbled.

"Not many people know I'm doing this, baby. In fact, until last night, I could count it on one hand and still have spare fingers."

Twisting to face me, with her leg now up on the bed, she asked, "Why don't people know? Does your family know?"

Leaning in, I shook my head. "No. Up until last night, only Tabby and Jose knew about it. I had to tell my brothers last night so that I could explain that I wasn't doing what you thought I was doing while they were trying to beat the shit out of me."

Her hand tightened on mine. "Shit, your brothers beat you up?"

Why were we getting off track?

"That doesn't matter, baby. What matters is that I'm telling you that there wasn't a woman or women physically in my home. What I was reading was from a book."

She looked conflicted when she looked away this time and started chewing on her lip.

"You never promised me anything, Jarrod, so you shouldn't have to explain yourself to me. I'm so sorry for putting you in this position."

I was fucking done.

It took all of two seconds to scoop her up off the bed and place her in my lap with her legs either side of me so that she was straddling me.

Holding her face steady, I dug deep for the words for this. "Katy, I don't mind explaining it to you because I want you to know this shit. Granted, I'd have liked to have waited a while to share my secret with you, but I can't say I'm pissed about it or about what happened. The highlight of my days has been hanging out with you, and before that it was catching a glimpse of you when you came out of your office."

Katy's jaw dropped, and she sat staring at me like I had two heads, and then said, "Sha da faa cup."

"What the fuck?" I choked, not sure whether to laugh or start testing the boundaries of my ability to explain shit.

"Mom used to get pissed at us when we were little and swore, so me and my brothers came up with something that we could say and she wouldn't be able to get angry about us for cussing," she explained blushing.

I did my best to laugh as quietly as I could, but it was one of the hardest things I'd ever done.

"That's fucking adorable," I told her, watching her eyes light up. Then I added, "But it's nutty and goofy as hell."

Shrugging her shoulders, she was unapologetic when she admitted, "That's me!"

It took a good while, but I finally managed to stop laughing. Sha da faa cup, how hilarious was that? This time when I looked at her, she had a soft look on her face as she watched me get some control over it.

"I like it when you laugh," she said quietly. "It's not just the way you look when you're doing it and the way your eyes light up, but the sound you make when you're doing it is one of the most beautiful things I've ever heard."

Fuck me!

Lifting my hands so that I was holding her face on either side with my fingers in her hair, I pulled her closer to me. "I like seeing you all the time, but when you get that hazy look in your eyes when Elodie does something or I say something you like, or when you're laughing at something and tip your head back, those are my favorite. Those are the ones I want to take a photo of so that I can see them over and over."

For once, the communication gods were with me. Happy day!

Glancing quickly down at my mouth and then back up to my eyes, she rasped, "Jarrod, what's happening here?"

Closing the inch that was still between us, I stopped with my lips about a millimeter away from hers. "I'm hoping it's the beginning of something between us. Something special that's just ours. Something where I get to know you better, learn what you like, memorize what you don't like, spend time with you…"

It was just as well that she cut me off by kissing me when she did because I was running out of things to list.

Letting go of the hand I was still holding, I lifted it up to cup the side of her neck, loving how silky soft her hair felt and how thick it was as I moved my fingers through it to the back of her head. With our differences in height, I had to bend over a good amount to reach her, but with her head tilted back it wasn't a painful amount. I'd always had a type – tall. Body shape didn't matter to me, but height did. The fact that she was so much shorter than me went totally against that, but I found I actually liked it. I liked that she wasn't like anyone from my past, it made everything between us new and special.

The only answer I had as to why that was, was that she was Katy. The chick who at a first glance I'd thought was cute, but I'd been too focused on life and what was going on with my friends. First there was Tabby's thing, then there was Jose's thing, then there was Rose's thing, and after that I was helping Raoul's brother Garrett get settled in Piersville. Add in my family and brothers, hanging out with the guys, narrating, and it didn't seem like a lot but it was.

Moving in next door had been a move I definitely wasn't regretting now as my tongue brushed along the side of hers and she mewled into my mouth.

Yeah, I was fucking happy, and I really wanted to see where this was going.

I was careful not to push her too fast, so we stuck to making out, but we didn't separate once, not even when I picked her up and put her in my lap to do it.

When her phone started making a noise, that's when we pulled away from each other, and I watched as she slowly opened her eyes and looked up at me hazily.

"Your phone's going, baby," I whispered, seeing it taking time for the fog to clear and for her to get her bearings back, and loving every second.

She jerked and looked down at it, only now noticing that the alarm was going off on it. "Holy cramoly, how long did we make out for? The last time I looked I had forty-nine minutes left."

Not wanting to be a smart ass but figuring it was prudent, I pointed out the truth. "Forty-nine minutes then."

She looked back up at me, rolled her eyes, and then just tipped herself off my legs and saunter-limped back through to Elodie's room.

Turns out the Tylenol helped, and her fever was dropping which was a relief. That said, it was an unspoken agreement between us that we would continue checking her temperature every hour, which is what we did until it was time for Katy to get ready to go to my parents' house.

I loved getting to play with Elodie and watch her inquisitive mind guide her through her toys after she woke up. And I have to say, I seriously fucking loved getting to make out with Katy before she woke up from her nap. Both Crew girls had something about them that sucker punched me in different ways, and they didn't even have to do anything big for it to happen.

Maybe peace was overrated? Maybe Crew mayhem was where it was at, because I was starting to look forward to getting it whenever I could.

CHAPTER TEN

KATY

Waking up the next morning, I rolled onto my back and stared up at the ceiling, remembering everything that had happened yesterday. The chat, Elodie not feeling well, the kissing, more of the kissing, the drive to Jarrod's with his hand holding mine resting on his thigh, the feeling of the muscles in his thigh shifting as he worked the pedal, the meal at his parents...

Jesus, the meal at his parents.

We'd arrived after my parents did, so they were already introduced, happy and relaxed when we got there. That lasted all of five minutes until Major and Ammon arrived with Maude, who was surprisingly well behaved until after beer number two when she told Gloria she would kill to do her hair.

So, while Jarrod's dad Dolf manned the BBQ and turned the jerk chicken, Maude worked on her hair even though Mom and I had tried to talk her out of it. Just as Dolf was plating the chicken on a platter, they walked back into the room and everyone just stopped and stared. I wasn't kidding when I said Maude liked big hair, and holy shit did Gloria have big hair after she was done with it. It looked like she'd teased, ratted, lifted, sprayed and fluffed it out until she had an actual beehive on her head.

Seeing it, Dolf almost dropped the platter. Bond – who had been chomping on a stolen piece of something called 'festival' – choked and Dad had to pat him on the back. Canon dropped his bottle of beer on the patio. Reid let out a yelped "holy shit". And Jarrod muttered, "Fucking hell."

Gloria, though, she loved it and asked Maude to come back to do it again. Major and Ammon were both standing facing the fence in the Klines backyard, their shoulders shaking as they laughed quietly, and Mom was glaring at Dad like it was his fault because it was his mother.

Me? I buried my face in Elodie's neck and started praying for some sort of time portal like the chick in *The Witcher* could conjure up. Now would be a great time for me to start tossing coins for a Witcher. In fact, I had a bunch of ones, five fives, and three tens in my wallet, too, I would throw those at him along with the coins, pass him my credit cards, and beg him to save me.

My sister had shown up after we'd finished dinner – jerk chicken, rice and peas, and something called callaloo with pieces of festival. I swear I could eat that every day and never grow sick of it, so much so that I'd asked Gloria for the recipes. It looked complicated, but damn if it wasn't worth the effort – and were sitting eating Johnnycake. It was Bond who'd let her in and who was the one to catch her when she tripped over her own feet when she saw Gloria's hair and had then shot a glare at Maude.

We'd all sat down talking and Gloria had filled my family in on where her family was from in Jamaica, the history of Port Royal and how half of it sank into Kingston Harbor in 1692, its links to Captain Morgan (*the* Captain Morgan and his pirates), and then how Dolf's family had fled from Germany to America during the first world war, and how his grandfather was named Adolf but changed it to Dolf after Hitler started his reign of terror and fucked upness, so he and his father were named Dolf without the A because of that.

Hearing this, my brothers had started bitching about my parent's choice of names for us and how they'd have preferred Dolf and Gloria to name us. And thus began the old Crew name conversation.

-

"This isn't fair," Major had snapped, glaring at Mom and Dad. "They all have kick ass names and we're stuck with our messed up crap."

Not realizing that she was opening a door that needed badly to remain locked tight, Gloria had innocently asked, "Where did you get their names from, Katherine?"

Maude had started laughing, and hadn't stopped when both my parents had glared at her.

"Major got Major because he's a *major* pain in the ass," Ammon had snickered, swallowing a mouthful of beer at the same time Major punched him in the arm.

Ignoring the impending war between her sons, Mom replied, "Well, when I was pregnant, we decided we wanted to merge my grandfather's name with Paul's grandfather's. Mine named Martin and his was Jordan, so we decided on Major."

"She just doesn't want you to know the truth," Ammon had snickered.

"Oh yeah, and what about your name? Did she have a craving for gammon? Or maybe she really preferred salmon and didn't want people to call you fishy," Major growled. "Here fishy, fishy!"

Ammon's whole body had tensed up through this, and I'd chanced a glance at the Klines to see them all watching it with amusement.

Like her sons weren't about to get into a smack down versus raw fight, Mom continued, "With Ammon it was a bit more problematic. I'd wanted to name him Ryan, but I had a hard labor with him and after he was born, Paul had gone out and gotten rip-roaring drunk. We're talking beyond snockered," she added, glaring at Dad. "Anyway, because I was still recovering, he filled in the forms and couldn't remember the name we'd chosen, so he looked up at the television and saw the reporter's name was Ammon."

Tipping his head back to look at the dark sky, Ammon had muttered, "Fuck my life."

Throughout all of this, Maude was sitting laughing herself silly as she continued drinking her beer. When she looked up and saw me watching her, she shrugged a shoulder and took another big mouthful from the bottle.

Gloria had been fully invested in this story at this stage, so she ignored my brothers who were trying to silently goad each other into a fight and asked, "What about Katarianne?"

"Dad was probably too drunk to spell catamaran," Major said sarcastically, and had then given me a small smile of apology.

"That one was on me, too," Dad sighed. "Katherine wanted Arabella because she said Katy was born looking like a fairy princess – which she was," he added, winking at me, "and that Arabella was a beautiful name for something so precious and beautiful."

Focus off of each other, Ammon crossed his arms over his chest and sent my parents a scathing glare. "I notice me and Major didn't get any comments like that."

Not even looking contrite, Dad returned, "That's because you both looked like miniature versions of that Winston Churchill guy."

Looking at each other in confusion, they had both lifted up a butt cheek to pull their cell phones out and looked the guy up on the internet. When they found a photo, the glares they'd given them that time were almost scary.

"Your retirement home is going to be in a basement," Major hissed, shutting his phone down.

"And you'll change your underwear once every two weeks," Ammon added. "Which'll be shitty because you'll only get cabbage water, so your asses will be active."

If it had just been us I'd have laughed, but because it was in front of Jarrod and his family – who I really liked and wanted to think good things about me – I buried my face in my hands and prayed again for a portal.

While I'd been doing that, the Klines had all burst out laughing, as in bent over and holding their guts types of laughing.

"I love this family," Bond wheezed, and then turned to Jarrod. "I'm thinking you need to name y'all's kids, though."

My head had shot up out of my hands and I was thinking that the portal could go fuck itself because I was just going to run and never look back, when Jarrod roared out laughing and pulled me into his side.

"Agreed."

"Anyway," Dad forged on. "I decided that I wanted to merge Katherine's name with Mom's name," he nodded at Maude who was sitting smiling at me proudly now. She loved that I was named after her and so did I. "So, I went with Katarianne."

All the Klines, including Bond, Canon, and Reid had all looked over at me with the same soft expression on their faces, but it was Jarrod who commented on it.

"It's as unique and special as she is."

Well shit!

Giving us a moment to just look at each other, Gloria got the attention off us from everyone else leaving us in our own little bubble.

"And Aura? How did you decide on that?"

Seeing as how she'd arrived by this point and had sat quietly throughout the conversation, it was a shock to everyone when she'd stood up and picked up Elodie, holding her like a shield. "I don't want to play this game anymore. Let's talk about something else."

"Oh, now I really have to know," Canon snickered, leaning forward and shooting Aura a shit-eating grin.

Dad had the good grace to look guilty as he'd blurted, "She came out looking like a fairy princess, too, so I gave her the name Katherine had chosen for Katy…"

"Even though I'd already said I wanted her name to be

Melody," Mom hissed. "Why don't you continue, dear, so they can hear how her name became Aura and not Arabella."

Throwing his arms up in the air with frustration, Dad said loudly, "Because I forgot what you'd chosen, ok? You got taken through to surgery because you were bleeding everywhere and I was holding this little fairy in my arms thinking I'd never see you again. I knew it began with an A and ended with one, too, so I went with Aura."

All the Klines sat blinking as they digested this, and I sighed, "Welp, there goes that then."

Leaning into my side, Jarrod whispered, "There goes what?"

I hadn't realized he was as close to me as he was, so when I turned my head my nose had bumped against his, making my brain short circuit for a second. "Huh?"

I watched up close as his beautiful eyes smiled at me and was slightly disappointed that with our positions I couldn't watch his mouth doing it, too. "There goes what, Katy?"

"Any chance that your family will think I'm normal and like me," I mumbled, still somewhat transfixed by his eyes and not realizing that it was silent enough for people to pick up what I was saying.

"Oh, we like you all right," Reid called across the table. "Y'all are fucking crazy crackers and it makes us look normal. I vote aye."

"Aye," Canon agreed.

"Total aye," Bond did too, nodding his head and slapping his hand on the table.

Tilting his chair back so it was supported by its back legs, Dolf stuck his thumb up in the air. "It's a thumbs up from me."

Getting up from her chair, Gloria walked around until she was behind mine and gently moved my hair off the back of my neck so it was resting over one shoulder. "You already had my aye, but this is me letting you know you've got it. I'm over the moon Jarrod found you," she told me, squeezing my shoulder for emphasis. "And your grandmother does great hair, so now I've got that, too."

My head snapped up to look at my parents in horror, and then over to Maude, who was sitting smiling happily. "Anytime, Gloria girl. Anytime. The higher the hair, the closer to God."

"Jesus," Jarrod muttered, looking horrified at the thought of his mom's hair getting any bigger.

I didn't even think it was possible for it to get any bigger.

"Him, too," Maude agreed.

Gloria had given my shoulder a final squeeze before she moved back to her chair, and as I'd watched her doing this, Jarrod's brothers had all given me a wink. Holy shit, that felt good.

Still, I leaned into Jarrod and this time kept my voice quiet enough that only he would hear it. "You regretting what you want to start with me yet?"

His head had jerked back, and he'd frowned down at me for a moment before he started chuckling and shaking his head. "Fuck no. I'm thinking I need to celebrate the fact I've made the best choice I've ever made in my life, baby."

This hadn't been said quietly, so all the women sighed happily, their eyes dreaming of romance, hearts and roses, while the men all made gagging noises.

Sofa. King. Great!

Even with that, it was a freaking awesome night, and I'd loved every second, aside from passing Elodie over to Mom. Leo was off work for two days, so he was collecting her today and would be spending time with his 'little pal'.

That left me alone and with time to think.

My family had moved to Piersville just after I'd started college, and it was only natural that we all gravitated back to them once we'd all graduated and were ready to live the adult life. This meant that I hadn't grown up with everyone here, so I'd had to work hard to get to know people – well, hard for me, seeing as how I wasn't the most social person. But the second I'd seen Jarrod when I got the job at Ren's garage, I'd been hooked. It wasn't just his height and looks that made him stand out, it was the fact that he paid attention. Whenever I spoke to him, I knew I had it and that he'd give it to me until I was done. Then he started to let down his wall, brick by brick, and I got to see the personality underneath. The whole mix was outstanding. Being shy and quiet, though, I never got to fully engage with him until recently, so the sudden change in our relationship and interactions was making me feel off center.

I was going to use today to get that center back, and the only way I knew to do that was to get so engrossed in one of my favorite things that I didn't have to use my brain for anything else.

So, jogging down the stairs with Duke on my heels, I opened the back door and then bounced from foot to foot, waiting for him to come back in. When he did, I slammed the door shut, locked it and jogged straight back up again before I bounced on my bed. Reaching under it, I tagged the Alienware laptop that I'd saved for for two years, and opened up *The Witcher* game.

Then obviously I had to attach my phone to my Alexa and play the song, too… on repeat.

Jarrod

Waking up to the song was funny. Hearing it the second time made me laugh harder. By the third time I'd begun to stop finding it so funny. By the fourth I was close to begging her to change it. By the fifth I actually got out of bed and walked through to the study to tap on the wall that separated us.

And then I heard a muffled scream coming from her bedroom and lost my shit.

Picking up my jeans from last night, I pulled them on and ran down the stairs, managing to grab the keys I had for Katy's house that she'd given me yesterday. Because we'd been helping each other out with shit, she had a spare set for mine, too, in case of an emergency. This meant that as I ran out the house and jumped over that fucking, *fucking* fence, it only took me five seconds longer than normal to get the key in her lock and turn it because I'd dropped it the first time I tried.

Not even looking around, I made my way upstairs and stopped when I came face to face with Duke, who was alert and looking pissed. When he saw it was me, he stood down and moved to the side, leaving the way to her room wide open for me – which is where I ran to.

I'd had many thoughts of what was making her scream, but not one of them was what I came across. She was so engrossed in what was on her computer screen, and the damn song was playing so loudly that she didn't even notice me come into her room. A quick glance around showed that nothing looked abnormal in the room, and then I looked back at Katy and made a different type of discovery.

TALK FLIRTY TO ME

She was sitting in bed wearing a tank top that had what looked like the line you see on a heart monitor in the hospital (I'd never had one done so I had no idea what they were called) that was attached to an Xbox remote. Covering the bottom of her body was a knitted green creeper from *Minecraft*, but it was like a sleeping bag that was split up the middle so her legs could go either side and not be joined together like a normal one.

There was absolutely nothing that could stop me from bursting out laughing, which snapped her out of her gaming fog. Her head snapped up, and she finally saw she had company, screamed, jumped, and somehow managed to place her laptop on the free space on the bed. Then she rolled to her side off the mattress and onto her feet and stood up, staring at me like I was a character out of a game.

I'd just opened my mouth to say something when the *Minecraft* creeper sleeping bag finally lost the battle with gravity and dropped to the floor, leaving her standing in her tank top and underwear. I want to say I was a gentleman, I also want to be able to blame it on anything other than the fact it was her panties, but I looked down and lost the war.

Any laugh that had ever come out of me out of me before had nothing on what came out of me then when I saw Mario from *Mario Bros* winking at me on her crotch with his thumb in the air.

And then it got better when she turned around to hide it, and on the back it said *Talk Gamer To Me* ...

Falling to my side, I tried to get air into my lungs while Duke took the opportunity to try and lick every inch of my face and neck, and when he couldn't do it, he started jumping either side of me like it was a game.

"Oh my god," Katy squealed, finally able to say something.

"Wait, which panties... Oh my god..." she shrieked and hurdled over me to where a pair of sweats were lying neatly folded on a chair. I'd only just started getting proper lungful's of oxygen when she spun around and pointed a finger at me. "You didn't see those. You walked in and they were pretty girly ones... with lace!" she added as an afterthought.

Rolling onto my knees and using my hands to push up as I gulped in air, I shook my head. "You're not taking that away from me," I wheezed. "Those were awesome."

"Shut up," she squealed again, covering her face with her hands.

"Are they all like that?" I asked as I got to my feet. "Wait, do you wear those to work, too?"

The thought of her wearing gaming nerd panties in her office was kind of a turn on if I was honest. It hadn't occurred to me before now that something like that would be, but then, it was Katy. She made things like that hot.

Before she could answer – or her head could explode judging by the redness in her face – there was a knock on the front door. Sending me a glare, she pivoted and walked out of the room, only just remembering that her ankle was still giving her grief.

Still chuckling, I followed behind her with Duke pushing past me to get to where his mama was.

"Don't be mad, baby," I called. "I'll show you mine if it makes you feel better!"

Seeing that I was now in the living room, she made a farting noise at me, and then swung the door open to show Maude standing on the other side with her hand up ready to knock again. Slowly, her eyes moved from her granddaughter to where I was standing, and I belatedly remembered that I didn't have a t-shirt on.

Swinging back to look at Katy, a huge grin took over her face, and she pushed past her and walked toward me with her arms wide open. When she got to me, she gave me what amounted to as much of a bear hug as she could give, and put her cheek flat against my chest.

"This is the best moment of my life," she sighed, not letting go.

Shooting Katy a look that begged for her to help me, I gave her a quick hug back and then patted her shoulder gently. When she just held on and stayed holding on, I mouthed, "Help!" at Katy, but she just stood there and shook her head.

"Uh, Maude…"

"You get extra points if you sing to me at the same time," Maude sighed – again. "Double extra points if you sing *Tears In Heaven*."

"Maude loves Clapton," Katy informed me, and then mouthed, "Karma."

"Katy loves Clapton, too," Maude added. "But her favorite is *My Father's Eyes*. Used to listen to it and play air guitar in the car with her dad all the time. Well, that was until he did it on a corner and took out a mailbox."

"No, he still does it," Katy sighed, making me wonder how into air guitaring someone could get to hit a mailbox.

"I see," I mumbled, looking down at the top of Maude's hair that was so voluminous this morning that it almost hit my chin.

Still holding on tight, Maude declared, "It's taken a couple of decades, but I've finally found my happy place."

Seeing how uncomfortable I was getting – I mean, a hug was a hug, but a five-minute hug? – Katy suggested, "Why don't we have a coffee, Maude?"

"I'm good."

"No, really. Why don't we have a coffee," she ground out this time. "In the kitchen."

"He has bumps on his tummy and I'm an old woman. I'm using them like one of those massage mats. It's therapy."

"Maude," she warned, walking up and tapping her on the shoulder. "I think you're good now."

Instead of listening, she just shook her head and sighed again.

"Um, Maude, can I go and get a coffee?" I asked.

"Sure, you can do that while I'm still like this. Maybe you could carry me? I have old legs."

Tipping her head back to glare at the ceiling, Katy snapped, "Ok, fine. There's an all-male stripper group coming to town next weekend. I'll take you if you let go of him."

Those were the magic words because she let go of me, gave me a pat on the chest and then turned around to hug her granddaughter, who looked now like she'd just swallowed acid. I could understand that feeling, because I kind of felt like I had, too.

"Male strippers?" I questioned, wondering why this was bugging me so much.

"Yes, dear," Maude said over her shoulder as she made her way to the kitchen. "It's at Sheeve's next Saturday. A bit like Thunder Down Under, but apparently they're hung like stallions."

Following slowly behind her, Katy asked, "How do you know that?"

"Because I wouldn't go to one where they weren't, Katarianne," she said simply, shrugging as she put a pod into the machine and hit the button. "Imagine the force field they make when they shake it about."

Leaning on the counter, I scrubbed my hands over my face. "Jesus."

This time when a face hit my chest, it was Katy's and not Maude back for round two. That meant that I had zero issues putting my arms around her. In fact, she could stay like that for as long as she wanted.

Looking away from her cup and taking our positions in, Maude asked, "So, by the state of undress, I'm taking it you spent the night, Jarrod?"

"No, I didn't."

"Mm hmm," she hummed, and then looked at Katy. "Please tell me you were wearing some of those pretty panties I got you and not a pair of those god awful ones with the characters on them."

Thinking back to Mario, I burst out laughing and told Maude. "No, they were definitely character ones."

"Was it the blue spiky hedgehog?"

"Nope, they were the ones with Mario on them."

Seeing that she was looking blankly at me, I winked with my thumb in the air like he was in the picture.

"Oh, Katy," she said disappointedly. "And I bought you all of those pretty ones. How are you ever going to get Jarrod's dragon in your dungeon if you wear that type of stuff?"

Turning her head, Katy hissed, "It's *Dungeons and Dragons*, Maude. I keep telling you that."

"Still sounds perverse," she sniffed back, pulling her cup out and heading to the fridge. "Like when they put that little mushroom on it with 'Eat Me' above it."

I couldn't help it, I had to know. "Is that the little Mario mushroom?" When Katy nodded, I tilted my head to the side and asked, "Have you got those?"

Katy turned her head in the opposite direction to where Maude was to look anywhere but at either of us, but it was confirmed when Maude closed the door to the fridge loudly and said, "She's got them in four colors."

Lace was hot, but a Mario mushroom with 'Eat Me' above it? Abso-fuckin'-lutely.

Waiting until Maude had walked back past us to the living room, I leaned down and whispered, "You wear those, baby, and I'll do whatever it says on them," and pulled away from her to follow behind her grandmother. "I'm just going to get a t-shirt. I'll be back in a second."

Patting her lap, Maude winked, "I'll keep your spot warm."

For the second time in the space of thirty minutes, I burst out laughing hard enough to wake the dead.

Fuck peace and quiet. I wanted Crew life.

CHAPTER ELEVEN

KATY

I'd been awake for the last twenty minutes, desperately needing the bathroom but too afraid to move. Why? Because apparently I'd fallen asleep on Jarrod again, except this time in my bed. At first when I'd woken up I'd been confused why my pillow was so hard, warm, and was breathing, but then it had all come back and I'd been frozen in place since, telling my bladder it could wait until hell had frozen over for it to get what it wanted. Moving meant possibly waking him up, which also meant that I could never blink again either so my eyes could make their peace with that, too.

Unfortunately, not being able to move gave me time to think, which gave me time to remember – some of it good, some of it embarrassing.

After he'd gotten dressed yesterday, Jarrod had come back over and spent the day with us. I'd been having issues getting the TV in my living room to attach to the internet, so he'd tinkered with it to see if it was a software issue or something. Alas, it looked like I needed a new TV if I wanted to watch

Netflix downstairs. Fortunately, the one in my bedroom was
newer so I could still watch it up there, but that was kind of a
pain in the ass if you wanted to be in the living room.

Finally, after what felt like ninety days, Maude had gotten up
and said goodbye to us. Apparently she was headed to a flower
arranging class and couldn't be late. She also told us that the
flower arranging class was the bachelorette party for her friend
who was getting married for the fifth time, at the age of eighty-
five, and that she was only going because there was going to be
good wine there.

I'd been dreading the moment we were alone, but as soon as
the door shut, Jarrod picked up his phone and said we should
order Chinese food. Not one to pass down Chinese ever, I'd
agreed, and when normal cable looked boring as hell, we'd
decided to go upstairs and watch the last episode of *The Witcher*
in my room while we ate the food. I quickly realized that one
didn't just watch one episode of the series and that to
truly enjoy it, you had to watch all of it all over again – so
we did.

That had started a discussion on the game versus the series,
and which was better. I was torn, like actually torn on this one.
I liked the series, the game was awesome, the Geralt character
in both was hot as hell... I couldn't make up my mind.

During all of this, I'd noticed how aware of my eccentricities
he was. He was overly careful not to drop food on the bed, he
didn't move stuff around, if he wanted to see something he
asked and then made sure I was ok with how he'd put it back,
then as soon as we were done eating he took the garbage and
leftovers downstairs and put it all away... it might not sound
like a lot, but not many people were like that. Because of that,
when he came back up, I'd told him about how things had been
out of place in my room and what had happened to my
pictures, and he'd tried to think back over the day everyone

was here. The only ones who were actually in my stuff were the twins, and he didn't think they'd do that because they were moving stuff to organize it properly, not to mess it around.

Not having answers bothered me, but I wouldn't have put it past my brothers to move shit while they were round here, so I'd just have to cause them pain when I saw them again.

After that, we'd settled down and had watched a movie called *Rampage* which I was now putting in the top five of my favorite movies ever. I'd started off resting back against some pillows, but soon enough Jarrod had pulled me down so that my head was on his chest and had played with my hair through it. I totally got what Maude meant about it being her happy place!

I hadn't realized how stiffly I'd been holding myself, though, until he muttered, "Relax, baby. I'm not gonna jump you."

That declaration made me somewhat disappointed as well as relieved, but it also made me focus on relaxing my muscles. Then I got a wild hair – something that I wasn't known for – and jumped on him and kissed him, a clean pair of Mario panties and all. There was only so much Jarrod chest on my face I could take, and it really was the only way to get rid of the tension… that was the excuse for doing it at that moment, at least.

Then we settled back into our previous positions, rewound the movie, and I fell asleep on his chest watching it.

Yes, I'd jumped Jarrod, literally. The poor guy was innocently watching an albino gorilla who could speak sign language and give the birdie to Dwayne Johnson (he'd also mutated along with a crocodile and wolf who'd killed the hot guy from Magic Mike – sad times) and I'd launched myself on top of him.

I wanted to die of embarrassment!

Figuring that maybe giving my bladder what it wanted and

then going on the lam (or maybe my bladder could hold out while I went on the lam? Not far, just three hundred miles or so) was the best way to escape, I slowly slipped away from him, freezing and watching him when he shifted slightly. When he didn't move again, I let out a breath and looked down, ready to continue on my way, and came face to face with a bulge under the blanket.

A bulge at his crotch under the blanket.

A blanket bulge.

A Jarrod penis blanket bulge.

And my head was right over the penis blanket bulge. Now, I'm not gonna lie, I'd obviously tried to picture it. Who in their right mind wouldn't have? It was Jarrod freaking Kline's penis. Any woman who even glanced at him probably thought about it and it was right under my face, under my blanket, in my bed.

Fuh. Ka. Me.

Glancing quickly up at him again to make sure he wasn't awake, I looked back down at it and studied it. If all of that was him, then holy shit. But, being rational here, the likelihood was that some of it could be his zipper sitting weirdly (disappointing), as well as the way his jeans had gathered while he was sleeping (doubly disappointing), and both of those could also have made the blanket lie slightly weird (totally disappointing). In an ideal world, it was all Jarrod, though, but I had to be slightly rational.

A deep chuckle snapped me out of my blanket bulge musings, and if I thought I was embarrassed before, it had nothing on how I felt right then.

"Babe," he rasped in a deep, sleepy voice. "It's not going to bite you."

"How do I know you didn't get any of the genetic stuff like George did in *Rampage*?"

This apparently was a hilarious concern to have, but I thought I had a point. "I don't think it's going to go around attacking people, Katy."

"But how do you know?"

His large hand landed on my shoulder and stroked the skin next to the strap of my tank top. "Because he's never done it before."

"How can you be sure?" I pressed. When all he did was laugh, I asked, "Just out of curiosity, how much of that blanket bulge is you?" This time when I looked up at him, he had a huge grin on his face, but all he did was raise an eyebrow at me. "Damn jeans, zippers, and blankets," I muttered, finally pulling back and moving to do what I'd needed to do for at least thirty minutes now.

It wasn't until I got to the door that he called, "Hey, Katy, can you pass me my jeans from the chair, please?"

Acting automatically, I picked them up and chucked them to him, and decided that I'd be more comfortable peeing in the spare bathroom than the one attached to my bedroom. I wasn't sure exactly how thick the walls were between the rooms, but I didn't want to risk him hearing me tinkle. That was just a bit too much out of my comfort zone, especially after I'd questioned his penis.

It wasn't until I sat down that it hit me. His jeans had been on the chair in my room… He didn't have his jeans on… *That wasn't a zipper and jean bulge at all…*

Staring at the wall, I felt a small shiver of something work its way over me. I'll call it *something*, because it definitely wasn't a bad shiver at all.

149

"No wonder he looked so cocky!"

Jarrod

Spending time with Katie wasn't a hardship at all, far from it. She was quiet, but what she had to say was usually funny, even if she didn't intend for it to be. I also knew that with what was building between us, I needed to guide her slowly and carefully. I'd given it some thought the night I'd asked her out in front of her parents, and I didn't think she was totally innocent, but I also knew confidence was a problem for her and so was shyness.

Katy was shy in a strange way. Normally, I'd think of someone blushing or hiding their face, but with her she showed it in different ways. She tended to withdraw and wait rather than act, and she was just... well, Katy. Sweet, beautiful, just like the fairy princess her parents had said she'd been born like.

So, I was going to have to guide her through this, which meant that I had to take my time – even if she jumped on me like she had last night. That along with her having the guts to question me about my dick this morning gave me hope that she was feeling the same things I was about what was happening between us – hope and fucking happiness like I couldn't remember ever feeling before.

One step at a time.

I was also finally taking her out on our first date today, which I was getting ready for. I'd waited until she was in the bathroom to yell it to her, and then I'd run downstairs to head back to mine to shower. It wasn't going to be anything huge, but it was going to be fun...

"I CAN'T BELIEVE YOU BROUGHT ME HERE ON OUR FIRST date," she gasped as she took in the displays around us. "It's... I..."

Stopping, I gently turned her to face me. "You don't like it?"

"Like it? It's the craziest first date ever," she said, still sounding shocked.

This time my voice was disappointed when I asked, "So you don't like it?"

"I love it. It's the best date in the history of dates," she told me in a tone that implied that I was the crazy one.

Turning her back around to face the room filled with gaming displays and people walking around in character costumes, I whispered in her ear, "Live it up, baby. Where do you want to go first?"

When I'd bought the tickets on Friday, I'd had second thoughts just as the 'Congratulations' message came up that confirmed my successful purchase. In fact, I'd been lucky as hell to even get the tickets this late and it was purely down to the fact that the gaming convention had been planned six weeks previously, but because of an influx of really bad weather and a norovirus outbreak, it had been canceled. The tickets I'd had to purchase in the end were all access, all day, VIP ones which had cost a fortune, but I'd done a ton of overtime recently so it wasn't impossible. Seeing her face now, though, I'd pay double what I had just to see that excitement again.

Before we could take the first step forward, she spun around, pulled my face down to hers and kissed me soundly. For a minute I forgot we were surrounded by people in cosplay outfits and gaming paraphernalia, and I also forgot my one step at a time mantra...

At least until I felt someone stop beside us and growl, "Fuck!"

Reluctantly, I lifted my mouth away from Katy's, and we both looked to the side to see a dude dressed up as Geralt of Rivia, aka the dude from *The Witcher*. *Of course it was, it wouldn't possibly be anyone else, would it?*

"Oh my god," Katy whispered, staring at him. "You even sound just like him."

The guy focused his amber eyes on her, growled and then stomped away before she could say anything else.

Shaking it off, I looked down to see her eyes sparkling up at me. "I just growled at by Geralt of Rivia. Best. Date. Ever!" she told me, leaning into me on the last word.

And there began the weirdest date of my life – and possibly the most expensive – but it was also the best date I'd ever been on, too. And not just because she was so excited, but because she was Katy.

Katy

Eight hours later...

Going out on a date with a tall guy was one of the bestest things ever. Three times we'd gone into a theater to see different actors/creators speak, and each time I'd had the problem I'd encountered my whole life – height. For some reason, even with heels on, the world was filled with gargantuan freaks of nature. Because the venue for the con didn't have fixed seats in the rooms, it was standing only which freaking sucked.

Then in came Jarrod and his height. Without even asking – although you couldn't not see me standing on tiptoe to try to see over the shoulder of the big ape in front of me (literally because he was wearing a gorilla suit) – he'd bent down, put his head between my legs (yes, it was as exciting as it sounds until I realized what he was actually doing), and had lifted up with me on his shoulders.

Fan. Fa. King. Tastic! And that was a new one that I was keeping all to myself. My brothers could get in shit for swearing because I was keeping it.

What made it even better – although it confused me how anything could be better than his head between my thighs, especially seeing as how a lot of it connected to my vagina – was that the guy on the stage saw me and started laughing, then called me up to meet him at the end.

When we'd gone to the second one, Jarrod had just done it again without me even having to go onto my tiptoes for a second, and the guy was at that event, too. He'd waved at me and yelled, "Hey, Katy!"

For the third one, I'd been ready and waiting, and we'd ended up having coffee with all the actors and creators after it was over.

And, and, *and*, I was now the proud owner of five bags of merchandise and signed swag that had been given to me by those actors and creators. Add all of this onto me having Jarrod's head between my legs and against my vagina three times in one day, and it *was* the best moment of my life.

The only time I was even mildly embarrassed was when a guy dressed up as Mario had come up to us (big costume head and all) and had held his thumb up to me. Of course the big shit head had to get a photo of the three of us (and Mario's thumb) together and had then texted it to Maude. She was kind enough to send a voicemail back of her cackling with laughter, which ended with her threatening to shove the roses up someone's ass if they touched her arrangement again. Jarrod looked alarmed by that and had asked if he should send his brothers over, but she played Bridge on the first Sunday of the month, and those old biddies were hella aggressive when they were losing.

We were now on our way home and I had a warm feeling in my stomach about how the day had gone.

"We should take Elodie next year," Jarrod mused as he overtook someone. "We could dress her up as baby Groot."

The warm feeling I'd been nursing turned into a blazing inferno. "Really?"

Taking his eyes off the road for a second, he looked over at me and grinned when he saw how happy that idea made me. "Yeah. We'll make it a weekend with her and get the Friday to Sunday tickets."

This made the inferno hotter than the sun. First off, he liked my niece enough to take her to something like that, and for the whole weekend. Second, he was thinking of ways to include her into things. Third, he thought we'd still be whatever we were in a year. Or wait, was he thinking that we could split up and survive it as friends? That was a sucky prospect.

"She loves Groot. I got her this baby one that dances to that Jackson 5 song, *I Want You Back*. I swear whenever it turns on, she does her best to moonwalk."

"Why doesn't that surprise me?" he chuckled, reaching over for my hand. "Hey, I have a question."

"Shoot."

"Now that I know where your names came from, how did Elodie get her name?"

Now this *was* a Debbie downer topic. "When she was born, Effie left it until the last second almost to get to hospital. When

Uncle Leo got the call, the staff said she'd practically crawled in, pushed her out, and left. They'd only just gotten her situated in a bed and had taken Elodie to have some tests done seeing as how Effie was high as a kite."

His hand tightened on my fingers, and then it felt like he forced himself to relax. "Was she born addicted?"

"No," I blew out a breath. "Being the *caring* mother that she was, Effie had stuck to pot once she knew she was pregnant. That said, we're not talking about a joint here and there, we're talking constant. Elodie was only just under five pounds when she was born, slightly premature, and it took them six weeks to let Leo take her home because she had some ups and downs because of it."

"Jesus," he muttered. "Poor precious girl."

"Anyway, Leo couldn't decide what to name her, but he knew he wanted to do something similar to Mom and Dad because he was torn between his dead wife's name, Ellen, and her mother's name, Melodie – with an I and E. He'd been thinking Mellen until I visited her and told him he couldn't call the poor baby something that sounded like melon. I mean, what's up with that?"

"People call their kids apple," he pointed out. "What about Mellencamp? He's a legend, so you could have given him the credit."

With my head still pressed against the headrest, I turned to look at him. "Does she look like a Mellen to you?"

He took all of five seconds to think it over and answer. "Point taken."

Damn right, doggy. "I suggested Elodie, and he loved it, so that's what we named her."

"What happened to Effie during all of this? Were CPS involved?"

"Yeah," I sighed, turning now to look out of the window at the dark around us. "It was a mess, but Leo's a great guy and CPS prefer to keep kids with their families, so after some red tape and cavity searches, they said ok. Then he had to track Effie down to get her to sign over custody to him which sucked."

"Why did it suck?"

Doing my best not to cry, I whispered, "Because by the time he found her, she was so high, she'd forgotten she'd even had a baby."

There was a tense silence, and then he growled, "What the fuck?"

Exactly. She was my flesh and blood, but I couldn't get my head around it a year later.

"Leo struggled with that the most I think."

Shaking his head, he asked, "So, what's with the purple teddy bear?"

This question hit on another sore point for me. "Three months ago when she did one of her fly by visits, she made a huge deal out of the teddy bear. At first Leo wasn't sure about giving it to her because of the quality and was worried that one of the eyes would fall off and she'd choke on it, but by the time Effie left, Elodie wouldn't sleep without it. He took it to a friend of his who was one of those rare doll fixer guys to check the eyes and he did something that made them uber safe."

"Uber safe?" he snickered, giving my hand a quick squeeze. "What kind of safe is that?"

What kind of question was that? "Uh, only one step down from as safe as Fort Knox."

Fortunately, we were at a red light when I said this because he threw his head back and burst out laughing. "Fort Knox is *secure*, baby."

"Exactly. Fort Knox is a big safe that's uber secure, so I'm right."

This answer got him laughing again, but this time he had to tame it down slightly because the lights had just changed back to green so we were moving away from them. "I don't mean to offend you when I say this, but it's..." he stopped and searched for a word, but I had one to hand.

"Ugly?"

"Well, yeah, but that wasn't what I was looking for."

"Gross?"

"True, but no."

"Cheap?"

On that one he sighed and shot me a glance, telling me I'd hit the nail on the head. Looking back at the road he mumbled, "Ever since I saw her with it, I've wanted to replace it. My grandparents bought us Steiff bears from Germany when we were born, so I had a look at their site to see what they had available. I'll understand if you don't want to give it to her, but I just wanted her to have something..." he paused and shifted uncomfortably, "better."

When I didn't answer him and just kept staring at him, he carefully reached behind him into the footwell and pulled out a bag. Placing it on my lap, he explained, "I don't want to take something her mom gave her away from her, so it can be an extra bear for her if you want. It's just the one she has doesn't look like it would last long either and with it being the only thing she has from Effie, maybe y'all should look at keeping it safe for her so she always has it."

Slowly, I opened the bag in my lap and saw a pretty box inside it with the word Steiff on it. Lifting the lid on it, I saw a beautiful bear that was the same color as the one Elodie had now. The difference was, as I ran my fingers over its face, it had eyes that you knew definitely wouldn't come off and choke her, and it was so soft even I wanted to cuddle it forever. The one she had now felt almost like industrial carpeting when you touched it, and if Leo hadn't had the eyes secured, one definitely would have fallen off and it just wasn't worth the risk.

What I had in my lap now was a thing of beauty fit for a special princess baby, and Jarrod had bought that for my niece.

When I didn't say anything, he said, "It was a stupid idea, you don't have to…"

"It's beautiful," I choked out, interrupting him. "It's the most beautiful bear I've ever seen, and it's perfect for her."

"Do you think she'll like it? You can always put the bear Effie gave her in the box or on a shelf, just so that it doesn't fall apart."

The thought that had gone into this from this man was mind blowing. Not only was he buying Elodie a bear like his grandparents had bought him (a German bear which to me linked to half of what made Jarrod Kline the man he was), and not only had he looked for something that was just like what she had, but he was looking at preserving what her mom – who'd abandoned her – had given her so that she had it for life because it was so cheaply made.

It all blew my mind.

"She's going to love it. I'll speak to Leo to see how we should do it, but I know he'd be onboard with the original purple bear disappearing. Maybe if we arrange it so that you're the one who gives it to her so she understands how special it is?"

"I can do that," he replied gruffly, clearing his throat afterward.

Reaching for the hand I'd been holding before, I was the one who squeezed this time. "Thank you so much for this, Jarrod. It's the most thoughtful gift I think I've ever come across. Well, aside from taking me to a gaming and comic convention. And letting me sit on your head."

"You were on my shoulders, honey," he chuckled, and then glanced over at me. "And trust me, none of it has been a hardship. Far from it."

That's when all of my energy left me at once, and my back hit the door with a thud. "Well, this sucks."

"What sucks?" he asked cautiously.

"Well, if I ever want to do anything for you, I have to think of something that's going to kick all of this's ass. I also want to kiss you and you're driving so I can't. See? It sucks!"

It was just as well my back was already against the door, because he flicked a glance at his rearview mirror, swerved off the road onto the gravel, and then undid our seatbelts and pulled me into his lap, kissing me before my ass hit his thighs.

It was quick by our standards, but it was the hottest kiss we'd had so far, which said something. And there, on the side of a road as we made our way home from the best date ever, with a purple bear from Germany beside us, Jarrod took a little bit more of my heart.

What I didn't realize was that I'd taken a whole lot of his, too.

CHAPTER TWELVE

KATY

O*ne week later...*
"This is the happiest moment of my life," Maude yelled across the table to me, making Maya, Isla, Ebru, Sabine, Sonya, Layla, Scarlett, Jose, Tabby, Rose and I laugh.

Yup, we were all here, but the difference was that only me, Maude and Layla had come honestly and hadn't had to sneak out of our house to do it. How the men all fell for their women having period pains at the same time I didn't know, but they had.

"I thought that was when you had your face against Jarrod's naked chest," Tabby shouted back.

Maude stopped to think about it as she watched a guy on the stage having a shower and then shrugged. "Ok, this is the second happiest moment of my life."

Putting her finger to her lips, Maya got up and walked through the darkened seating area to where a man in a suit was watching the show. No one else had seen her doing it, so it was only me watching out for her and wondering what she was doing. The man looked over her shoulder at the table as she turned around to point at us. After that, she gave him a hug and skipped back to us.

Leaning into my side she whispered, "Wait for it."

"Wait for what?" I whispered back, but all she did was shake her head and look back up at the stage.

"Do you know they wear cock socks?" Tabby asked us, her speech slurring slightly after her Sambuca challenge with Maude earlier, so it came out "cocksh shocths".

Finding this tidbit of information interesting, I tried to think of what kind of socks a man would wear on his pee-pee. I mean, I wasn't an expert in men's socks, I stuck to ones with Harry Potter, Alice in Wonderland, and retro gaming characters on them. They just looked cuter than normal ones to me. But I knew that Jarrod wore these thick ones that had what looked like extra padding on the soles and had a thick part that went up his ankle. Would that be suitable for a penis? Then a mental image hit me of one of the handsome, built guys on the stage pulling a sock on with the Cheshire Cat grinning on it over his schlong and I burst out laughing getting the attention of the table.

"Don't mind me," I snickered. "What kind of socks do they use? Like those sneaker footsy ones?"

"I dunno," Tabby shrugged, eyes on the stage. "All I know is that when they do something where they have to pull their speedos off, they have it all tucked away in a nice little cocky socky house."

"He looks like he'd wear a penis sock size twelve," Maude

guessed, nodding her head at the handsome blonde on the stage. "Maybe even a thirteen."

"If he keeps jerking it around like that, he's going to need one of those socks they wear on construction sites," Maya muttered beside me, making me burst out laughing again.

And then it happened, something funny to everyone else, but a total nightmare to me.

"I hear there's a blushing virginal bride in the audience," the MC said into his microphone as he pointed at our table.

Looking behind me and seeing a wall, I turned back and glared at Maya. "That better not be me," I hissed.

"Oh, it's not," she confirmed, grinning widely before she turned around and muttered something under her breath that I couldn't hear over the round of applause that filled the room.

"Maude Crew, where are you darlin'?" the MC asked, still staring at our table.

This didn't call for non-swearing swearing, this called for the mother of cussing. "What the actual fuck?"

Before I could stop her, she was up on her feet with her hands in the air, screaming. *"That's me, that's me."*

"Well, get your beautiful ass up on the stage, babe. We're gonna give you something you'll never forget," he told her, jumping off the edge and running up to hold his arm out to her.

Rather than say something like hi or that Maya was a big fat liar, she yelled, "Is your cock sock a size twelve or thirteen?"

"Oh, fucking shoot me," I muttered, sinking lower in my seat.

"Here, have a drink," one of the girls said and pushed a pitcher and a full shot glass over to me. "It'll help numb the pain."

And on that note, I shot back whatever was in the shot glass, and then stuck three straws in the pitcher and went to town.

"YOU KNOW," I TOLD MAYA, LEANING DRUNKENLY INTO HER side. "I read that strippers are like really smart."

Equally as drunk as I was, seeing as how we'd been competing to see who could down their pitcher first, then we'd timed what was quicker – two straws or three - then we'd done something else, and now I was sloppy. Sloppy, I loved that word, it should be used more.

"My name's sloppy," I snickered, holding my hand out to her.

"Mine's blottola," she giggled back.

"We need a lady up on the stage," the MC said this time. Maude had been up, she'd ripped the dudes pants off and screamed, then he'd rubbed all over her and got her to run a soapy sponge over his chest and back... After that I'd started drinking more because I was still feeling pain, so I missed out on what happened, but whatever it was the crowd screamed louder than they had all night. Now, they needed another poor, sloppy chump. "Is there a Katarianne Crew in the crowd tonight?"

Nudging me with her elbow harder than was necessary, Maya pointed to the stage. "That's you he's calling."

"No, it's not. My name's sloppy!"

"Katarianne Crew, we know you're out there gorgeous, and we also know you're as beautiful as your name. Now get up on the stage."

Maya shot up out of her seat and started pointing at me. "She's here, she's here."

There was no way you could miss her doing it, but there was definitely no way you could miss it when everyone else at the table stood up and yelled it too.

At the same time, three men jumped off the stage and jogged across the floor to me.

"Hey, babe," a guy with black hair said as he got to me. "Time to make you soar."

Through the drunkenness, I heard the word 'sore' not 'soar', easy mistake but totally different meaning. So, I did what any sane woman would do when a stranger said he was going to make her sore.

"I'm not into the red room of pain," I yelled, trying to back away from him and hitting a hard lumpy surface that grunted. Pointing at Maude I added, "Pick her, she'll let you do anything to her."

"Aiyeeeee," Maude screamed, jumping up and down. "Hell yeah I will."

Shaking his head and grinning, the guy picked me up and carried me up to the stage.

"I don't like pain," I told him. "I'm a gamer. That means I like my laptop, my Xbox, games with weird characters in them, cheese balls, Cheetos, and food that you can eat that doesn't make a mess."

"Cool," one of the other guys who'd jumped off the stage said as he walked beside us. "What games do you play?"

So I listed them. In a room where women were paying money to see the guys strip, and those guys were carrying me to the stage to whip the bejesus out of me, I listed all the games that I loved to play – and bonus, I ended up getting one of their gamer tags to add on Xbox because he played one of the games, too.

After they got me settled on the stage, I was trying to figure out which way I could run and my chances of getting to a door while I was seriously intoxicated, when the door I was staring at opened and in walked a bunch of pissed off Townsend men, Montgomerys, a sheriff, a tattoo artist, a deputy sheriff, a Jarrod, and three Klines who tripped over their feet and burst out laughing when they saw me sitting on the stage.

I was just about to point at them, scream, and run to the girls at the table when I remembered how they'd all stood up and fed me to the lions only minutes earlier. Instead, I crossed my arms over my chest and grinned at them.

The girls mistakenly thought I was having fun and started grinning back at me until the men arrived at the table. Even with the bright lights shining in my eyes, I could see their faces drop when they realized they were busted. This meant, though, that I also saw the expression on Jarrod's face when he saw me sitting on stage. He wasn't pissed – at least, not that you could see on the outside – he was what I'd guess was vaguely amused by my predicament. Then, his mouth slowly broke into a grin which confused me until two men wearing towels walked in front of me and cut my line of sight to the table off.

"Are you ready, gorgeous?" One of the soapy wet guys asked me, closing what little distance there was between us.

"No," I answered honestly, because I really wasn't.

"We'll be gentle," soapy number two assured me, but this just made my blood pressure go up even more.

My eyes flicked from soapy one to soapy two and back again. "Please don't whip me. I'm not sure what my friends told you, but I've got a really low tolerance for pain. This morning I accidentally hit my toe on the leg of my bed and I cried for an hour." Which was a lie, kind of. I'd only hopped around and whimpered for five minutes, then I'd spent twenty making sure it wasn't broken. It should have been broken if you ask me, but those freaky foot digits always survived.

Soapy one looked at soapy two, and then they both burst out laughing. "We're not going to hurt you, babe," soapy two chuckled. "When we're done with you, you'll be feeling the opposite of pain."

This I highly doubted.

Then they started loosening the towels. A tug here, a slide of a finger between the fabric and their skin there, another tug, then another, and before I knew what was happening, the towels were off and resting over their crotches meaning that the audience got an unencumbered view of their naked asses. Still, just in case they were going to drop the item onto the floor, I covered my face with my hands.

The audience went crazy around us, but I was struggling to join them in their naked hottie enthusiasm. I just wanted to go home, eat chips, and maybe watch Netflix with Jarrod - I was that basic!

A pair of hands gently gripped my wrists and lowered my hands and I realized I had a hottie number three now in the mix. "You don't wanna miss this bit, darlin'," he growled in my ear.

Blinking to get my eyes to focus, I looked to the side and saw that the audience was now standing up at the stage waiting for the finale. A movement in front of me got my attention, and in the next second, the towels went flying off to the side and the stage went dark as the lights cut out.

That didn't mean I didn't get to see something seeing as how they didn't cut off soon enough. I could now break the news to Maude that a cock sock was just a plain black skull cap for the penis and balls. I could also tell her that hottie number one had put it over his balls, too, but hottie number two was letting his vegetables roam free.

It was too much for my brain, so I blindly stumbled to the edge of the stage – not caring if I fell to my death now – and went to jump down. Just as I'd committed to the jump by tipping forward, a strong pair of hands grabbed me around the waist and I was being lifted through the air until I was gently placed back on my feet and terra firma. I knew those hands, and I knew that cologne, so I launched myself at the owner and wrapped my arms around him, freaking relieved that the torture was over.

I felt the rasp of stubble on my cheek before Jarrod chuckled, "I doubt they've ever come across a woman who's hidden from them when they've done that, baby."

Tilting my face so it was in his neck, I was inclined to agree with that. "It was the worst moment of my life."

With that, he straightened up and burst out laughing, getting the attention of some of the women who were now making their way back to their tables from where they'd been standing getting a closer look at naked, soapy butts. A small group of them stopped and stared at Jarrod with their mouths open and their eyes wide.

"Please tell me you're one of the stage guys," a blonde lady asked hopefully.

"Sorry, but no. I'm just here for my girlfriend," Jarrod told them, shaking his head and holding me closer.

"I'll give you a hundred dollars to get soapy," blonde lady's friend said, reaching into the purse that was dangling by a short strap on her wrist. "No, make that two hundred."

I felt it as the muscles in his back that my hands were lying flat on tightened up. "No, but thank you for the offer."

Not to be deterred, she said to her friends, "How much money have y'all got in your wallets. We'll put it together for him."

"Oh, good idea," a redhead agreed as she dug her wallet out of her clutch. "I've got four hundred," she told them, and then leaned in Jarrod's direction and winked, "in ones."

Deciding now was the best time to quit this, I tugged on his hand. "Come on, let's get back to the table. I need a lot more alcohol than I've had."

Blowing out a relieved breath, he walked us quickly toward where the men were now all sitting with the girls. That kind of shocked me because I was certain they'd hustle them out of the building, but instead they were sitting with bottles of beer.

Dropping my hand, Jarrod put his arm around me and tugged me into his side. "Was it that bad, baby?"

Shooting him a look that said it all, I decided he needed to know exactly how bad it was for me. "Maude was up there a while ago, and to numb the pain and embarrassment of it, I downed pitchers and shots. Then, Maya and I did some experiments on the speed of consumption via straws of the contents of pitchers. I was happily sloppy until I was taken on that stage and now I'm sober. Their skull cap wrapped penises sobered me up. To get over the pain I've just endured, I now need more alcohol, but I'm not sure there's enough to get rid of the image burned into my retinas of construction socked cocks."

Jarrod listened to all of this quietly, and when I was done he just blinked, then blinked again, then blinked again. I was just about to move around the table to where my seat was when he threw his head back and burst out laughing again, the cords in his neck standing out sexily as he did it. I vaguely noticed that the table had gone quiet as he did this, but I was enjoying this show too much to acknowledge why that might be.

When it left him, he tipped his head back down again, his face still holding a wide grin. "We should probably get you some alcohol then."

"Sweet Jesus, that was beautiful," Maude gasped, her hand shooting out to grab Tabby's.

"Jarrod's hot, but when he's laughing like that, he's seriously fucking hot," she added, her eyes still on him.

Stunned for other reasons, Ren said to Cole, "Jarrod laughs? I thought he just did a smile or those little huh huh chuckles."

Relieved that the focus wasn't on my trip to the stage, I moved to my chair and then looked around for another one for him to sit on. Unfortunately, the place had been full before, but with the men here now it was definitely full, so there were no free seats to be found. Jarrod didn't find this to be a problem, though, because he sat down and then tugged me until I was sitting on his lap, and wrapped his arms around me, holding me close.

"She needs booze," he told the table, and the women all held their hands up at the same time to get the waitress's attention.

The woman who'd been serving us all night did a skip walk up to the table and shot us all a huge smile. "What'll it be?"

She was seriously the happiest person I'd ever met in my life. All night she'd been friendly and skippy, and I had no idea how she was doing it. If I had to deal with a bunch of women getting rowdy over guys ripping their clothes off, I'd be hiding in a corner praying for it to be over.

Gesturing for her to get closer, I laid out my order. "Ok, I'm relatively shy and I got carried up to that stage with a sloppy buzz going on after a lot of shots and pitchers – which were drunk by just me, FYI. So, I need enough replacement booze to numb the pain and embarrassment of socky cockies. Can you do that?"

The woman's head jerked slightly hearing this, and then she looked at me wide eyed and nodded. "I gotchu, boo," she assured me, and then skip walked away.

And indeed she did have me. Within minutes she was back with two pitchers with straws in them and five different colored shots that were in glasses slightly larger than the ones before.

Placing them down on the table in front of me and passing Jarrod a beer, she explained, "Got Larry at the bar to put double in the pitchers and the shots are what I call brain blasts. They're double measures, too, but if you start from left to right and finish with the pitchers, you'll be a new woman."

Reaching into my purse, I pulled out a twenty and passed it to her. We were running a tab that we'd split at the end, but every time she'd brought us a round, we'd tipped her. "You're a good woman, a good, good woman. You deserve fifty of those for what you've done for me here, but I didn't bring that amount with me."

I heard her say thank you and laugh, but I was already making my way through the shots. The first one burned, the second one stoked the burn, the third one added more kindling onto the burn so that it started to flame, the fourth one was like pouring lighter fluid on those flames, and the fifth one – which was cinnamon – turned it into an inferno. Because of that, I reached for the pitcher and took large pulls on the straws to put the flames out. Also, because of all of this, my sloppy buzz came back, left the building, and was replaced by a blottola buzz.

Halfway through the second pitcher, Maude went up on stage to have her photo taken with the men who were now done with their show. As they picked her up and held her so that she was laying across four of them, she screamed, "Now *this* is the happiest moment of my life."

After she'd had about twenty photos taken in different poses, we paid the tab and the men helped us out to the cars. Because she lived close to Jose, Ellis was driving Maude home, so with dramatic farewells where we acted like we wouldn't see each other for five years – i.e. *"Oh my god I'm going to miss you." "You better call me, ok? Don't leave it as long as you did this time." "I can't believe I'm not going to be sitting across the table from you anymore. This sucks so hard!"* - Jarrod put me in his Explorer, and off we went with us all waving at each other until we were too far away to continue.

That's when I realized exactly how drunk I was.

"I can't feel my lips," I giggled, making 'puh, puh, puh' noises.

"Exactly how drunk are you, honey?" Jarrod asked, thankfully sounding amused by it all, but this was Jarrod – he found most things amusing.

"I'm sloppy."

Shooting me a quick glance, watching me play with a button that made my chair back go down, then come back up again, then down again. I'd thought it was the one for the window, so this was even more confusing for me. "Sloppy?"

"The sloppiest sloppy in the history of slop," I muttered, pressing harder on the button. Then something hit me and I burst out laughing, with the seatbelt digging into me because my seat back was so far forward. "I'm a slopapotamus."

And then I did something I didn't even know was possible – I laughed myself to sleep. The next morning he'd describe how he looked over and there I was, face hanging down as I used the seatbelt to support my body because of the forward position of the back of the seat. In fact, apparently I'd let out a giggle every so often, too, even though I was out cold. Because he was afraid I'd be sick in my sleep or fall down the stairs for some reason, Jarrod slept beside me again. This time I didn't sleep on top of him, but I did wake up the next morning lying on my back sideways across the bed, with my feet on his chest and my head hanging off the bed.

CHAPTER THIRTEEN

JARROD

One week later...

One week later...

It had been two weeks since our first date, and
since then I'd spent pretty much all of my time with
Katy. Working together and living next to each other might
have been a problem if we weren't so busy with our families
and friends.

On Wednesday, her uncle had dropped Elodie back because
he'd gotten called away on business. Katy had discussed the
bear thing with him prior to him coming over and he'd been
onboard with our idea, preferably ASAP. So, after work we'd
gone back to her place, and I'd sat on the couch waiting for
them to arrive. Normally he carried her in, but this time she
wanted to walk in on her own, which she did, carrying the bear
under her arm the whole way.

Duke had been stoked to have his little buddy back, which
was great to see because he'd been acting weird lately, almost
like he was on guard, and we'd found some blood around his

mouth but couldn't see any injuries on him anywhere. Apparently, having his bud back was what he needed because he turned back into the happy dog he was, instead of the tense dog who lay down watching the door all the time.

When she'd seen me sitting there, Elodie let out a little shriek and had run over to me, something that I absolutely loved and had shown her the same excitement at seeing her back when I'd picked her up and blown a raspberry on her stomach. Like all kids, she'd noticed the box immediately, so with Leo and Katy watching, I'd let her open it and held my breath for her reaction.

I really needn't have worried because she looked at her bear, down at my bear, back to hers, and then she'd lifted the new one out of the box, placed the old one in it, and had wrapped her arms around the new bear with her head resting on top of it. With those innocent actions, she'd stolen my heart all over again.

The bear issue was still getting to me, and I guess I felt guilty about taking her mom's bear away from her. I really wasn't doing that, it was just that it was rough, as in scratchy rough, and even though Leo had his friend fix the eyes, I was still scared she'd swallow one or it would fall apart and she'd be left with nothing of her mom's. Doing it this way guaranteed that she had a bear she loved to cuddle, she wasn't at risk of choking, and we could put the other bear somewhere safe so that nothing happened to it. Until Katy figured out where that was, it was in the box the Steiff bear had come in on top of the shelves in Elodie's room.

That was drama number one done and dusted. Drama number two came on Friday – my birthday. I hadn't told Katy it was my birthday because we were new, and honestly, I didn't really care about it. Somehow she'd found out, though, so that morning she'd woken me up by making me breakfast, then she'd given me my presents. We'd discussed our favorite cars one night while we were watching a movie, and I'd told her about my love for Vipers. So, for my birthday, she got me a t-shirt with a 2010 Viper SRT10 (in black because that was my dream car), a book that basically covered anything mechanical to do with a Viper, a keyring with the Dodge Viper emblem on it, a pair of pajama bottoms that had the mushroom from *Mario Bros* on them on them, and a book about Port Royal where Mom was from. She'd been worried I wouldn't like it, but I loved every last bit of it.

That night we'd gone to my parents for another BBQ, this time it was my favorite meal my mom made: Jamaican escovitch snapper, rice and peas, bammy which was a flatbread, patties with ground beef in them, and she'd made a rum cake for dessert. These were all the things that the four of us asked for every year on our birthdays because they were so fucking great. The only thing that came close to it was the seafood you got at a restaurant called Gloria's in Port Royal (not related to Mom) and a chain restaurant across Jamaica called Island Grill – we didn't tell her that, though. All that Mom needed to know was that her food was the shit.

Mom had invited Katy's family again, but this time only Major, her parents and Maude came because Ammon had gone to visit his friend in Colorado, and Aura was in Georgetown visiting one of hers, too. The night had gone well until Mom started reminiscing about the four of us – and to a parent, reminiscing means sharing the most embarrassing stories you can think of about your kids.

The one that made everyone laugh the hardest was the time she found a bra in Canon's bed and thought he was hiding his "inner woman". So, being the supportive mother that she is, she'd sat him down and started doing his makeup for him, and then added one of her wigs which was long and curly. After that, she'd decided that he suited fall colors better because they were warm and would bring out his eyes more. Amazingly, through all of this, Canon had sat still, wondering what the hell was going on, and because we all adored her, he let her get on with it in case she was sad about the fact she never had a daughter. Ironically, Mom had been thinking that she finally got a daughter, so she'd been close to tears with happiness.

When she'd made him sit down at dinner like that, all of us had been sitting staring at him while she was serving food onto our plates. Dad had asked what the hell was going on, Mom had explained which ended up in a food fight between us all because we called him a liar when he denied it, even though we knew the bra belonged to Jenny Briggs who he'd sneaked into his room two days previously.

Then she'd brought out the baby albums, and I'd lost the will to live and had gone inside to play with Elodie for a while. One of Mom's wigs was a freaking awesome afro styled one that she hadn't worn since 1989 (she claimed), and I'd put it on Elodie's head to show everyone along with these huge sparkly chandelier earrings. The women had melted, and from there they'd taken her back to Mom's dressing room (aka Bond's old bedroom), tried every wig she owned on the baby, and then taken photos of her wearing them with a pair of Mom's shoes.

As gratitude for my distraction technique, Dad had promised me half of Bond and Canon's inheritance on top of my own. The best bit for me, though, was all the photos we now had of Elodie laughing, so into it that the few teeth she had were on display as she did it. And never once did she let go of her purple bear.

Going into work this morning hadn't been fun, but I finished at four and Katy had finished at one, so it wasn't technically a full day because we hadn't started until ten. Katy hadn't mentioned doing anything together tonight, so for the first time I had nothing to do – and I didn't like it. I felt kind of lost without her.

At a red light, I pulled my phone out and looked for a song that had been on my mind since Maude had mentioned it. The one that Katy loved by Eric Clapton, *My Father's Eyes*. Finding it, I hit play and listened to the beginning with Clapton playing the strings of his guitar perfectly and I could see why Paul got carried away with his air guitaring to it. For the next five minutes and twenty-three seconds (I checked how long the song was on the screen), I got sucked into it. By the time it was over, I was singing and air guitaring my ass off. Totally got how Paul got carried away with it, it would be an insult to the legend of Clapton not to do it.

Next up, I put on *Tears In Heaven*. Normally I was more of a rock type of guy, preferably classic rock, but this song… there was so much said in it. I vaguely remembered it being written for his son who'd died in a tragic accident, and that got me thinking about Elodie. Ever since I'd heard about how uninvolved Effie had been, it had been weighing on me. Did I want to be a father one day? I hadn't ever really thought about it. I'd just taken the fact it would happen for granted, if I was honest. I loved my friend's kids and spent a lot of time with Olivia, but I'd never had that urge to have one of my own. Again, I just assumed it would happen at some point.

What got to me was the lack of appreciation it appeared Effie had for her daughter. Here was this beautiful little girl, so full of life and love, and she hardly saw her, almost like she was a blip in her life. Everyone has a different story; I came from a stable, loving home and family with parents who adored me and my brothers, and not once had we ever felt anything other than that adoration. Katy had the same with her family, and they all worshipped the ground Elodie walked on. How do you get to the stage where a hit is worth more than your child?

How do you push out a baby and then walk away from it without even making sure someone was there to look after it?

Addiction. I'd only ever smoked pot, and even then it was when I was in high school and did it because everyone else was doing it. What makes someone go for a drug that changes them and that they then rely on to survive? I understood how bad addiction could be because I'd looked it up after Katy had told me about Effie, but it made me wonder if something had happened to her at some point that she wanted to escape from? If that was the case, should I speak to the family and see if we could track her down to get some help? Leaving her to wander lost and reliant on drugs that could kill her at any moment didn't feel right, but I wasn't sure I was at the stage with Katy to raise something like this.

I was going to have to soon, though, because it was weighing on me.

Pulling into my drive, I looked over and saw Katy's car in her driveway and cut the engine. Seeing it sitting there, I said fuck it and decided to just go over and see her. Just as I'd climbed out of the car and was shutting the door, I got a text from her.

Katy: *Come over. I'm just doing something so you can use your key. K x*

Seeing as how her keys were now attached to my own, this was no problem.

With a grin on my face, I jogged around the fence this time, and then down the path to her door.

Katy

Oh god, oh god, oh god, *oh god*. This had seemed like such a good idea on Tuesday, but now I was so anxious it felt like I was about to have a heart attack.

Gloria had called me on Monday to ask me to Jarrod's birthday dinner… a birthday I had no clue was happening. Thinking on it, that was a stupid move of mine because obviously everyone has a birthday so I should have asked, but it just hadn't occurred to me that it would be anytime soon. So, I'd played it off like I'd known about it, and then freaked the fuck out. Literally!

Maya had told me this played into the GYMP perfectly, because it meant I got to do something special for him to make him feel special and show him I got him. I liked to think that I got Jarrod, but I had no clue how I was meant to show him that. By Wednesday I was a nervous wreck, I'd covered his gifts, but her words about showing him he was special kept going round in my head. Books, t-shirts and Viper stuff didn't show a man you got him and that he was special – although, I obviously wasn't a man, so what did I know? So the question was, what did? And that's when Maya had introduced me to her friend Tony, who'd been busy with his daughters up until then. Apparently he knew exactly what to do.

An hour later, I was standing in the middle of Scarlett Treasures wanting to die of embarrassment.

"You want something sexy slutty, not *slutty* slutty, you dig?" he'd asked, standing with an item that to me went with the latter of those descriptions.

"Not really," I'd replied hesitantly.

"Ok, so here we have a satin number which would hardly cover your vagina," he said patiently, getting a glare from Scarlett. "That says slutty sex. This one here," he picked up a burgundy one made of a stretchy transparent material that had a thick lace band over the boobs and on the hem at the bottom, "says sexy slutty and invites him to tear it off your body."

Scarlett apparently had to concede with this one. "It pains me to say it, but he's right. That one really does invite him to do that."

Nodding, he passed her the *slutty* slutty one, and then held the sexy slutty one against me and closed one eye as he looked at me. "That color is a hell yes with your coloring, Katy. And with you being all tiny and fit in your pocket like, he's gonna see you as his little sexy pixy wearing it."

Looking between the two of them, I'd gulped at that description. "If you say so."

With a long drawn-out sigh, Tony nodded slowly. "I do, I really do. Now, what else can we find?"

The answer was: the burgundy nighty, a pale pink version in the same style, a navy satin nighty that had slits up either side of the legs that were trimmed with lace, another one that again he'd gone for the same style but with burgundy satin, and a white satin one in the same style that had a wide band of transparent lace under the boobs, too. As if that wasn't enough, I'd also ended up with ten new pairs of panties in different styles, along with five bras that matched them (two styles of panty for each bra).

As we passed by a table, I'd seen G-strings which tied at the side with satin bows, and an idea had hit me. So, picking up a pair, I'd asked Scarlett if she could make an adjustment to them for me, seeing as how she did 'personalized wedding underwear' according to a sign on the wall.

When I'd told her my idea, she'd looked at me like I was whacked, whereas Tony had put his head on the desk and muttered, "So close, I was so close."

But, the adjustment had been me, and I thought Jarrod would appreciate it, so to heck with his dramatics – even though I wouldn't ever say that out loud because he'd saved my bacon and he was a really nice guy.

After that, I'd gone to the store with another purchase in mind. It took me five trips up and down the aisle to stop and get what I was there for, then it took me staring longingly at a bottle of tequila thinking I could drink it to get up the courage to actually go to the till point. Then I'd hidden the items under the huge amount of groceries that I didn't need but had picked up on my many journeys past the aisle the items were in, and then I had to act like nothing was amiss when the checkout guy scanned the items. I did, however, freak out when the kid who was packing the bags went to pick them up to put them in with my groceries. He looked about thirteen and no way did I want that on my conscience. I'd just shoved them in a bag that was already back in the cart when my brother had appeared out of nowhere, which was a semi-relief because I'd noticed Shane Perkins watching me from the end of the aisle nearest me.

Saying hi and bye, I pretty much ran to my car to put the bags in the trunk, and then drove home like I was a paranoid diamond thief.

All of that just for three boxes of condoms.

It wasn't until I'd hidden them away in my bedside drawer that it dawned on me – I could have just ordered them online and no one would have known.

And this led me to now, sitting on my knees on the bed, wearing the burgundy sheer number with my personalized G-string under it, my hair blown out, and my makeup sex kitten style (although, it could have been hooker style, I had no idea.)

Cue the heart attack at twenty-two.

Tony had given me his number and told me to call him if I had any questions, so on my way home this afternoon I'd done just that. After he'd thrown around some ideas – some of which made me blush so hard I could have roasted s'mores on my face – we decided that this one was the best one, i.e. it was the one I could do without dying of shame.

Hearing Jarrod's footsteps coming up the stairs, I raised up so that I was standing on my knees and widened my thighs slightly, eyes trained on the doorway. He was looking down at his feet when he cleared it, but then he stopped and his head lifted up to look at me. He slowly trailed his eyes from my face all the way down to my knees, and then back up again, stopping on my chest for a second before looking back up at my face.

"Baby, what…"

"I decided that we needed to celebrate your birthday all over again," I told him, praying that I sounded a level of confidence I definitely wasn't feeling at that moment.

Hearing that, he swallowed audibly and then looked down my body again, this time stopping on my crotch. Maybe I should have listened to Tony…

"Is that," he squinted, "Luigi from the *Mario Bros* smiling at me?"

Yes, yes, it was. "I thought after the whole Mario incident, this would be…" I paused and looked around the room – noticing that the books on my shelf were out of place again – at anything that wasn't Jarrod, "applicable," I finished lamely.

Slowly he took a five steps closer to me, his lips twitching slightly. I totally should have listened to Tony.

"It is applicable to us," he agreed, toeing off one boot and then the other while I watched frozen in place. Once that was done, he continued walking closer to the bed until his shins were almost against it, meaning that I had to tilt my head to look up at him. "Can I take a closer look?"

Like he had to ask twice.

My arms had been hanging loosely at my sides, so all I had to do was turn my hands to grip the hem, and I slowly pulled it upward.

"Stop," he ordered gently as soon as the material had cleared them, then sat down on the bed. "Are the bows there for decoration?"

My only response was to shake my head.

"So if I untie them, they'll show me your pretty pussy?"

The pretty pussy in question clenched, but this time I nodded.

Gently dropping down onto his side, he leaned on one elbow, leaving the other arm free to extend so he could untie one side. I felt it the second the ribbon came undone and then half of the material sagged.

"Never thought I'd say this," he rumbled in a deep tone I'd never heard from him before. "But the Luigi addition ratcheted up the sexy factor of this outfit."

Tilting my head to the side, I thought about that. "So, Luigi does it for you?"

Before I could make a mental plan to contact Scarlett and tell her I wanted Luigi panties in all colors in this style, he let out a soft bark of laughter. "Fuck no, baby. *You* in your ribbon panties with Luigi on them does it for me."

I was still getting more panties like this with him on it if that was the case. I might even look at what other gaming characters I could get put on them.

That plan again screeched to a halt when I felt him trail the tip of his finger from my hip down the crease of where my thigh met my vagina, making my legs tremble slightly.

Feeling it, he glanced up at me. "You scared?"

Shaking my head, I croaked, "Not even close."

His eyes heated as he got what I was saying, and then he trailed his finger back up again. "Are you sure about this, baby? Are you sure you know what you're asking for?"

"I'm not an innocent virgin waiting for you to come back from a lifetime of knighthood and chivalry, Jarrod," I snapped, albeit breathlessly.

His finger froze where it had been moving across my abdomen, tracing where the waistband would have been if half of it wasn't sagging down, and he glanced back up at me. "You're not?"

I went to drop the hem of the nighty that I was still holding up, but seeing what I was about to do, he ordered, "Don't. Leave your hands where they are."

It irritated me how I did it immediately, which then made the tone of voice I used to reply to his previous question that bit more growly, "No, I'm not. I've just never done this before."

Rolling his lips together, he resumed the movement of his finger until he was at the other bow. I braced, waiting for him to tug it, but the tug never came. The more I waited and wondered, the more tense I got. Then he finally – fucking finally – tugged the ribbon, and it was *hasta luego* Luigi, or maybe that should be *arrivederci*?

"Christ," he rasped, running his finger down the crease on the other side now. "Never in my wildest dreams would I have thought it was this pretty."

Ok, that was a nice thing to say, but what was I meant to say back? "Thank you."

Why was I such a freaking dork?

Running his hand down the inside of my thigh now, he grinned up at me. "You're welcome, but really it's me who should be thanking you."

Rolling my eyes, I smiled back down at him. "It's really no hardship, you know. Your hand feels really... Oh, Jesus Christ," I groaned, as he ran the tip of his finger through my cleft, stopping to circle around my clit once before stroking back through it again.

I felt the bed dip as he used his free hand to get up on his knees, and when I opened my eyes, he was right in front of me. "Before we take this further, Katy, where's Elodie?"

"She's at Neo's. He wanted time with his niece."

Nodding, he leaned in until our lips were almost touching. "So I can make you scream?"

He could if he wanted to, which is what I told him.

The next second, I felt a tug on the backs of my thighs, and I was falling onto my back on the mattress – screaming. "That wasn't what I thought you meant."

Reaching over a shoulder to grab the back of his t-shirt, he pulled it over his head and threw it to the side. "It wasn't, but it was the fastest way to get you into the position I've wanted you in for a while."

Now that was a great response, and also true.

Before he'd arrived, I'd placed electric candles around the room, and the flickering light that they gave off was making the bumps of his muscles more pronounced. With my eyes on them and the V at that was just visible above the waistband of his jeans, I didn't see the expression on his face as he looked me over. Maybe if I had, I'd have seen how much this meant to him. Then again, if I'd seen the depth of that, I'd have gone out and bankrupted myself buying lingerie from every proprietor I could find, so it was probably just as well.

As an FYI, none of that was what was going through my mind at that moment. Instead, I was wondering what that V and those muscles would taste like if I licked them. There was a shower at the garage that the guys used before they left for the day, just out of a personal need to be clean before they got in their cars. Ren and Cole I could understand seeing as how they had kids who would climb all over them the second they got through the door, but Jarrod doing it had always confused me. In fact, I could probably count on one hand the amount of times he hadn't done it. At this moment, though, I was supremely grateful that he showered there, because I was certain that I was going to find out how the areas tasted – sans engine oil.

"I would pay good money to know what's going through your head right now," he said gruffly, getting my attention away from his abdomen and onto his face.

"I want to lick the V you've got going on, and I was wondering how your six-pack would taste."

He blinked twice at this honest information. "Do you have any idea what you do to me?"

My eyes flicked down to his hard length that his jeans were doing a shit job at concealing. "Pretty much."

He let out a hoarse laugh, getting my attention back on his face. "That's only part of it, Katy. There's much more to it than that," he explained, slowly lowering down onto a hand fisted in the bed beside my shoulder, and closing the distance between our faces. "Every day you do something that takes me by surprise in a good way. Every day you look at me with this soft look on your face and it makes me feel ten feet tall. Every time I kiss you, I want to take you down on the nearest surface and fuck you until neither of us can move again. There's so much to you that just reels me in, and I've spent a lot of hours pissed that I haven't had you in my life like this from the day you were born." When I went to question that, he shook his head. "No, I'm serious. I feel like – even though we're both young still – I've wasted time, time that I want to have spent with you, and I don't understand it."

Well shit.

"And now I've got you dressed in the hottest nightie, having worn the sexiest panties I've ever seen in my life, and I don't want to waste any more time."

With that, he lowered down and kissed me, his mouth opening almost immediately so his tongue could caress mine. I got so drawn into the kiss, that I only barely registered him shifting to his side and his hand trailing down my thigh. Then his finger was delving through my folds. This time, he circled around my entrance before he plunged the digit inside me. It felt so full with just one finger that my head tipped back and I let out a strange mewling noise that I'd never made before in my life.

"Fuck," he groaned, "you feel like silk."

That sounded like a positive thing, so I didn't say anything – not that I could. The sensations hitting me were almost overwhelming.

Then he began to kiss down my neck, making his way to my breastbone, then down past that down to where my nipple was. Throughout all of this, he never once stopped moving that finger in and out, and I couldn't stop my hips moving slightly with each plunge and withdrawal. At the band of lace on my chest, he stopped to nuzzle it with his nose, and then he shifted and sucked my nipple into his mouth, the lace of the nighty still covering it, and I came. With just those two actions, I came. I wasn't a one pump chump because there'd been no pumping. I was just a chump.

Lifting my head up, I watched as he quickly moved down my body until his head was over my crotch, and then he lifted me up with his hands under my ass and swiped his tongue through my folds. Any strength to hold my head up still was now gone, and it fell back again as he continued to lick, stopping only to suck and flick my clit, which was so sensitive now that I couldn't stop my hips jerking each time.

Feeling another climax building, I groaned, "Jarrod, I need you."

"Busy," he muttered, punctuating it by sucking my clit into his mouth.

"Please!"

"Busy," he repeated, trailing his tongue down to my entrance, and then plunging it into me.

"Honey, please," I started, and then stopped when my breath hitched in the middle of the word and the end of it came out as almost a squeak.

That apparently was the key for him, because he moved away and I heard the clinking of his belt buckle. Rolling onto my side, I reached for the drawer that I'd kept the condoms in, almost hissing with irritation when I realized it was too far away to reach.

Seeing what I was doing, he leaned over me and opened it, taking out one of the boxes. Our positions meant that I came face to face with his penis and I was too taken with how beautiful it was to be scared by the size of it. It was like the rest of him – perfect. Moving back so that he was on his knees, he tore the wrapper of the condom with his teeth, and then rolled it down his length – and that sight was awesome. An act like that was a private moment, something that I wouldn't have thought that I wanted to share with anyone, until then. Now I wanted to see it each time that we did this.

Once it was in place, he lifted me up off the bed with his hands in the middle of my back, and I wrapped my legs around his waist.

"We're going to do this slowly," he said softly, holding my eyes as I felt him position himself.

Shaking my head, I tried to push down to get him inside me, but his hands kept me in place. "I don't want to go slow."

"Katy," he growled. "Slowly. I don't want to hurt you."

Lifting my eyes to look at his face, I saw the worry there and my head cleared slightly. This time I nodded and took a deep breath in.

And then he was slowly pushing inside me.

Such was his strength that he controlled my descent with just his arms around my waist. When I was halfway down his length, he stopped and rested his head in my shoulder. "Are you ok?"

Wrapping my arms around his shoulders, I moved so that the tips of the fingers of my right hand trailed up through his close cut hair. I could feel the strain in his body and realized how much this was costing him. "I'm fine, you can keep going," I whispered, angling my head so that I could kiss his jaw.

With a shaky breath in, he raised his head, and lifting me off his length slightly, he raised his hips at the same time as lowering me down. With our eyes connected now, he sank me down the rest of his length until I'd taken all of him.

Ok, all right. Ok, all right. This is a lot, but it feels fantastic. The feeling of fullness and being stretch was overwhelming and looking into his eyes while feeling this and knowing he was inside me at that moment... un-fucking-believable.

Still looking at each other, he lifted me back up again, and then dropped me back down. Slowly he repeated this move until he knew I'd adjusted to him, and then he started to do it a bit faster.

Dropping my legs so that I was now properly astride him with my knees in the bed, I took over control of the movement. The glides up felt good, but nowhere near as good as the drops back down felt. Seeing the effect it was having on him, I took the opportunity to grind into him on the next downward slide, getting a loud groan out of him when it made me clench around him.

That apparently was a trigger for him, because he tipped me backward onto the bed and started thrusting into me as he leaned down and took my mouth again. I used the change in positions as an opportunity for my hands to roam, and skimmed them down his back, feeling the muscles bunching with each thrust.

Never in my life had I imagined it would be like this, and when he moved to put all of his weight on one arm and I felt the thumb of his other hand on my clit, I realized that it was possible for it to feel even better.

Roughly thirty seconds later, every muscle in my body froze, and I screamed as I came, clenching around him as he continued thrusting, making it go on even longer.

"Fuck," he grunted, his thrusts getting harder and faster.

Wrapping him up in my arms and legs, I felt it now as the muscles in his back went into overtime with the wildness of his movements.

Then he had his head in my neck and he let out a growl as it hit him. A fucking *growl*! Through it all, he continued to move in and out until the power behind each thrust lessened as it left him. After a while, once we'd gotten control of our breathing, he lifted his head up, skimming the stubble on his chin up my neck and across my jaw until his mouth was over mine.

That's when I opened my eyes and saw his gorgeous greeny-hazel ones smiling down at me.

"To use a Maude phrase, that was the best moment of my life," I told him breathlessly, and then froze when I realized what I'd just done.

I'd named my grandmother and quoted her while he was inside me.

Fortunately, I discovered that things could feel even better-er-er-er (because it warranted creating a new word for the English vocabulary as better didn't cut it). Jarrod burst out laughing, full on belly laughs that moved him around inside me. Something about this made me come again and hard. Totally better-er-er-er.

CHAPTER FOURTEEN

JARROD

I t was after round three, and now we were lying in bed. Well, I was lying in bed and Katy was using me as her mattress, which I had zero issues with. As someone who'd always liked their space and who hadn't embraced the whole cuddle mentality, this should have irritated me, but I was enjoying it.

She'd been tracing over the tattoo that went all the way up my right arm, across my chest, and ended at my left elbow. It was meant to have been the same as the left one, but I'd run out of symbols for it, so I'd decided to leave it as a work in progress rather than blindly pick things on the internet.

"Do these mean anything," she asked, rubbing her finger over one of the symbols.

Lifting my arm up, I pointed at them, starting with the one on my wrist. "This one is a Mayan symbol that means a shield, the one above it here is a Viking rune that meant strength." Twisting my arm so she could see the inside of my forearm, I continued, "This is an ancient Egyptian symbol for family, the one here on the inside of my bicep is also an ancient Egyptian one that means destiny…" I trailed off when she sat up. Then again, she was naked, having lost the nightie completely during round two, so that was why.

Moving so that she was straddling me, she leaned in and squinted. I'd had ancient symbols from all over the world that meant something to me tattooed, and then we'd filled in the blanks with tribal tattoos, dark slashes that joined them all together. With how they'd been done, you had to look carefully to see some of the symbols, but I knew what was where.

"How long did all of this take?" she asked, lifting my right arm to look at that one more closely.

"About a year. I could have probably had it done sooner, but it cost a lot so I wanted to break it up."

Nodding, she skimmed her hand over the area on my right forearm that was still blank. "What about here?"

"Still looking for inspiration, I guess," I shrugged. "Because all the symbols mean something to me, it's hard to find the right ones. I figured I'd wait until I turned forty and I'd have a new phase of life that symbols applied for to complete it all."

Tilting her head slightly, she thought about this. "I could always help you look."

Images of *The Witcher* and gaming characters hit me and I burst out laughing. "I don't know if Henry Cavill's face with his long white wig on would fit in with the rest of the ink, baby. Or even Luigi smiling out at people."

"Drat," she muttered, making it clear her disappointment was her joking. "And there was me thinking of the cute little mushroom from Mario."

She was too fucking cute and a total dork.

Running my hand over her unmarked skin, I thought about a tattoo that would suit her. There were a lot of ancient symbols that came to mind, but at the same time I kind of liked her skin free of ink.

With her lying with her chest on mine, the top of her tits were visible, like if she was wearing a corset. Somehow my dick still had it in him to start rising, so he did even though I figured she had to be sore and it would make me a nicer guy to ignore him.

Apparently she didn't want me to be a nicer guy, though, because the second she felt him, she looked up at me at the same time as lifting up so that she could slide her hand down my stomach. Once she was at her target, she wrapped it around him and started to move it up and down.

"Fuck being nice, I'll start that tomorrow," I growled, pushing up and shifting us so that she was now the one on the mattress and I was braced over her. "How many condoms did you get?"

Her eyes rolled up to look at the headboard of the bed as she counted, and then she rolled them back down again. "Three packs of ten, so thirty."

"We'll get some more next week."

Katy

Walking into work on Monday was problematic, but not because of all the sex I'd had over the weekend (although that didn't help). My pain and stiffness was because yesterday we'd decided to go out to pick up some Thai takeout – regardless of the amount of groceries I now had sitting unused in my kitchen – and just as we'd pulled out of our development, a car that hadn't had its headlights on hit the side of Jarrod's Explorer, and then roared off.

Fortunately, Jarrod had just started to move into the road, so the car hit the front of his vehicle, but still. Also fortunately, he'd called Ren, who'd called through to the tow company that the garage used, and someone was out within thirty minutes to tow his car to the garage.

I was slightly bruised from the seatbelt and slightly sore from the impact, but it would have been worse if Jarrod had been further into the turn he was making onto the road that ran along the side of where we lived, because it would have hit his door.

This also meant that we'd had to drive my car in today. After a five-minute argument over who was driving it, with Jarrod telling me he had a dick so he was driving and me arguing that vaginas ruled the day, I'd given him the keys and stormed round to the passenger side. All my pissy-ness was forgotten as I watched Jarrod try to get his long body behind the wheel of the car. Obviously I could have helped him by pressing the button to move the seat back, but after ten seconds of watching it, I'd realized that it had to be witnessed by everyone, so I'd videoed it with my phone. In the end, he had to put the soft top down, move the seat as far back as it could go, lean the back of the seat back, too, then sit behind the wheel with his legs either side of it. Fortunately, I had an automatic because I had no idea what he'd do if he had to use his left leg to push the clutch to change gears constantly, seeing as how it was trapped between the wheel and the door. His right one wasn't so bad because the center console didn't take up that much space in my Mini.

So, we'd driven into work with the wind in our hair, but especially in his because his head was so high in the air.

"You need a new car," he'd growled as soon as we'd left the development, after he'd pulled onto the road more carefully than I'd ever seen him do it. Not that I blamed him, even I was paranoid now that someone was going to hit us even though you could see clearly either way at the turn.

Still, he'd just insulted my baby. "No, you need to chop five inches off the top of your head. Or better still, chop your ankles off."

"How is that better?"

I hadn't actually realized I'd said that, so I had to think up an excuse on the fly. "Because you have big feet so your shoes are double the price of normal ones."

Letting out a frustrated sigh, he stopped at a red light. "They don't cost more. In fact, you wear more expensive shoes than I do."

I could say I doubted that with some of my shoes, but I definitely couldn't say that with all of them. I liked shoes, I'd always liked shoes, and we had an outlet mall not far away from where we lived. Those shoes were heavily discounted, but not all of them were classed as *cheap*, we'll just say that.

Looking down at his boots, I tried to guesstimate how much shoes that big would cost. Surely with the extra acreage they had to cost more? I mean, it was a lot more leather than a pair in my size would be, and then there were the soles. I was a size seven, and he had to be a size thirteen or fourteen. Did that mean they put more holes for the shoelaces than they would on a pair in my size? If that was the case, more holes meant longer laces, too. Ergo they'd be more expensive – which an argument I laid out for him.

This time he looked at me like I'd gone insane until a car behind us beeped to let us know – oh so kindly – that the light had changed to green. Figuring that we were best to ride the rest of the journey in relative silence, I turned on the radio and hit play on one of my favorite songs.

Leaning back, I closed my eyes and listened to the opening guitar part of it, smiling like I always did when I heard it.

"Is this Clapton, too?" Jarrod asked, ruining the silence part of my plan. Then again, I guess I'd said relative silence.

"No, it's George Harrison."

He listened a while longer, a smile breaking out on his face, too. "This song's awesome, what's it called?"

"It's mine and Maude's song," I told him, smiling when he just chuckled and shook his head. "It's called *Cheer Down*."

Shrugging, he signaled to turn onto the road that the garage was on. "It suits the two of you. I'm a huge Harrison fan and I've never heard it."

"Now you've heard it once, you'll listen to it a thousand times and still not get sick of it. In fact, I bet you'll be sitting with your guitar trying to figure out how to play it later on."

Slowing down to turn into the garage, he shot me a look that made 'little Katy' twitch. "I'd play it for you a thousand times if you wanted me to."

There was absolutely no way in hell or heaven that I'd ever say no to that. "You're on!"

My happy bubble was back in place... at least until Cole and Ren spotted Jarrod's head and then my car (which was how it went in my head when I played the scene out again later on).

"Holy shit," Cole howled, holding onto the frame of the entrance. "Where's the rest of your car?"

Seriously, his head did clear the top of the car!

"Fuck!" he growled, sounding so much like Geralt in *The Witcher* that I sighed and shifted in my seat. Realizing immediately, he shot me a glare that softened when he saw the happy smile on my face and then he just shook his head.

Getting out of the car was just as amusing as getting into it, and Cole and Ren got a show as he had to wriggle out from behind the wheel. What was even better was that Duke was in the back seat, and just as Jarrod bent over to stand up, his leg still next to the wheel, Duke jumped and landed on his back, using it as a trampoline to get out.

Realizing that it would be a good idea for me to get to the office, I skedaddled as quickly as my sore body would let me, and scurried past the two Townsend men who were still laughing. Just as I passed where they were standing, though, I whispered, "I've got a video of him trying to get in."

Both men stopped laughing and then followed behind me to watch it.

And then the day went a bit weird when I went down to the forecourt and saw that creepy guy Shane again, standing with his arms crossed in front of him, watching me with a look on his face that didn't exactly scream happy things. In fact, they were so far from happy things that I turned around to tell Jarrod, but when we came back out again he was gone.

Easy come, easy go, I guess!

Any thoughts of creepy Shane fled, though, when other members of the Townsend family turned up at the end of the day to watch Jarrod getting back behind the wheel of my car. That shit was totally going viral.

ONE WEEK LATER...

"You'd tell me if it was one of my brothers who kept moving

my stuff around, wouldn't you?" I asked him as I walked out of my kitchen with two plates of leftovers that Gloria had dropped round.

"Absolutely," he replied with zero hesitation.

"You'd tell me if it was one of your brothers doing it, too, wouldn't you?" I asked this time as I sat down beside him and passed him his plate.

"I'd kick their asses myself."

Balanced on the edge of my plate was a pink plastic bowl with the same food we were eating for Elodie, and as soon as she saw it she came toddling up to me. I didn't normally let her eat in the living room, but Jarrod had bought her a purple place mat to put on the coffee table and had spent the last week teaching her to eat sitting on her knees beside it. Initially, she hadn't liked this because his plate was bigger, so now he had a blue version of her bowl in the cupboard and tonight was his first night as a big boy.

On that note, I decided to point it out in my own special way. "Is your food too hot?"

Lifting his head up, he glanced over at me. "No?"

"I see," I mumbled, looking down at my plate. "Do you need different cutlery, or would you like me to put a cork on the fork?"

"Katy, why the hell would I need a cork on my fork?" he asked, sounding totally confused now.

"So you don't hurt yourself, honey. Those are sharp edges."

"You'd have to check with Mom, but I'm pretty certain I've never caused myself an injury with a fork," he replied with forced patience.

"Ok, be careful with that plate now. It's heavy and if you break it you could hurt yourself," I pointed out helpfully.

Placing it down on the coffee table, he turned so that he was facing me now. "Do you need a cork on your fork?"

"Nope," I replied before shoveling in a mouthful of Gloria's heavenly delights, my eyes on the kid's movie playing on the television.

"Then did you hit your head when I wasn't looking?"

"Nope."

"So why don't we put this bizarre conversation to bed and finish our dinner?" he suggested, and I had to swallow down the laughter that was building inside my chest. I'd only just managed to do that when he went to reach for his plate and let out a little growl. Looking down, I saw my niece sitting on her knees in front of his plate, happily feeding herself from it. "Petal, that's my plate," he said softly, calling her by his new nickname for her.

Turning around, she frowned at him and shook her head. "My!"

"No, baby, it's mine," he told her and held his hand out. "Can I have it back?"

The glare on her little face reminded me so much of her mother's when she was little. "No, my!"

Before he could say anything else, she picked up her pink bowl and passed it to him, then turned back to the plate.

I only just made it to the kitchen before I started laughing.

Reaching into the cupboard for his 'special plate', I lifted it down and emptied the rest of the Rubbermaid containers that

I'd heated the food up in onto it, and then carried it through to him.

Retaking my seat beside him, I lifted up a forkful of food and asked, "*Now* do you need a cork on your fork?"

The rest of dinner passed silently with only little squeals of excitement from Elodie breaking it. Then, just as I was picking up the plates to take them through to the dishwasher, she walked on her knees to where the big man was sulking, climbed up onto his lap and wrapped her arms around him. "Wuv cawot," she whispered, unable to say his name and figuring carrot was close enough.

His reaction to her eating off his plate might have seemed like he was pissed, but seeing it in first person, he'd been proud of her for her ingenuity and for eating off an adult plate. There was nothing that either of us did that ever truly pissed him off even if he acted like it, and seeing him wrap his arms around Elodie and hold her tighter to him, I knew that the perfect I'd thought he was, was nowhere near the perfect he actually was.

Saying I'd fallen in love with him was an understatement, and I didn't need any GYMP to make it happen.

Walking around the back of the couch, I headed toward the kitchen, pausing when I heard him say back, "Cawot loves 'Lodie, too."

I'd had a lot of dreams about Jarrod in the months after I'd started working at the garage, fantasies that ranged from tame to downright dirty. Not one of those dreams had even come close to the reality of being part of his life, though. When your dreams pale in comparison to the reality of your man, you know you've found the needle in the haystack.

THREE HOURS LATER...

I was face down on the bed, my hands gripping the sheets to stop my body being pushed up the mattress with each thrust.

We'd started with me kneeling at the side of the bed with him on his feet because of his height, but then he'd shifted me further up the mattress and had joined me on his knees. This had also posed a problem because his legs were so much longer than mine, so he'd had to lift the lower half of my body off the bed to do what we were doing now. This meant that with each thrust there was a real danger of me sliding forward, so my grip was fierce on the sheet and I hoped it didn't ping off the edge of the mattress each time he plunged into me.

"Can you stay quiet?" Jarrod taunted on a hard thrust, and a small groan left me.

Deciding honesty was the best policy, I shook my head. "No, no, I can't."

Chuckling at my response, he slid his hands from where they were gripping my hips down my ribs and in so that he now had one of my breasts in each hand. Gently, he pulled me up until I was sitting upright on my knees in front of him, with him still inside me.

Leaning down so that his mouth was next to my ear, he whispered, "Then I'll help you."

Those words really didn't fill me with confidence that he'd succeed, but they sure as hell sounded ominous.

The first thrust in the new position was a hard thrust upward that made me reach back to hold on to him, digging my nails into his side. With a growl, he moved me up and down so that I was riding him, periodically adding a hard thrust of his own. No matter how many times we'd done this, I still felt overwhelmed by the size of him as he moved in and out of me.

Even thinking about the fact that he was inside me at that moment made me clench - as it always did - around his length, earning myself a harder thrust than previously from him.

It might have been the position, it might have been the thrusts, or it might even have just been because it was Jarrod, but in a matter of seconds I went flying over the edge. He only just managed to turn my head and kiss me in time, swallowing down the loud moan that came out of me as I clenched around him.

When he felt it leave me, he lifted his head and smiled down at me. "Told you I'd do it."

I didn't have it in me to get irritated at his cockiness, I was too absorbed in how it felt being so sensitive after coming so hard, with his thick length still moving inside me the way it was. I did have one thing to say though. "When you come, I want to be kissing you, too."

His eyes flared slightly, and then he doubled his efforts, lifting me up and dropping me down more quickly and thrusting up constantly now. The ironic thing was, I was waiting for him to come when another one hit me. At the same time, we moved to kiss each other, and I swallowed his growl while he took my second moan. It was phenomenal.

The connection that I felt to him at that moment didn't surpass how I felt to him normally, but it made it feel stronger and deeper.

That's why, after he'd gotten rid of the condom and had slid into bed beside me, I didn't even wait for him to pull me into his side. Instead, I moved so that my head was on his bicep with my arm around his waist – aka, my happy place. We'd discussed me going on the pill, so I had a doctor's appointment next week to discuss it. I would have thought I'd blush and dread going, but in reality it excited me that we were dispensing with condoms. Just him and me, it felt... *more*.

"Are you happy?" he muttered, just as I was starting to fall asleep.

"Happier than I've ever been in my life."

If I'd been more awake, I might have realized that the fingers he'd been running through the long strands of my hair paused. "Really?"

Tipping my head so that I could give him a kiss on the chest, I mumbled, "It's why I love you so much," just as I fell asleep.

CHAPTER FIFTEEN

KATY

A lot can happen in two weeks. Stuff that's organized just so can get messed around, things can get put out of place, my uncle can get news that at the end of the month he can work from home which meant I wouldn't get Elodie as often. And those three things were just top of the list of things that had happened. Jarrod's insurance company had also sent him a check for his car, which meant I got dragged car shopping with him, and I'd found out that Gloria had a twin – which had just happened.

Maude had come over thirty minutes ago for a catch up while Jarrod was out helping his brothers with something, and we'd been sitting discussing her wanting to buy wigs like Gloria's.

"What would you use them for, though, Maude?"

Thinking about it, she just shrugged and reached for a cookie. "Don't know, don't care. I think it would be awesome to have an array of hairstyles and colors to suit my mood, don't you?"

"An array?"

"That's right," she nodded. "An array. Gloria always looks so beautiful in hers and the height I got on that first one was phe-nom-en-al!"

And there we had it, that's why she wanted wigs.

A knock at the door got our attention seeing as how I hadn't been expecting anyone at all today, and while I was walking to answer it, I asked, "Why don't you ask her to go shopping with you for one then?"

"I did and we've been. I've got three waiting for me at home."

Rolling my eyes, I opened the door and came face to face to the lady herself. When I looked at the woman beside her, I did a comical back and forth between the two of them – at least, it would be comical to them. For me, what I was seeing was confusing the hell out of me.

"How's there two of you?" I asked, still looking to see which one was the real Gloria.

That question was answered when she gently nudged me aside to get in. "This is my sister Rita. She's over from Jamaica for a couple of weeks and wanted to meet her nephew's woman, so here we are."

Smiling at Rita, I shut the door behind them and watched as Gloria picked up Elodie who had come running to see her.

"Oh my god, she's beautiful," Rita sang, walking up to see her.

Elodie's face went bright and then the smile dropped as she looked back at Gloria. Then she looked at Rita and pushed the top half of her body away from Gloria with a hand on her chest.

"What's wrong, little button? She's doing that because you're ugly," Rita told Gloria, giving her a smack on the arm for good measure.

Elodie looked over at me and let out a little squeak, her bottom lip wobbling slightly.

"This is my sister, Elodie. Her name's Rita, can you say Rita?" Gloria asked her, and Elodie looked back at Rita and shook her head.

"She calls Jarrod cawot," I told the duo as I walked past them to the kitchen. "If she can say Rita, he's going to be so mad."

Following behind me, Gloria gave me hers and Rita's coffee orders, and then reluctantly let Elodie – who was now warming up to the fact that there were two Glorias in the room – go to her sister.

Once the coffees were made, we sat down in the living room with Elodie excitedly showing Rita every single toy that she had.

Looking between the two, I was shocked at how much alike they looked even after seeing Jarrod with his brothers. I mean, I looked like my siblings, but not to the extent that this family did.

"I didn't know you were a twin?" I asked. "That's pretty cool."

Putting her cup down on the table, Gloria shot Rita a look. "My twin is a pain the ass and we definitely do not get along."

Maude shot me a wide-eyed look that reflected what I was thinking at that moment, too – awkward AF – and her lips pressed tightly together as she kept in the questions she no doubt was dying to ask.

"Yup," Rita agreed, stroking Elodie's purple teddy and grinning at her. "Gotta take her in small doses."

Well, it was probably best that they lived in different countries then, I guess. When the silence dragged from 'reflective silence' to 'awkward as hell silence' I started to think of questions to ask that would be diplomatic and neutral.

"So how often do you see each other then?"

"Once every five years or so," Gloria replied, watching Elodie with a warm smile on her face, which threw me seeing as how she was in the presence of a sister that she apparently didn't get along with. If that was me, I'd be struggling to smile and be tense.

"Last time I saw the b…" Rita stopped and looked down at Elodie who was now holding a fabric ball out to her, "burned out piece of trash was two years ago," she said, then glanced over at Gloria. "And she looked like a burned out piece of trash. Bright pink spandex leggings, highlighter green tight top, tits bursting out, and her hair looked like she'd been dragged through the streets and then swirled in a toilet. It was during Carnival, but still."

Gloria pulled a face and then pointed at Maude. "She does good hair. You know my wig with the hair to here," she pointed just past her shoulders and got a nod from Rita. "She styled it so perfectly, I didn't want to wash it."

Maude had been thinking about something through this, so she didn't hear what was said. Instead, she tilted her head and said to Gloria, "I didn't see any spandex or bright clothes in your wardrobe. That would totally suit you, and I could rock a hairstyle to match them. You need to get some more because that wig you've got with the auburn highlights in it would kill with those colors, and then we could put some curls through it, give it volume on top…" she trailed off, lost in her hair fantasy. "Oh, what about that wig at the shop we went to that had the long bangs at the front like Katy's? We could totally make it look like Cher in that Turn Back Time video when she's in the tiny little leather swimsuit thing with boots up to her thighs."

Rita had stopped playing with Elodie through this and was now looking at Maude with her mouth open. Gloria on the other hand was mulling this over. "I don't think I want the spandex and bright colors, but I could totally do a tank and those jegging things."

"Depends on the colors, though," Maude pointed out, putting her finger to her lower lip.

"Obviously," Gloria agreed, her mind stuck on the potential new look.

There was another silence, but this time two of the people in the room were lost in thought and not feeling the horror/awkwardness that the other two people were feeling at the mental image that had hit us at the description given by my grandmother.

"Do you…" Rita started, her eyes flicking between her sister and Maude's hair, "do you do your own hair?"

Patting the side of her bouffant, Maude grinned at her proudly. "Of course, great ain't it? If you've got an hour this week, I'll do yours for you. The higher the hair, the closer to heaven and all that."

Seeing that Rita didn't want to be rude but also had no intentions of her hair reaching heaven before she did, I cut in. "I'm amazed at how much y'all are getting along given that you don't normally. Which one of you was born first?"

It was a desperate grab to save poor Rita, but it was also a stupid grab because it brought up the tensions that we'd been trying to bury after their tales of dislike for each other. Stupid, stupid me.

"Oh, we've always been close," Rita replied, waving her arm in the air dismissively. "Gloria's fifteen months older than me, so I'm the baby of the family."

This information confused the hell out of me because I wasn't a mathematical genius, but fifteen months would be a hell of a long time to wait for the second twin to be born, right? It's not like their mother popped one out and then lay there waiting for the other one to come out for fifteen months.

I was busy thinking this, but it was my grandmother who said it out loud. "Wait, so your mom had to stay pregnant for fifteen months after Gloria came out? Didn't they say they'd do a caesarean or anything? I know things have changed from the days when I was born, but still, I would have assumed they'd be worried about you and your mom enough to not make her wait that long."

The two women looked at each other and then back at Maude. "Um, she wasn't in labor for fifteen months with me," Rita said slowly. "She got pregnant with me after Gloria was born."

Maude's head jerked slightly, and she looked quickly between the two of them. "So how in the ever loving hell are y'all twins?"

Both women burst out laughing, finding this hilarious for some reason. I was relieved that I hadn't been the one to ask the question, but at the same time I was struggling to figure out the answer to it, too.

"We're not twins," Gloria chuckled, waving it off like it was a ridiculous notion. "My twin's in Jamaica still."

Now that blew my mind and broke my silence. "How do y'all look identical if you're not twins? I've seen it with Jarrod and his brothers because those guys look like quads..."

"I don't think they look that alike really," Gloria mused. "They've got similar features, but everything else is different."

"Are you high?" Maude screeched, slamming her cup down on the table and making us all jump. "Those boys look so alike that I got them to show me their driving licenses to make sure they weren't talking shit."

"Shih!" Elodie yelled as she held both fists up in the air, making all of us flinch.

Uncle Leo was going to kill Maude for teaching his daughter to say a cuss word as one of her first words. There was no way that was going in the baby book I'd started for her after she was born either. I had no intention of sitting with her first boyfriend in seventeen years' time (and he'd better be her first boyfriend, and one who had no interest in doing anything else because holding hands was racy enough), showing him her achievements as a baby. When we got to the page about first words, there'd be a list of them including the word shit at fourteen months old.

Shooting a glare at Maude who was now inspecting her shoes, I crouched down in front of my niece and stroked the back of my finger down her face, getting a goofy grin in return. "We don't say that word, 'Lodie. It's a mean word that only big people say, not pretty little babies."

Apparently at that age, those words meant nothing because Elodie just shrugged and repeated it. "Shih!"

Glaring over at my grandmother, I snapped, "You're in so much trouble with Leo. And how am I going to put this in the baby book?"

Sensing that this could escalate, Gloria interrupted us by taking us back to the original conversation. "Maybe it's because they're my sons that I don't see the fully how alike they look. But then again, I don't think I look anything like Rita and my twin, Anna, and we're meant to be identical."

That made sense, I guess, but it was still hugely inaccurate. Jarrod and his brothers looked more alike than I'd ever seen any siblings look and given the age differences it was testament to the strength of, it seemed, Gloria's DNA. It stood to reason that a mother would see her kids as each being unique as well as not seeing the visible similarities between her and her siblings, but as an outsider, trust me, it was blowing my mind that they weren't all from the same fertilized egg.

"I agree with the ladies," Rita said. "Those boys look like they were all in utero at the same time, and that some paranormal event occurred where one tiny egg the size of a pinhead split into four massive babies." Getting a glare from her sister, she then decided wisely to start talking about Port Royal, telling us about different places in Jamaica that we should visit. The more touristy parts had no allure to me in any country, I preferred to go off the beaten track, but when she told me there was a place called Fern Gully, I made a mental note to break the beaten path rule and go visit it. That movie had seen me through a lot as a kid, and who wouldn't want to go to the place it was named after?

As we were talking, Elodie made the red pooping face that she always did, and then started clapping her hands. This was something she'd done from the minute she could do it after she'd been constipated for three days as a baby, and when she'd finally broken the poop force field, we'd all clapped for her. Now, every poop was celebrated with a red face and a round of applause – even if you had company.

Picking her up, Maude took her upstairs to change her.

"I really need to start potty training her," I muttered, making a mental note to get a book on how to do it. I wasn't sure if there was a book that dealt with a psychological approach to potty training, but I was adamant to find the closest thing I could to it.

"Jarrod, Bond, Canon and Reid were all using their potty by

the time they were sixteen months old," Gloria told me, like this was information I needed to know about these grown men. "It was Canon who took sixteen months, though. The rest all figured it out pretty quickly and were using it by thirteen months."

The fact that it was my boyfriend and his brothers aside, this was actually kind of intriguing information. I also needed the answer to something. "Who was the fastest to learn it?"

Not even hesitating, Gloria said, "Jarrod. He got a green potty the day after his first birthday, pooped in it that same day, and a week later was ripping off his diaper to sit on it."

Holy shit!

"He could do that when he was just a year old?" I asked, double checking she had the age right.

"Of course. Jarrod started walking at ten months and was advanced for his age, too."

"Boy basically uncurled after he was born and started playing music," Rita snickered. "I swear he was born at thirty-nine weeks, but he came out a twenty-year-old man."

That I could see, but still...

"Do you think Elodie's delayed with her development?" I asked both women. "Her mom is an addict, but she stuck with marijuana while she was pregnant. Elodie was tiny and a bit premature and it's always worried me all of that would affect her."

Leaning forward, Gloria said seriously, "Every baby is different, Katy. I get so annoyed with those baby books because they don't take that into account and it makes new parents worry."

That was true. I had three of the books upstairs so that I could figure out how to look after her when she was born. When she hadn't hit the milestones by the stage that they'd stated in the books, I'd freaked and taken her to the pediatrician to get checked over. Fortunately, she was confirmed to be 'healthy as a clam', but it was hard to switch off the worries given Effie's history.

"Your niece is good, honey," Rita added, backing up what her sister had said. "My daughter didn't start walking until she was nineteen months and she refused to use a potty until she was almost three. Then, at the age of nine, she decided that she was old enough to wear a bra and took one of mine and stuffed it with apples. After that, it was makeup at ten that she applied with a heavy, heavy hand, and she was borrowing my wigs. She'd gone from taking her time to being impatient for time to move more quickly. I was never worried, though, because she's her own person and kids personalities and will power differ from child to child."

"You worry a lot now, though, Rita. That child is wild," Gloria pointed out, shaking her head at the thought of what her niece got up to.

Letting out a frustrated sigh, Rita adjusted herself on the couch, no doubt trying to get more comfortable during an uncomfortable subject. "That's putting it mildly. She's a hellion who makes an impact wherever she goes."

"Shoulda had boys," Gloria muttered, shooting a smirk at her sister. "My boys have always been sweet and easy."

Rita and I shared a disbelieving look before we looked back at Gloria to see her glaring at us. "They're angels," she snapped, and I almost choked on air.

"Katy," Maude called from upstairs. "You're almost out of diapers, honey. There's only one left."

That's what I'd meant to get when I went to the store – diapers. I knew I'd forgotten something.

"I better go get some," I sighed, getting up to get my purse. "Are you guys ok to stay here with Maude? Jarrod should be home soon, so I can always text him to come here so he can see Rita."

"How far away from the store is the garage he works at?" Rita asked. "I might go with you and head in to surprise him there. He can drive me back here when he's finished."

So that became the plan. Maude and Gloria would stay here to look after Elodie, and I'd drop Rita at Ren's garage and head on to the store, which was exactly what we did. During all of it, I thought about how much more secure the world felt having the Kline family in it. In the grand scheme of things, they'd only known me for a matter of months, but it felt like I'd known them my whole life.

I knew I loved Jarrod, even though I was too scared to say it to him, but I still struggled to understand what he saw in me. I was plain and liked gaming. He was hot, narrated erotic books, worked out, was hot again, and sang like a god. We just didn't seem to fit, but we did at the same time. I'd never believed in soul mates or people being fated for each other. Looking at it from a different perspective, I was starting to think maybe I was wrong about that.

And on that thought, I parked up in the parking lot for the store and hustled my ass into it to pick up diapers, thinking as well about how I'd approach ever telling him how I felt.

Jarrod

Three hours later...

I was late leaving work after Rita showed up because we'd been talking while I was working, so it took me longer to finish the car I'd been assigned. Not that it mattered, though, because Ren and Cole were both in shit with Maya and Ebru, so they were delaying going home and had hung out at the garage with us, and Hurst had finally admitted defeat with his car and it had been written off, so he'd come to hide with them. My aunt was a blast, so there had been a lot of joking and laughter going on until we realized the time and locked up. Now we were home, and I was heading into Katy's with Rita walking beside me.

I was just about to ask her if we should all go out for dinner when I noticed that Katy's door was wide open, something she never did in case Duke or Elodie got out.

Holding my hand up, I silenced Rita, who'd been talking about my cousin, by putting my finger to my lips. When she saw my expression, her mouth snapped shut audibly, and she nodded.

Walking quietly up to the door, I put my hand flat on it and pushed it open all the way. It looked like there'd been a struggle by the door and the table Katy kept a glass dish on for loose change and keys was shattered, glass and coins spread out across a large area. Just behind that was the television lying face down and at least eight feet from where it should have been. Looking over at the couch, I saw a pair of feet that I knew well only just poking out.

"Call 911, Rita. We need two ambulances," I barked, moving quickly around the edge of it to where Katy was lying on the floor with her back to me.

I knew the basics of what you were meant to look for, but all of it left me as I leaned over her and saw the small pool of blood under her mouth.

"Katy, baby," I whispered urgently, putting a shaky hand on her neck and hoping I was in the right place to feel her pulse.

The fluttering under my fingers was a relief, but I wasn't sure if it was coming from me or her. I'd done a first aid course in high school and I remembered the guy saying something about us being able to feel our own pulses in our fingers, but I couldn't remember why he'd said it.

That's when I thought about checking to see if she was breathing – which, at a later date, would hit me as the first thing I should have looked for.

Seeing her chest moving, I carefully moved around so that I was now in front of her, next to her arm that was outstretched on the floor.

Leaning over her so that my mouth was next to her ear, I called, "Katy."

 When nothing happened, I reached for the hand on the floor and gently lifted it up. That got a reaction in the form of a pained groan.

"Jarrod," Rita called, sounding like she was crying. "Her grandmother's over here."

Reluctantly taking my eyes off Katy, I looked over my shoulder and realized immediately why she'd sounded like she was crying. The ever vibrant Maude, so full of life, was almost unrecognizable. Her eyes were already swollen, and her face was bruised all over.

"Did you call 911?" I barked, turning back to Katy and panicking because I didn't know what to do.

What if one of them stopped breathing? With the bruising on Maude, I wouldn't know if it was safe to CPR. With Katy, I'd probably break having to do that to her.

I didn't know what to fucking do!

"No," she whimpered. "I saw Maude and… and…" she broke off and started sobbing.

Pulling my phone out of my back pocket, I unlocked it and hit a number I'd never had to dial before in my life.

"911, what's your emergency?"

Four words I'd never expected to hear in my life, and then I said some words I'd never even thought about saying, but once I had, I never wanted to say them again.

"I need an ambulance. My girlfriend and her grandmother have been beaten and are unconscious."

With Rita crying hard in the background, I felt something deep inside of me start to crack, but then Katy twitched and something hit me. She needed me to be strong for her, and so did Maude. If I did that, I could follow the instructions that the lady on the phone was giving me while we waited for the ambulances to arrive. If I cracked now, I wouldn't be able to do that and it could cost them their lives.

The lives of these two beautiful women, who'd made such a big difference to me in such a short space of time, were potentially in my hands.

So, with that epiphany, I took a deep, shaky breath in and did what the woman said.

CHAPTER SIXTEEN

KATY

I felt it as soon as I began to wake up, but it didn't make sense to me. There was just so much pain all over. It wasn't unusual for me to wake up with aching thighs or a pain here and there, it happened to everyone and I liked to think I was an *Avenger* while I was sleeping, but this was different. Whatever I'd done through the night had left me feeling like I'd gotten in the ring with the late and great Mohammed Ali.

Surfacing more from slumber, I took in a painful breath and couldn't stop the moan that followed it. *Holy shit, that fucking hurt.*

"Katy," a deep voice whispered beside my ear and a hand gently picked up one of mine. "Wake up, baby."

Moving to roll onto my back, I almost screamed with the pain that filled me with those movements. My elbow, my back, my side, my shoulder, my head... everything felt like it had been crushed.

"Baby, you're in hospital. You were in an accident," the deep voice rumbled, and that's when my eyes opened as it all came flooding back to me.

"Where's Elodie?" I whimpered, needing to know he hadn't taken her.

"We don't know, Katy. And if you wake up a bit more, maybe you can tell us," Mom's voice said from the opposite side of the bed to where Jarrod was sitting, and I looked at her without moving my head and causing myself more pain.

Seeing the tears in her eyes, I looked back to the other side and saw that Jarrod looked like he hadn't slept in a week.

"It was freaky Shane," I rasped, closing my eyes as it all played out in my mind. "I dropped Rita at the garage and went to get diapers. When I came back, I heard Elodie screaming from the driveway and ran into the house because it sounded like she'd hurt herself. Gloria was sitting on the couch with her on her lap, and her face was bleeding. I didn't even get to ask what happened because something hit me on the head, and when I fell down he started kicking me," I stopped to lick my lips, feeling how dry they were.

Every word, every replay of what I remembered was draining me, but the panic... the panic *hurt*.

"I was trying to crawl away from him, but he grabbed my arm hard and pulled it up behind me. I turned onto my back and then Shane put his hand around my throat and squeezed. He kept asking where the shit Effie stole from him was, but I still don't know what he was talking about. I told him I didn't know, but he squeezed harder and then started punching me," I whimpered, the tears falling out of the corners of my eyes and trailing into my hair.

"You've done well, Katy," a new voice that I recognized

instantly told me, and I realized Jarrod and Mom weren't the only two people in the room with me. "Did he say anything else to you?" Dave asked.

Closing my eyes, I replayed the look on his face as he punched me, how he'd called me a "fucking slut" as he did it, the rage he was feeling as he punched me.

Then I remembered, and my eyes shot open as I sucked in an agonizing breath. "He said if Effie didn't bring it to him, he was going to kill Elodie." On the last word, saying my niece's name and thinking of her being in pain, I started sobbing, big chest wracking sobs that made me want to scream in pain.

I wasn't sure what injuries Shane had caused me during the assault, but I knew for sure that each sob felt like someone was stabbing me with a spear in my abdomen and head.

I'd put up with that pain every day for the rest of my life if I got Elodie back, though.

Large hands gently held either side of my face, and I looked up and saw Jarrod looking down at me with tears in his eyes.

"Do you trust me?" he asked, his voice sounding rough and raw.

I didn't even need to think about my response to this question, but I needed to calm my crying to answer it. When that proved impossible, I gasped out, "Absolutely," my voice breaking in the middle of the word.

Closing the distance, he ran the tip of his nose down mine. "I'm going to get her back, Katy. I'm going to make him pay, but she's coming home."

And with that, he pulled his head back, and I saw how serious he was. The easy going light that his eyes always had was gone and in its place was a darkness I wouldn't have thought he was capable of. He wasn't just saying the words to make me feel better, he was actually going to make it happen.

I tried to raise my right arm to grab his hand, but the pain in my elbow was too much to be able to do it, so I had to use my left one instead. Wrapping my fingers around the wrist of his right hand, I clipped, "Make it happen and bring her home."

With a nod, he lifted up and turned around to Dave, who was watching us. "Get her dad to call Leo. Tell him I want Effie's number."

"I've got it," Mom offered, pulling her phone out of her purse and pressing the screen a couple of times. "Here," she passed it to him.

Looking from the screen to me, he gave me one final nod before turning to Dave. "Let's go."

How could something like this happen? How was it even possible?

I didn't understand why Shane would think I had whatever he wanted. I never saw Effie, none of us did, so why would he assume she'd given me something of his?

My little niece's face, her mouth grinning, popped into my head and I took in a shuddering breath thinking about how scared she must be.

When he'd been attacking me, I'd seen Maude lying on the ground and knew she'd have done everything she could to protect her great granddaughter. I also knew she would no doubt be pissed and trying to get Jarrod to let her go with him to get Elodie right now, so I needed to speak to her and hold her hand until they brought her back to us.

Rolling my head to look at Mom, I asked shakily, "Where's Maude?"

That's when it got even worse – if that was even possible –

because her eyes closed slowly as her lips trembled, and tears started trailing down her cheeks.

Jarrod

Taking in a steadying breath, I looked around all the friends and family that were sitting in the waiting room and stopped on Leo.

"Your daughter has something that belongs to the fucker who did this. He's taken Elodie and if she doesn't give it back to him, he'll kill her," I growled, watching as his face turned from shocked to horrified.

Normally, I would probably have felt sympathy for him, but right now I was disgusted. I knew I was directing my anger in the wrong direction, but it was his daughter who'd caused this.

"I'm going to call her, it will not be nice, but I want whatever the fuck it is he wants in my hand in the next hour, and all of this shit is because of her. Her daughter's life is at risk because of her. Maude's life is hanging by a thread. Because. Of. *Her*!" I roared the last word, watching as his head jerked and he got even paler.

"Jarrod, man," DB muttered, coming up behind me to hold my shoulder.

Shrugging him off, I shot him a glare and moved closer to Leo. "Are you with me on this?"

"Of course," he replied immediately, looking confused about the question and why I'd be asking him it. I

if I'd been feeling even remotely rational instead of pissed, it might have dawned on me that this was because his mom was lying in ICU, her outlook unknown at that moment, and his granddaughter's life was hanging in the balance all because of his daughter, and the second he'd found that out any lingering loyalty he had to her had disappeared in a cloud of dust. I wasn't rational, though, so all I saw was a man who might stop me from getting the information out of Effie, so I didn't trust him one bit at that moment, which was why I'd laid it out. Another reason I'd done it in the way I had was so that DB could stop him if he went to grab the phone from me.

Hitting the number on the screen, I held the phone to my ear, my eyes not leaving his once. When no one answered the number, I rang it again and again, putting it on speakerphone so DB and his men could hear it. Finally, on the fourth try, she picked up.

"What the fuck?"

"That's the wrong way to answer right now, Effie," I clipped.

"Who the fuck is this?"

"Right now your grandmother is clinging to life by the skin of her teeth after being attacked by an acquaintance of yours who took Elodie. This means that your daughter is most likely terrified out of her tiny little mind and my mother is missing because he took her, too. And it's all because of you."

There was the sound of rustling and then she snapped, "How's that my fault? I'm not even there."

Jesus Christ, she hadn't even asked about Maude or sounded worried about Elodie even after what I'd laid out. Why the fuck are people like that in the world?

"Because the man responsible for all of that and putting your cousin Katy in hospital after beating and choking her, says you've got something of his. His message to you is that if he doesn't get it back, he's going to kill your *daughter*," I hissed, stressing the last word to try to trigger some level of human decency and compassion in her shriveled black heart so she'd give us the information we needed.

There was a pause and silence on her end, and then she asked impatiently, "And who's saying all of this?"

There was no fear or sadness in her voice. It was empty and uncaring, just like her, and sounded almost like she was bored by it all.

Glancing quickly at Garrett, who'd shifted to stand closer to where I was and mouthed the word calm to me, I took a deep breath before I replied to the bitch. "Shane Perkins is saying this. He passed the message on while he was assaulting Katy and your grandmother was lying on the floor fighting for her life."

I'd expected her to hear the name and realize how serious this was and that it wasn't a game, regardless of the information I'd already laid out for her, which should have triggered her into offering up information immediately but hadn't. But, proving she was an even bigger piece of shit than I thought she was at that moment, she snorted. "Shane? Really? He won't do anything."

Looking away from her dad and staring unseeingly out of the window of the waiting room, I asked incredulously, "That's seriously your answer? I tell you that your grandmother - that *Maude* - might die, that your cousin who's helped look after your daughter is in hospital after the man you claim wouldn't do anything beat and choked her, that your daughter's life is in danger, and that another woman – my mother – is missing, and you laugh and dismiss it?"

Not picking up on the barely banked fury in my voice, or just not caring about it, she replied, "Yeah, 'cos it's Shane."

Those four words broke the fragile hold I had on my anger.

"*Are you out of your fucking mind*?" I roared into the phone. "Tell me what he's looking for, Effie, or I swear to God I'll make your life a living hell. The dealers that you go to will send you away or give you flour to snort, the tricks you're turning to fund your habit will dry up, and the people you hang around with will lock their doors on you. You'll be dried up and strung out, living on the streets like the piece of shit you are." I stopped and then lowered the tone of my voice to a level of sinister I didn't even know I was capable of. "Don't think I won't make that happen. You don't know who I am, but I promise you, I know who you are."

I don't know where the words came from because I didn't have that kind of sway in the world, but I would give everything I had to make it happen if she didn't give me what I needed right now, and I knew targeting her habit and what she used in life to keep it going would be a trigger. The death of her grandmother, the violent beating her cousin had endured, the fact a woman had been kidnapped because of her, and her daughter's life hanging in the balance hadn't, but drugs would.

Fucking Christ.

There was a silence that stretched on for so long that I thought for a second that she'd hung up on me, but then she whispered, "In the purple bear. It's in there."

The fucking purple bear? Whatever was worth her daughter's life was in that piece of shit bear that she'd given to her daughter. She had to have known it would put her life in danger, but she'd done it, anyway.

Fuck. *Fuck me!*

And that's when all the remnants of the pity and ideas of helping save Effie from the demons that were controlling her and driving her to live a life of drugs I'd had left me. She'd *knowingly* and deliberately put her daughter's life in danger.

Looking back at Leo and seeing him looking ashen and devastated, I hissed, "Right now your father is looking like his world has just ended finding out his daughter deliberately put his granddaughter's life in the hands of a psychopath." When she went to say something, I snapped, "Shut the fuck up and fucking listen to me. Your grandmother is in a bad way – Last Rites kind of bad way," I clarified, listening to her gasp. "Your daughter will now know that her mother not only didn't care enough about her to raise her and give her the world she deserves, but she'll know that you cared enough about yourself to dangle her over the edge of a cliff. If anything, *anything* happens to that baby or my mom, I'll deliver you to Perkins myself. Now, the last thing you do for your daughter – in fact, it'll be the only thing you've ever done for her – is you text me the number you have for Perkins. If you don't, I'll find you and get it myself, and trust me – you don't want that to happen."

Before she could say anything else, I hung up and gestured to the men in the room who were all now standing. Apparently I'd been so absorbed in the phone call and dealing with a real-life version of Satan, that I hadn't seen the new arrivals to the group.

"I don't know what it is, but whatever he wants is hidden in that bear because the toy itself is worth jack shit."

"I'll go get it," Bond offered, Canon and Reid nodding and standing close to him. "Is it still on the shelf in her room?"

Shaking my head, I went to push past them, but DB caught my arm. "You're not going. The house needs cleaned up, Jarrod. You seeing that again with this new information will fry your brain and we need you."

Seeing the wisdom in this, I swallowed over the lump in my throat and then cleared it so I could talk. "Yeah, it's in the

Steiff box that the other bear came in. We'll meet at the garage and I'll call Perkins with the news."

Not needing to be told what to do, my brothers turned and left to get it. They'd just cleared the door when a hand grabbed my other shoulder and I turned around and saw Leo standing there, his face wearing what I figured was a similar expression to mine.

"If anything happens, I want her dealt with. I'm thinking you don't have the power you made her think you have, but whatever needs to done I'll help you with."

The conviction and determination in his voice shocked me, and then I got why he'd looked so confused when I'd asked him if he was with me before. "This is your daughter we're talking about. I'm not sure it's possible for you to do that to her, man."

"No, my daughter wouldn't do this to her family or her daughter. My daughter wouldn't have walked out of the hospital after she pushed Elodie out. My daughter wouldn't set her baby up to the possibility of having her life taken from her by giving her something that belongs to a man who'd take lives to get it back. So *that* isn't my daughter, that's a fucking nightmare and I want her stopped."

Nodding at him, I shifted the angle of my body to include him in what I was going to ask the men to do.

"We meet at the garage and wait for them to come with the bear. As soon as I've got it in front of me, I'll call Perkins to arrange a meet." All the men nodded at this plan, but there was more. Focusing on DB and his men, I said, "You're the law enforcement in this, so I need to know what you can do and give you the lead once we've got the bear."

As the sheriff, the onus on this fell on his shoulders. "Get the area for the swap. We'll look at it and figure out where we can go and not be seen. The more people we have around him the better because we don't know what he's carrying or how many people he has behind him, so the rest of you," he addressed the remaining men, "will have to act as backup. You act within the law, do you understand? Failure to do that risks Elodie and Gloria's lives and puts getting justice for what's happened at risk."

The normally light-hearted and easygoing Townsend family remained silent and serious as they all nodded.

"I'm going to call Carter and tell him what to bring to the garage," he continued. "We do this tight, men. And by tight I mean sticking to the plan unless we move to Plan B."

All of them confirmed they got it, and then we were moving. As I was walking out the door, Dad caught up with me.

"We'll get them back," he muttered. "And your mother's going to be pissed."

I didn't have the heart to tell him what was burning in my gut after seeing what Shane had done to Maude and Katy, and that was the likelihood that he'd done the same thing to her. If I thought about that for too long I'd lose the control I had and, not being experienced in this sort of thing, I needed that control to get them back.

This morning everything had been laid out ahead of me. I was in love with Katy, she was in love with me, I had my family and hers around us, we were all healthy and happy, and Elodie had fed me toast, pinching tiny pieces off at a time. As I'd left to go to work, she'd called out, "Love cawot!" and my gut had clenched in a good way hearing it.

Fuck, I wish I'd taken the time to stop and appreciate it all more. I also wished I'd have woken Katy up when she'd said she loved me as she fell asleep and said it back.

CHAPTER SEVENTEEN

JARROD

"Yes?" the sick son of a bitch answered, sounding like he had nothing going on.

"Shane, it's Jarrod Kline," I clipped, making a point to talk quickly. "I've got what you wanted back."

I'd learned from DB on the way to the garage that it was apparently no secret Shane had many bad attributes. He was a racist and at one stage it looked like he was bordering on being a white supremacist, too. He'd been investigated over the sexual assault of quite a few women – women who'd withdrawn their statements shortly after he was questioned over the incidents – but he'd always been released due to lack of evidence. Yesterday they'd found his car abandoned just outside of town and it looked like it had been in an accident and they'd already been looking for him when all of this happened to find out what had happened. I hadn't ever paid much attention to him, so I didn't know any of this, but now that we had all of this information it didn't take a genius to put two and two together about his car and the hit and run we'd been involved in.

"Is that a fact? Seems I've got two of what you want right here," he said in a singsong voice which put me on edge.

This fucker was crazy crackers, and he had two pieces of my world in his hands.

Taking a deep breath in to try to stay calm, I made eye contact with DB and nodded when he mouthed "calm" at me just like his brother had earlier. I could see the wisdom in them saying it because losing it wouldn't get us what we wanted, but it was starting to fuck me off.

"Well, you've gone to a lot of trouble to find what I've got now, Perkins, so it seems to me you're wanting this badly, bad enough for us to not fuck around and risk it getting lost. You with me?"

There was a pause on the other side of the phone followed by a clanging noise like a metal door shutting.

"Meet me at the lake. There's a cabin two miles up the slip road just past the entrance."

With that, he hung up, proving that he had no clue what he was doing. This is why boys shouldn't play with big boy toys, kids. At no point did he tell me to come alone – even though I definitely wasn't – and he sounded too confident. His confidence was irritating, but the fact he didn't know what he was doing concerned me because it meant he was acting on instinct now and that instinct might tell him to just say fuck it and kill Mom and/or Elodie if shit didn't go his way.

My role in this done for now, I looked over at DB and his team who began giving out orders.

"I'm sending the coordinates of the cabin to your phones. Cut and paste them into a search and one of the map sites online will bring up the area," Raoul shouted, tapping the screen of his phone. "DB, where do you want people to be?"

Squinting at the screen of his phone, DB assessed the area around the cabin with Garrett looking over his shoulder. "What do you think, Garrett?"

"You've got dense trees around it. If they split up into groups of two, spread them out around here," he suggested, making a shape like a C around the area behind the cabin. I don't know what ground foliage we've got, but there should be enough cover. We'll come in from the front with Jarrod. He's expecting him and thinks he's got this, so if we go here and here, we can come in behind Jarrod and get him while he finds Elodie and Gloria."

Nodding at his brother's suggestion, DB split the group up into twos, with me being teamed with Leo. With a final nod to everyone, we got into our cars and headed to the lake. It felt like it took forever to get there even though it was only ten minutes outside of town, and by the time we parked up I'd sung *Swing Low, Sweet Chariot* so many times in my head that I was now calm and focused.

"You ready?" DB asked, walking up beside me as we started making our way to the cabin.

"You have no idea how ready I am."

Gloria

I was sitting on the floor in a tiny pantry that had a thick metal door on it, but there was enough room for me to rock Elodie who was still whimpering.

The things I'd seen this man do today would haunt me for the rest of my life. The cold brutality that he'd beaten Maude and

Katy with was unnatural, and the look in his eye was like the devil had taken him over.

"Yeah, man, I need it. No, I don't care where you have to get it from, I need a hit," he shouted as he spoke to someone. Through the gap between the door and the floor, I could see his shadow moving back and forth as he talked into the phone. I knew he'd been speaking to Jarrod earlier when he'd pointed his gun at where I was sitting with Elodie in the living room and had then pointed it at the door to where we were now, slamming it shut behind us once I was inside and only giving me a second of light to glance around the space. "Look, I'm just waiting for a delivery and then I'll be down. Make sure you've got it."

After that he was silent, but the shadow continued moving like it had been until I heard him walking away. I couldn't sit here and do nothing.

Gently putting Elodie on the floor, I leaned down so that my mouth was beside her ear. "Don't be scared, ok, 'Lodie. Auntie Gloria will get us out of here."

Any other one-year-old would be screaming or panicking, but not Elodie. Like the precious cherub that she was, she whispered back, "Yeah."

I'd seen the handle of something poking out of a box in the far right corner of the room before he shut the door, so I slowly reached over and grabbed it. It was attached to something much heavier than I thought it would be, but when I felt the flat circular surface of it, I smiled.

A cast iron skillet – one of the old style ones that weighed a ton.

Getting up onto my knees, I whispered again, "Stay here for Auntie Gloria. I'll be right back."

I didn't want to leave her, but I didn't want to risk anything happening to her, so I had to do something and this was all that I could think of.

Leaning against the metal door, I almost rolled my eyes when it opened. The guy didn't have a clue what he was doing!

It took a couple of blinks to get used to the light, but then my eyes adjusted and I looked around the room for a place to wait. On the left side of the small living room was a cabinet with a small gap between it and the wall. Because he'd enter on the opposite side of it, he wouldn't be able to see the space until he was in front of it. That's where I was going to go.

Walking as quietly as I could across the floor, I thought of all the times I'd had physical fights with my sisters. My twin really was a bitch, so those fights had been intense and heated. I was going to imagine her face when I hit him, that way I knew my swing would be a good one.

Jarrod

"He can't be fucking serious," Leo whisper hissed at me as we looked at the cabin. "This guy's a complete moron."

I knew what he meant – it was totally open, and he hadn't even chosen a place where he had a good chance of escape, even in the dark – but there was still the matter of what he'd already done today.

"He's also wanted for the attempted murder of Maude and the injuries he gave Katy," I reminded him, turning to look at him in the little amount of light that we had where we were crouched down. "Let's not underestimate him."

"Fucker," he growled, almost making me laugh, but I wasn't sure if I'd be able to ever do that again after this.

Just then the screen of my phone lit up with a text from DB.

DB: *Go up and knock on the door.*

Yeah, that gave a good indication of how weak this man's plan was because that's all I had to do.

Passing it to Leo, I got up from my crouched position and made my way to the door. Just as I was about to knock on it, I heard a scream followed by a shout from inside. Moving back, I kicked the door open just as Mom hit him around the head with a skillet while he was on his knees.

"You're a nasty man," she screamed as he fell face down on the floor. Lifting it up again, she brought it down on his ass. "Nasty, nasty man."

Not even sure what I was looking at, I yelled, *"Ma!"* watching her bring the pan down again in the same place.

"Jesus Christ, is your mother spanking him with a skillet?" DB called as he ran across the room.

Confused and, I'm not ashamed to admit it, terrified out of my mind, I scanned the room not seeing any sign of Elodie, and that scared me even more.

"Ma," I shouted again, finally getting through to her.

With the pan lifted above her head, she looked over at where I was standing with DB now beside me and Garrett behind us.

"Officers, arrest this man," she ordered, lowering her arms and dropping the pan on the back of his thighs.

The heavy thud it made when it hit the floor afterwards told us all we needed to know – she'd hit him with a motherfucker of a pan. If his ass wasn't broken, his head definitely would be, and I didn't have it in me to give one shit about that.

"I'll call for an ambulance," Garrett offered in a tone that made it clear he didn't want to, as DB pulled his cuffs out and made his way over to the asshole who was lying unconscious on the floor.

Stepping toward Mom, I started panicking over the fact I couldn't see Elodie anywhere. "Where's Elodie?"

Looking up at me with tears building, she opened her mouth to say something but was interrupted by a high-pitched squeal that came from behind us.

"*Boo*!"

DB had just been bending over to give first aid to Shane, and the scream made him jump up and grab for his gun. That was joined by a clatter behind us and the word "fuck" was shouted as Garrett dropped his phone. Me, I froze and battled back the tears I wanted to cry at seeing her unharmed but also at seeing evidence of how truly unaware she was of the gravity of the situation she'd been in.

Christ.

"Phone's out," Garrett barked, picking it up off the floor.

Pulling mine out, I made my way over to where she was clapping her hands at DB who was holding his chest now. Hitting 911 (even though the last thing I wanted to do was save the bastard), I reached her just as the operator answered and asked what service I wanted.

"Cawot!" she squealed, watching as I crouched down in front of her.

I'd be her cawot for the rest of my life if she needed to me to be, so long as she was safe and smiling.

Unable to talk, I passed my cell off to DB to carry out the checks and shit the operator wanted and lifted her up, closing my eyes as she tried to strangle me with an overly enthusiastic hug. It was the best hug I'd ever had in my life.

"Clear," Garrett bellowed to the others outside the cabin, before he came back in and crouched down beside us. "Cawot's a hero, baby, so you hug him tighter, ok? Heroes need hugs when they conquer a dragon."

I wasn't a fucking hero at all. Right now Maude was lying in a hospital bed fighting for her life, my woman was in pain and scared out of her mind, and it was a miracle that Mom and Elodie weren't in the same way. So, what I was was a man hanging on by a thread who wanted to rip the fucker lying on the ground's head off.

I'd take the Elodie hug, though, every day for the rest of my life.

CHAPTER EIGHTEEN

KATY

W e passed the room that Shane was being treated in as Jarrod wheeled me through to Maude's room. Thanks to Gloria's efforts he had a severe concussion, a hairline fracture on his skull, and a broken coccyx, and was recovering in what looked like a nice room. For what he'd cost my family, he deserved to be dumped in a swamp.

Looking away from it, I focused on breathing as deeply as I could for what was about to happen.

After they'd returned from wherever Shane had been holding Gloria and Elodie yesterday, the doctor treating Maude had asked to meet with the family in my room. Apparently, after running tests on her, they weren't sure if she was going to survive, but they'd be monitoring and assessing her constantly over the next twenty-four hours.

The good news was that she'd survived.

The terrible news was that after looking at her file, they'd found out she'd been diagnosed with terminal cancer three months previously. She also had an injury to her head, and even if they relieved the pressure inside her skull, it was unlikely she'd regain consciousness. It was too severe, and her body was too weak from the cancer.

Apparently, after she'd been feeling unwell for a while and had delayed going to the doctor thinking it was just a bad flu or old age catching up with her. After a barrage of test and scans, they'd discovered cancer in her lungs and that it had spread to her brain. It was so far gone that treatment would have been useless, so she'd told them she accepted it and was just going to live life to the max while she could.

Well, she couldn't, not anymore.

The doctor who diagnosed her rang Dad last night and said he'd never met a braver and stronger woman in his thirty years of practice, and that's what she would have wanted. We had the choice to agree to them drilling holes in her skull to release the pressure and they'd keep her on life support, or we could let her die with dignity - which again would have been what she'd have wanted. So they moved her out of ICU and into a private room where she could slip away when it was time.

Looking up from my lap, I saw that Bond, Canon and Reid were standing sentry in front of her door, and as soon as we got close enough they opened it for Jarrod to wheel me in.

I never wanted to say goodbye to her, and I sure as hell never wanted it to be like this. She was meant to be around forever because nothing could defeat the power and strength of Maude Crew. When the doctors had updated us two hours ago on her condition, all the medical information they'd relayed had fallen on deaf ears, apart from their opinion that it was almost time...

I was going to have to say goodbye to my best friend and my

rock. Before that, though, the priest from the church she went to was giving my grandmother her Last Rites.

I'd had a choice – be here or stay away and come and say goodbye afterward. I'm not going to lie, I'd been leaning toward the latter, but then I'd asked myself 'what would Maude do' twenty minutes ago and I knew she wouldn't have missed it. She'd have wanted to be there for the rest of the family and to say goodbye to me properly. I might not be religious, but she was, so this would mean something huge to her. I couldn't let her down.

So here I was. Listening as she was given her Last Rites. Looking at the body of a woman who was too frail to look like Maude, but who was my larger-than-life grandmother no matter how much I tried to convince myself otherwise. I listened as she was given the final blessing, silent tears streaming down my cheeks.

I couldn't let her go, I couldn't even bring myself to say the word goodbye like everyone else was. One by one, they all went up and kissed her, whispering to her as they let her know she wasn't alone.

I wanted to be strong and do it, too, but instead I sat there numbly staring at her face, only just aware of people moving about around the room.

But then the most beautiful sound filled the room, the unmistakable opening notes of *Tears In Heaven* coming from right next to me. Slowly, I looked to the side and saw Jarrod sitting on a chair beside me with his guitar, and then he started singing my grandmother's favorite song. The guitar playing itself was flawless, but the way his deep voice carried the lyrics… there were no words for it.

Halfway through it, I had a moment of hope, something out of Hollywood, that she'd hear him playing and wake up. Even after it ended, I kept looking from the monitor beside her to her eyes, begging silently for her to just wake up.

I begged anyone who was listening for that miracle.

I begged even as Jarrod said to her, "I promised I'd sing it for you, Maude. I hope I did it justice."

I begged even as we sat with her for two hours, still letting her know that she wasn't alone.

I begged even as I kissed her goodbye and lay my head next to her hand on the bed.

Miracles happened, and Marianne Crew was too strong to give in.

Jarrod

12.43am

Katy was finally asleep, so I picked up my guitar and walked back down to Maude's room.

Opening the door, I pulled up a seat next to her bed and started strumming on my guitar again. I'd been listening to the song for two hours now and I could see it being played in my head, so I hoped I could do it justice for her.

"Katy told me this was a special song for both of you, beautiful girl, so I figured I'd keep you company."

And then I closed my eyes and started playing *Cheer Down*. I can't say I was even close to Harrison or Clapton when it came to playing the guitar, but the lyrics to both songs were more important than anything. I could picture her nodding her hair, her big hair not moving with it, and saying it was the happiest moment of her life. I got what the lyrics to the song meant, and to me they were perfect for the relationship she had with her granddaughter.

When I got to the end, I went straight into my favorite Clapton song, *Running On Faith*. Right now it was the only thing I had - faith - so singing it was also my plea for faith to help us.

Unfortunately, the type of faith that I'd been thinking wasn't to be, so instead I had to have faith that she was at peace and knew I'd keep her daughter and granddaughter safe and happy.

I sat with her in silence for twenty minutes once I was done, until a nurse came in to check her over. Giving her a smile, I walked back out and down the hallway to where Katy's room was. There hadn't been any need to keep her in the ICU after they'd come to their conclusions, and the family knew she wouldn't have wanted it to be like that anyway, so they had moved her as close to her granddaughter as they could. If you asked me, it was still too far, but while we'd been in with her earlier they'd moved Perkins off the ward, so that was something at least.

Getting back into the uncomfortable recliner beside her bed, I closed my eyes and tried to sleep, but I couldn't switch off.

That's why when I saw a doctor running down the hallway with two nurses behind him thirty-three minutes later I knew she was gone.

Katy was going to need me to be strong for her, so I spent the hours between then and when she woke up and heard the news letting it all out and getting myself together to be her rock.

CHAPTER NINETEEN

JARROD

F*ive days later...*

I was just putting the cufflinks into the holes in my shirt and looking at the time on the clock in Katy's bedroom when she got home. All she'd said as she left this morning was that she and some of the ladies were going to get something for Maude, nothing more than that. Seeing that we only had twenty minutes left until we had to leave, she was cutting it close.

And then she came up the stairs as fast as her bruised and battered body would allow, her arm still in a sling from where the bastard had dislocated her elbow. She was healing, she was alive, but physically and emotionally she was still very broken. The day that Maude died, I'd told her that I loved her and I was going to get her through this. After hearing her say she loved me back, even as her heart was breaking over the loss of her best friend and grandmother, I promised her I'd get her through this and she'd given me that burden to shoulder for her by assuring me that she knew I would and could. Any

249

man who loves his woman as much as I loved mine would move mountains for their woman, but her belief in their ability to do that was worth more than any word would ever be able to describe – and she'd given me that.

So, day by day, I was working at fulfilling that promise, even if it took the rest of our lives.

Throwing her purse onto the bed from the doorway, she walked quickly to the closet and pulled out a black dress.

"I need help," she begged as she carefully pulled the sling over her head with a wince, panic now taking over. "I can't get the zip on my dress done up with a bum arm. God, I can't even get dressed or undressed in under an hour because of it."

It was a slight exaggeration, but only by a few minutes.

Walking calmly over to her, my lips didn't start twitching until I got to her. Seeing what she'd done from a relative distance was one thing, but it was a whole other thing up close.

"Don't say a word," she warned as I carefully pulled her top over her head and then gently moved it down her bad arm.

"I wasn't going to say a word." That didn't mean that I didn't have at least seventy of them to hand, just in case.

"It's for Maude."

TWO HOURS LATER...

We'd driven to her parent's house first, my family meeting us there before we set off for the church. It was only meant to be five cars that left the Crew's house, but after I pulled up, car after car pulled up on the sidewalks around us.

When they'd gone to her apartment, they'd found a letter she'd written with what she wanted today to be like. In it she'd told them she didn't want a funeral cortege, and that they were to do it, leave, and then have a party to celebrate. If they went against that, she would "haunt them and fuck up their hair every day for the rest of their lives".

It wasn't until we drove through town toward where the church was at the far end that we realized that almost every resident had come out to bid her farewell, all dressed in bright colors, standing with their right hands over their hearts and their heads bowed. There were banners with sentiments like 'Gone but not forgotten', 'The higher the hair, the closer to heaven', 'Miss you, Maude!' and finally a huge banner that read 'We're glad you had so many best moments of your life. Loved you here and we'll love you in heaven'.

Seeing it, Katy drew in a shaky breath and reached for my hand, holding on as tightly as she could as she watched people in the distance bow their heads as the first car carrying her parents reached them.

"She would have fucking loved this," she croaked. "Especially that sign about the hair."

Speaking of…

As we parked up in front of the church and got out of the vehicle, I looked at all the women from our families. "Are y'all sure about this?"

"It's what she would have wanted," they all said at the same time.

They were absolutely right about that. Somewhere up in the sky right now, Maude Crew was probably grabbing onto someone's hand and laughing her ass off at the bouffants that every woman walking into the church had done to their hair.

I WAS PLAYING *TEARS IN HEAVEN* AGAIN, THIS TIME AS I stood beside her casket as it was lowered into the ground. All around me were huge bouffants swaying from side to side as every female who'd attended the funeral – including my Aunt Rita who'd extended her stay to say goodbye to a woman who'd made a huge impact in only a matter of hours – got caught up in the song and swept away by the words.

Beside them were the male attendees – all with their hair at a normal height – who were openly crying.

That's when I knew, somewhere up in the sky right now, Maude Crew was definitely grabbing onto someone's hand and laughing her ass off.

CHAPTER TWENTY

Katy

Sixteen months later...

In the grand scheme of things sixteen months was nothing, but yet so much could happen in that nothing period of time.

It had started with Shane being charged with a long list of things including (but not limited to because he was a bad bastard) murder, attempted murder, assault, breaking and entering, and kidnapping. It had taken a year for him to be tried and sentenced, but he was finally behind bars and unlikely to get out.

The judge had felt strongly about the fact he'd inflicted injuries on a terminally ill woman which had led to a slightly more premature death and had then kidnapped and threatened to kill a one-year-old while the woman in question lay dying only feet away. He'd also taken offense to the fact that he'd done his best to inflict life altering injuries on me seeing as how he'd told the jury that he'd felt something pop under his hand while he was choking me and had assumed he'd broken my neck so I'd be "too paralyzed to go after him". What he was too stupid to know was that it was only my larynx moving under his hand.

It turned out that he'd been the one breaking into my house, too, looking through things to find a thumb drive that had a recipe for a new type of LSD that Effie had stolen from him. Duke had bitten him on one occasion – the time when I'd found blood on him but couldn't find any wounds – and after that he'd taken to locking him in the kitchen. That would be horrifying if it wasn't for the fact that he'd bragged to DB and Garrett about having a protective body suit that he'd used after the bite because he wasn't "a fucking idiot" - something which evidence proved he actually was. Apparently, he broke in wearing it with a t-shirt of mine tied around his wrist confuse him, and would then push him through to the kitchen, locking him in.

The whole case had left me with anxiety and I had PTSD nightmares from the assault, too. It had taken a year of therapy to help me learn to live with the PTSD, but the case had made the nightmares come back, and the anxiety that followed them was almost crippling until I was prescribed Paxil and given a prescription for Xanax if I needed to take it. So far I hadn't, but it helped to know it was there if it became too much.

My inability to organize my things in a way that appeased my OCD at a time when I needed that order and control the most had also fueled part of my anxiety. I'd shuffled things around, tried different tactics for the order I put them in, shuffled again, taken shit out of all of my shelves and moved it around, but none of it had been right. One night, after a particularly bad day, Jarrod had told me he'd fix it and to trust him to do it right. The next day I'd come home to Isla and Luke's twins working away in the living room, and immediately what they'd done soothed the rough edges inside me. The order wasn't something I would have thought of, but it was perfect.

They'd enjoyed it so much that they'd continued to come over with their parents and had organized my bedroom, Elodie's bedroom (who we still had for a week every three weeks), and the rest of the house. Through this, we became close to Luke and Isla, and I owed their twins a huge debt of gratitude. On the flip side of this, Isla said they owed me a huge debt of gratitude because the twins loved doing it and had calmed down, which was hilarious. But my anxiety became more controllable thanks to what they'd done, and that meant I hadn't had to take the Xanax for it – something which meant a huge deal to me. Then Jarrod had moved in and the twins had begged to come back to help merge our belongings together, so even that had been a relatively stress less event.

The other big change for my family was that Effie had turned up at my parent's house the day of Maude's funeral looking broken and devastated. She'd told the family that she was going to get help and had apologized to all of us for what had happened. Unfortunately, even for Leo and Neo, it was too little too late. It wasn't just that we'd lost Maude months earlier than we were going to, it was so much more than that. As if the death of an amazing woman wasn't enough, she'd taunted Shane with the fact she'd hidden the drive in something we had and he'd never get it back, and she'd put her daughter in danger, an innocent one-year-old who'd had the fortune of having a family who'd loved her when her mother hadn't. Apparently she'd gone to rehab and was back at school studying for something, but I had no interest in what she was studying for or what she was doing anymore.

Last month, on the day that Perkins had finally, fucking *finally*, been sentenced, Jarrod had given me an envelope with printouts of our tickets to Jamaica. Ren had given us both eight weeks off, so we flew into Kingston, stayed a week, traveled to a place called Discovery Bay, went to Negril, traveled to Montego Bay but only stayed two days because of the tourists, then we'd driven to Ocho Rios staying outside it in a rented house for three days, and had then driven back to Kingston via Fern Gully. Last night we'd been up at a place called Strawberry Hill, and in a couple days we were going to the Blue Mountains for three days. After that we had a list of places we still wanted to go to, and we had the time and a car so we were going to try to see as many of them as we could.

It was a whirlwind of activity and excitement, and I was loving every second of it. That said, even with every beautiful part of Jamaica that I'd seen so far, I felt most at peace and comfortable in Port Royal. We'd made it our base and because the owner of the hotel we were staying in was a friend of Gloria's twin – who didn't have anything bright pink on whenever I saw her, and in fact looked fucking phenomenal in everything she wore like her sisters did – they held a room for us to come back to whenever we needed it. We also spent a lot of time with Rita whenever we were in Kingston, and I'd finally gotten to meet her daughter. All I could say was that she looked exactly like her mother and had a personality similar to Maude's – I wished Rita the best of luck with that.

And I needed it badly.

I'd sat on the shoreline of Kingston Harbor last night, trying to hear the bell that had been in the city before it was swallowed by the sea. Many of the residents swore they still heard it ringing under the water some nights, but so far I hadn't been able to. While I'd been sitting there, I'd thought over some of the stories I'd read about the earthquake that had taken half of the city in 1692, and I thought about three of the graves in the church's graveyard here.

An archaeological team had found the bodies of two children while they'd been on a dive years ago and had buried them together at the church. There were claims that they'd found them wrapped around each other, but only the people who'd brought them to the surface would ever know the truth of that. Regardless, they now had a beautiful headstone and a grave that was looked after by many of the residents of the city, and it had been decided that all the other bodies still underwater in the city would remain there, using the remains of it as their graves.

There was also the grave of a man who'd been sucked down with it when half of the city collapsed into the sea, but through some miracle, the suction that had dragged him down had broken and it was said he was "spat up, back onto the land". There was a museum with some artefacts from dives to the remains, but it was the counts of the tragedy and the graves that had the most impact for me because it was a catastrophe and act of nature that had ugly results, ones we couldn't see up on land, but miracles had happened out of it.

There was also the fact that Port Royal was now joined to Kingston by a long highway called the Norman Manley Highway, which had been built to allow traffic from the airport to get into the city. Originally, there had been small islands dotted between them, but it was claimed that they'd sunk ships between them and covered them in rocks, sand, dirt and asphalt to create what was once known as the Palisadoes.

The whole area had me hooked, and it was crystal clear why the Klines felt the way they did about the place. Maude would have loved it, even though in the heat and sun her hair would have wilted.

This morning Jarrod had brought me out to an island called Lime Cay. We'd woken up and caught a small boat out here, enjoying the peace and quiet of the short ride and island once we'd arrived. At the weekend, it was surrounded by yachts and boats with loud music, lots of alcohol and laughter, but right now it was deserted and we had it to ourselves.

This was where I'd found the first true peace in sixteen months.

I was sitting, letting the water lick my toes before it retreated and enjoying the warmth of the sun, when I felt him walk up behind me. Getting down onto the sand so that he was pressed up against my back with his legs either side of mine, he leaned in and wrapped his arms around me.

"You happy?"

For the first time in a long time, I truly was. "I think I needed this vacation to recharge the batteries I haven't been able to charge in a long time, honey," I replied, keeping my eyes trained on the sun glinting off the water. "So yes, I'm happy. Happier than I've been in a long time."

He'd been my rock over the last year and four months. Even on the nights when I'd woken up screaming or crying, he'd patiently hold me, giving me his strength, until I went back to sleep. That's not to say that I hadn't laughed and we hadn't had fun, we absolutely had, but it hadn't felt like I was living and enjoying the fun, whereas now it did.

"I know, baby," he whispered, kissing the side of my neck before he moved his hand so that his fingers were linked with mine. Then he moved again, and his left hand started fiddling with mine, which felt nice, so I relaxed into him even more.

There was silence for a long moment until he held the hand he'd been fiddling with up. "Hold that for me, will you?"

Looking down at what he was talking about, I froze as my finger glinted just like I'd been watching the sun do on the surface of the water.

"What?" I breathed, still staring at the large diamond on my finger.

"Hold on to it for me," he repeated calmly. "I'm thinking for at least seventy-five years."

"What?" I rasped, sounding like I'd been winded, which technically I guess I had been.

Carrying on like he wasn't holding a marble statue of his girlfriend, Jarrod murmured, "And when I add the other ring to it, you can hold on to that for at least seventy-five years, too."

I blinked repeatedly, wondering if I was seeing things. There'd been no discussions about the future yet, no hints or indication that he was going to ask me to marry him, so this had come out of nowhere.

I wasn't prepared, I hadn't even said yes yet.

"And what will you be holding onto?"

"The ring that you give me," he replied like the answer was simple, and then added, "and you. Every day, every night, for the rest of our lives."

"Are you asking me to marry you?"

The vibrations and movement of his chest as he laughed made my toes curl in the sand. "No, I'm telling you we're getting married, because asking implies you have a choice."

Ok, that was arrogant, but it was also one of the hottest things I'd ever heard, and I'd listened to all the books he'd narrated.

Figuring that words were now cheap and had no place in the conversation, I turned around and launched myself at him, taking him down onto his back on the sand.

Wrapping his arms back around me, he lay there grinning up at me as I stroked his cheek. "Is this you saying yes?"

"No, because that implies that I have a choice in the matter. This is me thinking that sex on the beach isn't just a cocktail and we have this whole island to ourselves for the next four hours."

There were some trees on the island, so to hide away from the fishing boats and the odd yacht that floated by, we hid amongst them and had the real-life version of the cocktail. And it was fucking awesome!

EIGHT MONTHS LATER...

I was officially Mrs. Kline now, and it had been the happiest day of my life. I hadn't cried, I hadn't tripped as I walked down the aisle to where Jarrod was waiting for me in his black suit with a black shirt under it – sans tie, which looked freaking amazing on him. I hadn't messed up my vows, I hadn't dropped his ring. Nothing had gone wrong, not even the smaller details.

Of course I wished my grandmother was here to see it with her big hair, but I was wearing some of her jewelry so I liked to think that she was a huge part of it because she made the way I looked even more special.

Tony had helped me choose my dress for the day, and we'd decided on a plain white strapless one that had a lace overlay with long sleeves. Scarlett had designed my bridal underwear and what she'd come up with was the most beautiful corset and panties I'd ever seen in my life in white lace with light blue stitching at the seams. It might not be as funny as my character panties, but for this one day I wanted to stick with a level of sexy hot that he'd never forget and what she'd designed absolutely gave me that sexy hot factor.

Elodie was one of my bridesmaids – *not* a flower girl. We'd tried to get her to do that, but she wanted to hold a bouquet not a "dumb basket of petals", and she'd stood beside me the whole time, grinning at Jarrod like it was the best show ever. Isla's daughter and Olivia had also been bridesmaids, and it had just looked fabulous with them carrying mini versions of the adult bridesmaids bouquets, with Kali in his smaller version of the suits the men were wearing as a page boy, that I had to thank Elodie for putting her foot down.

Then, when Jarrod had kissed me after we were pronounced man and wife, Elodie had squealed with excitement and then thrown her bouquet at the people sitting on the right side of the church, almost knocking Cole out. That just added to the day for me in all honesty.

I'd sat blushing and laughing through Jarrod's brothers speeches, and I'd refrained from throwing a pitcher at my own brothers for what they'd said in theirs. They'd brought up all of my childhood transgressions, sharing how I'd once dropped a pair of scissors on Ammon's foot that had ended up with him needing twelve stitches (accident), how I'd also thrown a bag of flour to him just before the scissor incident that had burst all over him so he'd had to go to hospital looking like Casper (also an accident, but we'd been baking cookies and I couldn't be bothered to walk across the kitchen to pass him the flour), the CD incident (his fault), how Major had needed stitches in his head after I'd accidentally dropped my encyclopedia over the bannister of the stairs as I was skipping down them (kind of an accident), and finally how he'd ended up with a buzz cut when I'd spilled wax into his precious hair (not an accident). By the end, I wanted to crawl under the table and hide because it made me sound like a wreck, but Jarrod had kissed me while he was laughing, and it felt so good that I couldn't have cared less if they'd recounted even more stories than they had.

There had been a discussion last month about what the first dance would be – the dad/daughter dance, or the first husband/wife dance. Jarrod had insisted that it would be the dad/daughter dance. So here we were, slowly moving to *My Father's Eyes*.

Pulling me a bit closer, Dad rested his chin on the top of my head. "I'm proud of you, Katykins, so very proud of you. And she wouldn't want you to be sad anymore." When I pulled back to say something, he just shook his head. "She's sitting up there on her cloud right now watching all of this, honey, and she's loving every second and screaming at you to live your life."

He was right, and until that moment I hadn't realized that I wasn't giving myself permission to actually live my life. I was happy – so fucking happy – but I was still living in the shadow of what had happened.

"Now, take a deep breath in," he told me, waiting until I did it. "And let it out along with all the bad shit."

The breath came out of me in a peal of laughter, and that final cloud lifted. It was only a year later that it would hit me that I hadn't had another anxiety attack after that talk with him, and that I'd only had two nightmares. Even my OCD had gotten better.

After the song ended, Jarrod walked up to us, and Dad held my hand out to him. "There's still time to run, Jarrod," he told him seriously. When Jarrod just held onto me, he looked at him like he was crazy. "Seriously? You're not even tempted? I've been married to her mother for thirty-one years, man. The ink on the certificate isn't even dry yet, so you've got time to escape. See the height of those heels? You've got an easy getaway."

Jarrod's response was a deep rumble of laughter. "I've seen her run in shoes, Paul. Trust me, there's no getting away."

Shrugging, Dad started to make his way off the dance floor. "Don't say I didn't warn you."

Pulling me into him, he looked over to the DJ and nodded. Then, as the opening notes of *Cheer Down* began, he said something that broke the tight tear control I'd had all day. "Thought I'd give her one of the most important jobs today."

One by one they fell down my face, more than likely ruining my makeup and staining my dress with whatever foundation was dragged with them. The difference was, these were happy tears, ones that knew he was right because she was loving every second of this being our wedding song.

If you dissected the lyrics, it would probably shock most people that it was our first dance, but to me they were some of the most beautiful words ever written and revolved around loving someone unconditionally. To cheer down – to me – meant that you didn't have to act happy if you weren't. If you added that into the words written by Tom Petty, it meant that you didn't have to act happy for the other person to love you. Jarrod had stuck with me through the darkest moment of my life, not expecting me to just be the happy-go-lucky person I was before it, and bringing me back to the person I'd been before. And I knew now what I'd known when the GYMP plan had been drunkenly jotted down on those napkins, I would take him however he came, unconditionally, so it was applicable from me to him, too.

My anxiety might have ended that night, and I might have almost conquered the nightmares, but it also *started* my life, feeling complete and happier than I'd ever been before.

"Farewell to the GYMP," the girls screamed at the end of the song, making me burst out laughing.

What was even funnier were the expressions on his brothers faces as we walked past them, their eyes looking him up and down like he was a freak of nature. "Never had you down as a gimp, man," Canon muttered, and then looked at me. "And you – it's always the quiet ones."

It probably wasn't the best idea to call it that, but in our defense alcohol does funny things to your brain. What's also funny was, the GYMP had meant nothing to me because we'd come together naturally. But if the girls wanted to believe our match was down to them, who were we to tell them otherwise. We knew the truth, and that was all that mattered.

The wedding wasn't about the attention and flash decorations (although we had all of that, too), it was about us. And when the food was served, I grinned over at Gloria, who'd been helping the caterers perfect it for the last couple of days. They didn't know what was in her rice and peas because she'd ordered them to leave the kitchen while she prepared it, and watching everyone inhale their food and go back for more, I was even happier that I'd gotten her to make our favorites today – Jarrod's (and now mine, too) birthday meal.

Beside her in its own seat was the last wig that Maude had ever styled for her. After she'd passed away, Gloria had put it in a special Perspex case so that it wouldn't get ruined. There were so many little additions that our families had done to include her, and that was definitely one of my favorites.

But then my husband gave me one final gift for the night – well, no he did that in the privacy of our hotel room, but this one was the final gift fit for public consumption. He walked up onto the stage and picked up a guitar that I hadn't noticed on it and nodded at the DJ.

He's sung to me so many times and I never got tired of it, but hearing him sing *Soul To Squeeze* by the Red Hot Chili Peppers? It made a perfect day even more perfect which I'd thought was impossible.

And the videos of it went viral, but because people also sent them to me, I got to relive that moment whenever I wanted to.

EPILOGUE

JARROD

ne year later...

O   We hadn't intended on having kids for another five years until Katy was thirty, but when that little test showed the surprise we had coming, we immediately adjusted our plans and celebrated.

What followed, though, was nine months of hell. Morning sickness, cravings (mostly putting pineapple on everything, including pizza which was a hard limit for me), afternoon sickness, food aversions, swollen feet, cankles, tears followed immediately by laughter, the boy-girl argument, the name argument, the gender revealed or kept secret argument, the nursery color scheme argument...

And then her water broke as we'd sat down to lunch with our families, ruining Canon and Major's shoes and only just missing Duke, who was sleeping by her feet. Proving that she was special, she went against the grain for a first time labor and within an hour our daughter made her way into the world, pissed and letting us know it. Fortunately, our son had made a quieter entrance *after* we'd arrived at the hospital, and he'd just looked around and had gone back to sleep.

Now I was sitting beside my wife who was sleeping, with my daughter Melody in one arm and my son Barker in the other. The name argument for our daughter had been over in a minute because as soon as I'd suggested Melody, she'd jumped on it. The one that had last four months – and had only ended because she'd seen him and decided it didn't suit him – was naming our son Anakin because Katy loved *Star Wars*.

There was no way in hell I'd have called him Anakin, so when she'd said her second choice was Barker, I was relieved that I didn't have to carry him out to meet our families saying, "Meet Anakin Kline." I wouldn't have survived the fallout from it, especially with him having an uncle called Bond.

As soon as Barker had left her womb (literally because he was still dangling by his umbilical cord), she'd told me these were the only two kids she was ever pushing out because, even with them being twins, they were on the long side and had come out at turbo speed with no time for drugs. The nurses kept telling her that she'd forget the pain, but she was adamant that she wouldn't forget her vagina tearing in two *ever*. Seeing as how she'd given me a life that was richer than my dreams, I could give her that.

With my eyes on the babies, I watched as not-Anakin Kline but Barker Kline and Melody both blinked their eyes a couple of times, and then looked up at me with different expressions on their faces. Barker's was content and sort of 'imma lay here and just be cute'. whereas Melody's warned she was about to lose her shit – which she did right then.

"Are they awake?" Katy mumbled sleepily.

Uh, gee, ya think?

"Your daughter is a hellion," I told her, watching as she pulled herself up to sitting in the bed. "And I think she's hangry."

Passing over the harpy, Katy fiddled with her top and then winced as Melody literally pounced on her and started feeding, growling when she got it. "Christ that's fierce," Katy gasped, looking up at me wide eyed. "The nurse said we'd need to top up with formula for a couple of days, maybe even always depending on how my udders do at producing a glass of milk for them."

That was an analogy that made me shudder at the mental image it brought. Not the milk production because there was nothing gross to me about that, but picturing udders on her chest.

"Yeah, she dropped that stuff off after you passed out. Once your harpy's done her thing, we can swap and I'll give her it, if you want?"

And just like that, we made the life changing adjustment from just the two of us to parents, as easily as we'd made the adjustment three years ago when we'd gone from people living independent lives to us.

After the feeding was done, diapers had been changed, and baby bootys were sparkling, I sat back down holding them in exactly the same way as before and started singing The Calling's *Wherever You Will Go*. Barker was the first to close his eyes and slip back to sleep, but Melody watched me with eyes that were the same color as my own until the song was almost finished, making me wonder if her path in life would be one that involved music.

Just as I finished the song, Katy sat bolt upright in bed and squealed, "I knew you sounded like someone, but I couldn't figure out why."

Being likened to the lead singer of the group was far from a bad thing, seeing as how his voice kicked ass. In fact, I remember back when the group released that song and people saw the lead singer, heard the depth of his voice and went 'huh?'.

"Yours is a bit raspier and a smidge deeper," she continued, holding her thumb and forefinger about a quarter of an inch away from each other in front of her face. "But that's it. Shit, how long has it taken me to figure that out?"

"Three years?" I suggested grinning at her.

She dropped her hand down to her blanket covered lap and her expression changed from excited to soft. "I saw you before that, honey."

Carefully getting up to put the babies in their fishbowls, I walked back over to her and sat down on the edge of her bed, planting a fist in the mattress either side of her. With our mouths now about an inch away from hers, I laid it out. "Six months before you became my GYMP, this beautiful gamer chick moved to town and started working at the garage. She intrigued me, and I wanted to get to know her better. So, when my lease was up, I moved in next door to her and got to know her and her huge dog, too."

"You did that on purpose?" she breathed, looking shocked.

"How else was I going to get you to talk nerdy to me?"

Laughing quietly, she lay back, watching me with sparkling eyes that were taking longer to open when she blinked. It might not have been a bad labor, but she'd given birth to two babies so she was exhausted.

Laying down beside her, I pulled her into my side and lay there staring blankly at the ceiling. Three years ago I never knew I'd have this, but now I couldn't imagine my life without it. Every night I went to sleep with my wife wearing one of her nighties and a pair of hilarious but sexy character underwear, with Duke watching out to keep her safe.

And now I'd fall asleep with two little humans who were half of me under my roof, too.

Two years later...

Using the money we'd saved and her inheritance from Maude, we'd bought a house in the same development. Detached, sitting back from the road, fenced in front yard and large backyard, perfect for a family of four and two dogs – Duke and Deloris, our German Shepherd. Sitting in pride of place in the living room were the photos taken of Maude being held by the strippers that night at the club.

I was still narrating audiobooks, but now I'd branched out into thrillers as well. The money was good, the work was steady, and with our jobs earning us a good salary, too, we were comfortable. While she was pregnant with the twins, Katy had given in and gotten rid of the Mini, replacing it with a black five door Mini Countryman this time that I could fit behind the wheel of and sit in without needing to angle my head so that it was up through the sunroof.

All of this was great and made for a happy family, but today for their second birthdays, Katy's parents had bought them a piano, and my parents had bought them both guitars. Bracing for the onslaught of key hammering and manic guitar strumming, we'd smiled through the dread, only to be shocked to shit when – at the age of fucking two – they'd played a made up tune on the piano that made you want to listen to it repeatedly, then they'd strummed on the guitars and tried a few different cords. It had ended with Barker on the piano gently moving his fingers over the keys while Melody tried to keep tune on the guitar.

We'd all sat listening to them, only tearing our eyes away from the pair to glance at each other once, and when they'd finished, we'd all stood up and clapped – meaning it, not just because it was our duty.

"Your kids are so going to science camp," Reid muttered to me out of the corner of his mouth, getting a glare from Katy who was standing with her arms around my waist.

"They're going to music camp," she corrected, more than likely wondering if there were any that accepted two-year-olds.

"You want your kids to go to band camp? Didn't you ever watch American Pie?" he shot back, making the rest of our siblings who were all close to where we were snort.

"Yes I watched it, who didn't? But there's a difference between band camp and a Mozart or Beethoven retreat," she snapped, putting her hands on her hips.

My brothers lived to wind her up. Over the years, we'd all become close, as had our siblings, and now they all acted like brothers and sisters – apart from Reid and Aura who steered clear of each other – so her reaction made his eyes light up.

Seeing that he was about to say something else, I held my hand up. "No. Not today, not about this."

Sighing, he walked over to the piano and sat down to touch the keys, finally giving us the plinky plonky noises that we'd braced ourselves for from the twins. Walking up to him, Melody and Barker watched him playing with frowns on their faces as he grinned down at them.

"Look at Uncle Reid playing just like you two," he chuckled, going back and hammering down on the keys now.

At the same time, the twins reached up and shut the fallboard that covered the keys down on his fingers, getting a shout of pain from him and high fives from the rest of their uncles and aunt.

Sighing, Katy leaned into my side smiling proudly at our children who walked away afterward shaking their heads and talking to each other.

Leaning down so that my head was resting on the top of hers, the sweet scent of her hair going up my nose, I asked, "Happy?"

"Yeah."

"Me, too. I wouldn't change this for the world."

There was a long silence where I swear she hardly breathed, and then she finally broke it. "That's a shame, because I'm pregnant again."

I was never getting that fucking Dodge Viper.

But ask me if I cared.

ABOUT THE AUTHOR

I'm a British author who grew up all over the world. My parents were diplomats, so we were posted to all of the corners of the earth and it was a *blast*. Some wouldn't seem so awesome if you heard about them, but my parents always made it a fun experience and it molded my brother and I into who we are today.

I live in Wiltshire in the west country of the UK. At random times of the day, I'll hear a moo from the fields around me, or get a whiff of that…uhhh…'country air', and I love it! I might not have grown up in the UK, but I'm a British girl to the bone (regardless of the suspicious whiffs coming in from the fields).

I'm a single mother with a son who is nearing his teenage phase. Maybe he's reached it early? Who knows. But he's awesome and has a personality and sense of humor that I can only attribute to my family. We're slightly bonkers, we have a wicked sense of humor and we find the positives in every situation. I'm so proud to be his mum and to watch him grow and mature.

Writing was something that I'd always done. I had a teacher in the third grade who always set us the task of writing a story and making it into a book every weekend. After I left school, I kept this up and wrote as often as I could or just plotted out books. This evolved into me taking the plunge and publishing my first book in 2016 and I've been typing ever since.

I'm proud to be an Indie Author, and I absolutely love writing out my crazy Providence characters and the more complex ones in my other series'. It doesn't matter if it's romantic comedy or something with more suspense – so long as it has a HEA I'll do it!

I've got so many more planned, so the best is yet to come.

Want to hear more about upcoming releases and hear from characters from the Providence and Providence Gold Series? Sign up to my newsletter:

https://landing.mailerlite.com/webforms/landing/n6g2k1

Wanna join in on the crazy unicorn loving tainted romance shenanigans? Come and join my group on Facebook, 50 Shades of Neigh!

https://www.facebook.com/groups/144042859588361/

Printed in Poland
by Amazon Fulfillment
Poland Sp. z o.o., Wrocław

59192177R00174